Was he going to watch her?

"No ghost can see you unless you want to be seen. I promise," Ryan said, seeing Monique's hesitation.

The decision was up to her. Before she had a chance to change her mind, Monique crawled out from under the covers. Walking around the bed, she turned so she stood directly in front of him. Then she crossed her arms in front of her chest and ran her fingers under the tiny straps of her nightgown. "And a ghost cannot tell a lie," she asked. "Right?"

"That's right." Ryan's voice faded, losing its steely edge as his hands gripped the fabric of the comforter.

Monique's eyes never left his as she slowly shifted a strap down one shoulder, then the other, and let the soft fabric caress her body as the material dropped to the floor.

A blue mesh thong. She stood in front of him wearing *nothing* but a blue mesh thong.

"So, Ryan," she said, turning slowly to ensure maximum impact. "What do you see now?"

Blaze™

Dear Reader,

"I see dead people."

Got your attention, didn't I? Well, the movie *The Sixth Sense* got mine (and most of the world's, too—it grossed over $600 million worldwide!). When Haley Joel Osment whispered those now famous four words, I admittedly had goose bumps marching down my arms...and an idea for a titillating book series firing up my brain.

What if, in order to have some semblance of a normal existence, a family was required to help ghosts cross over? The ghosts who had unfinished business, or couldn't find their way. And suppose the current mediums for this family were six twentysomething cousins, trying to live their own lives, while constantly on call to help those whose lives were gone? That's the basis for my first Harlequin Blaze miniseries, THE SIXTH SENSE. I hope it gets your attention, too.

Please visit my Web site, www.kelleystjohn.com, to win a fabulous New Orleans vacation giveaway, learn the latest news about my recent and upcoming releases, and drop me a line. I love hearing from readers!

Enjoy!

Kelley St. John

KISS AND DWELL
Kelley St. John

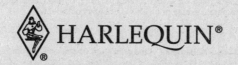

HARLEQUIN®

TORONTO • NEW YORK • LONDON
AMSTERDAM • PARIS • SYDNEY • HAMBURG
STOCKHOLM • ATHENS • TOKYO • MILAN • MADRID
PRAGUE • WARSAW • BUDAPEST • AUCKLAND

ISBN-13: 978-0-373-79329-7
ISBN-10:   0-373-79329-4

KISS AND DWELL

This edition published by arrangement with Harlequin Books S.A.

® and TM are trademarks of the publisher. Trademarks indicated with ® are registered in the United States Patent and Trademark Office, the Canadian Trade Marks Office and in other countries.

www.eHarlequin.com

Printed in U.S.A.

ABOUT THE AUTHOR

Kelley St. John's previous experience as a senior writer at NASA fueled her interest in writing action-packed suspense, although she's also got a weakness for steamy romances and quirky women's fiction. Since 2000, Kelley has obtained over fifty writing awards and was elected to the board of directors for Romance Writers of America. Visit her Web site, www.kelleystjohn.com, to learn the latest news about recent and upcoming releases and to register for fabulous vacation giveaways!

To the sexiest Cajun on the planet.
You know who you are!

Laissez Les Bon Temps Rouler!

Prologue

IN THE Louisiana bayou, the temperature is hot, the accents are thick and the sex is phenomenal. The Vicknair family knows; they've lived in Cajun country since their Acadian ancestors stepped off the boat at Lafayette. The generations since have done their part to maintain that thick Cajun drawl, have adapted well to the stifling heat and naturally, have enjoyed their share of superlative sex. But the Vicknair descendants acquired a bit of *lagniappe*, a little something extra, as well. From the moment the family entered Louisiana, each member merged with the other side. Not the other side of the state line, or even the other side of St. Charles Parish. Oh no, they traversed the boundary between the living and the dead. They quickly realized their only chance of living a seminormal life was by aiding those spirits who were having difficulties crossing over, helping them make what was wrong right, so they could find their way to the other side.

The newest generation of Vicknairs understands their duty to continue the family tradition and protect their secret. True, Louisiana is known for ghosts, vampires and voodoo. But so far, the Vicknair mediums have kept their penchant for the nonliving a secret. They live normal lives, for the most part. And the youngest Vicknairs want to keep it that way.

Perfecting their talent with every crossing, these mediums

are slowly but surely learning how to determine a spirit's dilemma and help fulfill that spirit's needs. Moreover, the six cousins currently performing Vicknair medium duty realize that when a lavender-tinted envelope materializes on the infamous tea service in the Vicknair plantation's sitting room, it's time to get down to business. Time to help a spirit. And woe to the cousin who ignores an assignment. While Adeline Vicknair may be dead, her feisty temper lives on, and when she assigns a spirit to one of her grandchildren, she's not just whistling Dixie. She wants it handled—or else.

Thankfully, the Vicknair grandchildren usually heed her call. They understand the simple rules associated with helping spirits, rules that have been handed down from generation to generation and that have never been questioned by preceding Vicknairs—as far as they know:

- A medium must heed a spirit's call and handle a spirit's needs in a timely manner. Failure to do so will result in unfavorable—if not painful—repercussions.
- Once a spirit is assigned to a medium, the two are emotionally bonded until the spirit's requirement for crossing over has been fulfilled. This bond should never be abused nor taken for granted in any way, shape or form.
- A medium should never lie to a spirit; likewise, spirits are physically incapable of lying to mediums.
- A medium may not touch a spirit. Period.

Three girls—determined Nan, wild Monique and sweet Jenee—make up the female half of the Vicknair mediums. Strong-willed Tristan, playboy Gage and tenderhearted Dax are their male counterparts. While the young mediums are repeatedly reminded of the rules, this new breed of feisty Vicknairs is under the distinct impression that rules were made to be broken—especially Monique.

1

MONIQUE VICKNAIR spooned sautéed crawfish tails from the black cast-iron pot, inhaled the spicy scented air, then turned toward Pierre and smiled. "Okay, bring me that bowl," she instructed, pointing a red-tipped finger toward the large dish. She'd had her nails done today at her salon. Nails done, brows waxed, skin moisturized, hair trimmed—the works. And tonight, she planned to put *the works* to the test with Pierre Comeaux.

"This bowl?" He lifted the white ceramic dish embellished with a thick blue ring around its bulging middle. Green onions, yellow onions and chopped bell pepper towered above the rim and added another tantalizing scent to the kitchen. He held the bowl out of her reach. "Do you need this, *chère*?" he asked, green eyes glittering with mischievousness. He knew she wanted him, and from the cocky smirk on his gorgeous face, he probably knew how much.

"Yes, I do." She swallowed thickly and prayed that the summons from Adeline Vicknair would wait long enough for at least one time of hot-and-heated with Pierre. Over the past six months, her deceased grandmother had single-handedly managed to keep Monique from any sexual activities whatsoever. Well, any sexual activities involving males. Monique had sure given her stash of vibrators a run for the money. Thank goodness Grandma Adeline didn't have the power to stop a charged battery, a steamy romance novel and a determined imagination.

But Adeline did have the power to make Monique miserable if she didn't heed a spirit's calling. In other words, when Monique's skin started burning, signaling she had a letter waiting, she should return promptly to the Vicknair plantation to start her assignment. Do not pass Go; do not collect two hundred dollars.

However, the operative word in that sentence? *Should.* She *should* return. But why now? Why this time? Why couldn't Grandma Adeline give her a little more time, just until Pierre made her toes curl? It never failed that the minute her libido experienced that exquisite elation, at the telltale moment of orgasm-here-we-come, some distressed specter decided to pay Monique a visit. Not exactly what the doctor ordered for a woman who enjoyed sex.

Take tonight, for example. Pierre Comeaux's invitation to a "cozy dinner on my terrace, beneath the whisper of mighty oak branches and a warm July breeze" had started Monique's sparks burning hotter than a levee bonfire at Christmas. Naturally, the image that came to mind was of the two of them sprawled on the veranda, their stomachs sated from a delicious meal and their sexual appetites equally sated from a delightful tango beneath a limitless blanket of stars.

Unfortunately, Monique had had a hell of a day at the beauty shop, with nothing going quite right, particularly in the color arena. And double unfortunately, she knew what that meant. It was only a matter of time until Adeline sent a summons that would warrant the attention of her middle granddaughter.

Middle. Middle girl in the list of cousins and middle child in her own family, with Gage the playboy serving as big brother and Dax the tenderhearted forming her younger bookend. Middle children were known for demanding attention, right? Well, she was ready to demand some now—from Pierre. Time was wasting. Flesh was stinging. Ghosts were coming.

She took a deep breath and prepared to ask the most gorgeous combination of dark-haired, tanned and muscled Cajun she'd seen in quite a while if they could skip dinner completely and get naked, but before she could make the request, he inhaled the tantalizing scents in the kitchen, emitted an extremely male guttural growl, and grinned.

"I've wanted to share a dinner with you—share a night with you—for a long time," he said. "You, me, delicious food and an entire night to explore possibilities." His smile broadened, his eyes smoldered with desire. He obviously saw all of this heat in the kitchen as enticing foreplay, and she did too; she just didn't know if she had time for it.

As it was, she'd botched three color treatments today at Monique's Masterpieces, her salon in nearby Ormond. Not completely botched, she supposed, but the auburn had ended up a bit too red, the blond a bit too platinum, and the black a bit too Elvis. That, in and of itself, told her she had a ghostly visitor on the way. Add the stinging growing stronger and stronger on the back of her neck, and Monique knew her minutes were numbered. If she did happen to get things started with Pierre, she wasn't planning on it being a quick encounter. Have mercy, she prayed he wasn't a minuteman. A marathon man was what she needed after going this long without.

Pierre moved behind her, wrapped his arms around her waist and tilted the bowl to pour the vegetables into the seasoned butter bubbling in the pot. He pushed closer, and the impressive bulge in his jeans nudged her bottom. "Is that what you want, *chère*?" he asked against her ear.

"Oh, yeah," Monique breathed, her desire mixing with the scent of spicy onions and peppers to create a hot, sizzling lust. However, her neck also sizzled, and regrettably, Monique knew why. She decided to fight it, just a little while, long enough to get Pierre out of his clothes.

No doubt about it, she wasn't heeding the call in a timely manner. Pesky rules. She was a healthy twenty-four-year-old woman who wanted—needed—sex. *Real* sex, as in the kind that didn't require batteries. Was that too much to ask?

"Have you got the garlic powder and paprika ready?" she asked, anxious to get this meal moving, and to get those clothes dropping.

Pierre moved his mouth behind her ear and nuzzled her hair out of the way while distributing hot, wet kisses against her skin. "Your hair is so soft, Monique, and the color—it reminds me of a sandy beach."

Monique blinked. *Sand?* Her hair reminded him of sand? And he thought this was a compliment? She cleared her throat, with the total intention of asking him to clarify his statement, but before she had a chance, his kisses moved a fraction lower, and her thighs clenched in anticipation of those spine-tingling kisses in other places.

"What about that paprika and garlic?" she managed, deciding she couldn't afford to waste time talking about the color of her hair.

His low laugh tickled her nape, due to its already stinging state, the sensation made her neck practically flame. Have mercy, her grandmother wasn't cutting her any slack—again.

"We have to let the onions sauté first," he said. "They need to be clear. How about a glass of wine while they're simmering?"

"How about a heap of sex instead?" she asked.

Another deep laugh rumbled against her neck as his

erection pushed her bottom and his hard chest pressed against her back. "*Chère*, we'll need longer than the time it'll take those onions to get tender, and I'm not about to have my first time with Monique Vicknair run short. On top of that, I promised you a mouthwatering dinner, and there won't be anything delicious about it if we leave that pot on its own." He nipped her right earlobe, then cruised slowly beneath it, until his lips nuzzled the sensitive indention where her neck curved toward her shoulder. "Nice to know you're so anxious, though," he said, his voice a husky whisper. "Trust me, it'll be worth the wait."

Monique glared at the onions that refused to lose their color. The burning had moved beyond her neck to settle in her chest and make her nipples ache. She knew good and well that Pierre Comeaux, with his mesmerizing green eyes, bulging biceps and bulging other parts, could sure enough put out this fire, or perhaps send her into a true bout of spontaneous combustion.

What was he waiting for?

"I—I really think we need the garlic and paprika now," she mumbled, losing herself in the feel of his mouth on her shoulder and his teeth working the tiny strap of her red tank dress down her arm. Consequently, the top swell of her right breast pushed above the soft fabric, and Monique wanted to cry from desperation. "Don't you?" she asked.

He laughed again. "Oh, Monique, who'd have thought you would be so eager? I promise, before the night's over, I'll take you right there, in the center of my kitchen island. Push your soft skirt up to your hips and give you exactly what you're wanting. First with my mouth, then with my—"

Monique's flesh burned hotter than the burner making the vegetables sizzle. It flamed, the fire raging forward from her chest to blaze through every limb. Her breathing hitched and every nerve ending bristled in anguish. She *couldn't* wait. If she stayed any longer, the pain might be too much to endure, even for the short drive home. Have mercy, sex with Pierre would have been good, but it wouldn't be tonight.

Damn family curse.

"I've got to go," she said, squirming out of his embrace and trying to control her madly racing heart. She was scorching, so fiercely that she honestly didn't know if she could maneuver the car back home, but she had to. The longer she ignored the calling, the worse it would be. She could only imagine how irritated her grandmother was that she had disregarded her summons, probably nearly as irritated as Nanette.

Fleeing the kitchen, Monique sprinted through Pierre's house and bolted through the front door, sucking big gulps of thick Louisiana humidity as she grabbed one of Pierre's big white columns for support. And, just super, the huge white cylinder reminded her of other things that were, from all indications in Pierre's jeans, long and thick and hard.

"Granny, I do not like your sense of timing," she announced, as the object of her current long, thick and hard fantasy lazily stepped onto the porch.

"You gonna explain what just happened in there, *chère*?" he asked, easing his mouth into that cocky, sexy grin. "Because I'm not into teasing, Monique, and when a woman asks me one minute if she can move on to getting naked, then the next minute she decides to leave, I have a tendency to think she's a tease." He leaned against the door frame and lifted one brow. "Are you, Monique? A tease?"

Monique shook her head. A tease? No, the one teasing here was Adeline Vicknair, but Monique couldn't tell him that. Trapped in this family-induced hell once again, she simply took a deep breath, started down the steps toward her car and called to the guy who'd almost given her the first male-induced orgasm she'd had in half a year, "I'm not a tease, Pierre, but I do have to go." Then she got in her car and sped away, wincing as the wind whistled through Pierre's matured oaks with a melodic resonance way too similar to her grandmother's laughter.

Monique punched the accelerator to the floor while her skin continued to flame. If the coming spirit was as strong as the burning sensation on her flesh—and that *was* the way it usually worked—this particular ghost would be a doozie. Probably male, she'd guess. And with Monique's luck, probably another cranky old geezer, bald with no teeth, who would proceed to cuss Monique out because he couldn't find the damn light.

No, she'd had that kind of spirit last time; Granny wouldn't give her two ornery old farts in a row. Would she? And what did Adeline Vicknair have against sex, anyway? Or rather, against Monique having sex. "You weren't a prude," Monique said, glancing upward and knowing her grandmother was undoubtedly listening. "And you know good and well this would have been phenomenal. What did I do that pissed you off?"

Monique glanced in her rearview mirror and saw Pierre, his muscled frame leaning against one of the big white columns as he watched her drive away.

"*Mon dieu*, Granny, this better be good."

Oddly enough, at that very moment, the wind in the trees changed direction, producing an echoing sound through the swaying limbs. Monique's ears pricked at the new reverberation, and she *knew* she heard Adeline's voice this time.

Oh, chéri, it is, the whistling branches hummed. *C'est si bon.*

NANETTE VICKNAIR stood on the front porch of the Vicknair plantation and cast an evil eye down the magnolia-lined drive leading out to River Road, along which her cousin should by now have returned from her date. "Where is she?" she muttered. Then she looked toward the darkening sky and turned her head toward the house. "And where are those roofers?"

Dax, Monique's younger brother, and the youngest of the male cousins at twenty-three, pushed back from his perch on one of the porch rockers and grinned. "My sister isn't known for her punctuality," he said. "You know that, Nan. But she always shows. Give her time."

"She needs to take her responsibility seriously. When we're called to help, we're supposed to help right then. I don't know why it's so hard for her to understand that what we do is important." Nanette wondered why she repeatedly had to give her twenty-four-year-old cousin the same lecture that she often delivered to the ninth graders she taught at Lutcher High. She called it the apathy speech, as in a soapbox spiel where she attempted to get them to care about something. Anything at all. Not that her speeches ever worked on the kids, or on her cousin, or on the roofers that should have been here two hours ago, for that matter. "And those construction guys need to take their job seriously, too," Nanette added.

"The Historical Society won't take us off their list unless the house gets worse," Dax said. "That's what they told you in the last letter, right?"

Nan released an exasperated breath. "The Parish President would like nothing better than to see this place torn down, and he's on the Board of Directors for the society," she reminded him. "Charles Roussel has made it no secret that he wants this 'eyesore' removed from his parish, and the Historical Society has made it no secret that they won't even consider giving us restoration help if it gets any worse. And right now, they're still busy working on the historic homes in New Orleans. Jefferson Parish homes take priority over St. Charles Parish, since that's where all the tourists, and their money, go."

"But they did say they'd get to St. Charles next, and that they'd help us with fixing the place up, as long as it doesn't get worse."

"That's just it," Nan said. "Our roof is barely hanging on, and I told the society that we'd make those repairs on our own. Actually, I listed several things we'd do on our own, if they'd say that we'd eventually get those restoration funds, but the roof has to come first."

"And why did you tell them that again?" Dax asked.

"You know why. So we wouldn't have to ask for so much money. That gets your project moved up on the list of houses needing funds."

"But now we have to prove we're actually making repairs," Dax reminded.

"We *are* making repairs," Nan said. "Working our behinds off every Saturday. Or haven't you noticed?" She didn't mean to sound so curt, but this home was near and dear to her heart, and the fact that the repairs were going so slowly, and that the committee would come out to review those repairs in a mere two weeks, was keeping her on edge.

"We need more money, Nan. That roof isn't gonna come cheap, you know."

"I know," she said, grimacing.

"We could always ask our folks for more money," Dax began, but Nan's glare cut him off.

"I tried to call my parents, but they're currently cruising to Jamaica for a three-week vacation, which they truly need. Plus, I really don't want to ask for help if we can deal with this ourselves. My parents, your parents—all of our parents—did their part as mediums and in working together to keep up this plantation. Now they've moved on, retired, so to speak, the same way we'll move on when we all have kids and they become adults. It's a chain of responsibility, and they did their part. I don't want them thinking we can't do ours."

Now it was Dax's turn to glare.

"What?" Nan asked.

"Well, I haven't said anything about it before, but it seems my parents believe the plantation did fine through Hurricane Katrina. They said as much to me, and they told Monique and Gage the same thing. Wonder where they got an idea like that?"

"You know I told them," Nan said, annoyed. "Just like I told my folks, and just like I told Uncle Jim and Aunt Clair."

"Yeah, I know you did," Dax said, rocking slowly on the porch, "but I'm not overly proud of lying to my parents every time they call, Nan. Or of convincing them to meet us at Gage's place in New Orleans when they visit, instead of coming out here. And it's been nearly two years. Don't you think they'd want to help if they realized the shape this place is in?"

Nan bit back her tears. She loved this house, loved its history. "I told you I tried to call my folks, but I couldn't get through. And don't you think if the spirits really thought we couldn't handle this they'd somehow let them know to get back here and help? They were mediums, too, but they haven't been contacted or felt the need to return. In my opinion, that means we're meant to handle this on our own. Besides, we aren't lying. The house did do fine through the hurricane. It's still standing, isn't it?"

Dax chuckled softly. "Yeah," he said. "That's about all we can say about it, but it is still standing."

"And we *can* fix it if we all work together," she whispered. "We can."

The rocker creaked as he upped his tempo moving back and forth, then he stopped and cocked a suspicious brow at his oldest cousin. "You think the ghosts will stop coming if the house is gone, don't you?"

Nan swallowed thickly. "I don't know. But what if they did? That's our family heritage, Dax, and I won't give it up without a fight." She took a deep breath, blew it out slowly. "And I really don't want to ask all of our parents for help. Surely we can fix things around here on our own. There's six of us—that's plenty, don't you think?"

He grinned. "Hell, I guess it is."

Satisfied with that answer, she sighed, then looked toward the darkening sky. "What are we going to do if we get another big storm tonight? We can't afford to lose more tiles off the roof."

As if hearing her question, a low, rumbling thunder echoed over the Mississippi River, churning steadily on the other side of the levee. Then Nanette paused, knowing she may not have heard thunder after all. "Dax, did you hear it?"

Dax, obviously knowing what she suspected, nodded. "Yep, that one was real. No ghosts for you tonight, I guess."

Nanette swallowed. The cousins all had different identifiers that preceded their spirit visits. She heard thunder, deep, rolling thunder, exactly like what she heard now, except this thunder was real. And she'd much rather this had been an apparition, since she wasn't at all sure that the new tarp Gage and Dax had attached to the roof this morning would hold. Tristan, the oldest male of the bunch, hadn't been able to help, since he'd been on duty and assisting with a fire at a LaPlace apartment complex.

Nan stepped off the porch and squinted toward the blue

plastic that would supposedly protect the house from additional water damage. Hurricane Katrina had done a number on the old plantation, and unless Nanette convinced the Historical Society to help, they were liable to lose the fight to save the place from demolition. She wasn't about to let that happen.

Carving a few green slivers off the end of a sugar cane reed, Dax grinned at his fuming cousin. "Calm down, Nan. It's a storm, not another hurricane, and the tarp can take it. I promise."

"But that's just it. Another hurricane will come, maybe not today, but someday, and we're not ready. The foundation isn't as strong as it used to be, the roof is barely hanging on and the first floor still fills with mud and water every time it rains. There's no way we're going to keep the house from being torn down if we don't get things fixed, and fixed right. And the next thing we have to fix—and soon—is the roof. *When* the roofers decide to show," she added.

"You really think they're going to keep coming out here to do those mini-patches? It doesn't pay enough, and they know we haven't got the money for new tiles yet," Dax said, stating the obvious.

She frowned, her throat tightening at the thought of losing the sugar cane plantation that their family had nurtured over two centuries, the place where so many spirits had found their way home. Would the demolition of the house mean the end of Vicknair mediums? And could she ever forgive herself if she didn't keep that from happening? It'd taken all of the insurance money to dredge the sludge from the bottom floor after Katrina, and they still hadn't removed it all. Now more could easily come in, and they were tapped out.

"We need that money from the Historical Society," she said. "Unfortunately, at their last meeting President Roussel decided to proclaim this place an eyesore and a potential disaster area, which made them move our roof inspection up. Now we only have two weeks, and that's if they don't decide to come sooner."

"How cocky Roussel got elected Parish President is still beyond me," Dax said.

"He got elected because, cocky or not, he brought the females of the parish out in record numbers to vote."

Dax simply shook his head. "I don't get it."

"He's nice on the eyes," she admitted, then held up her palms defensively when Dax raised his brows. "Not that I care. He's still the jerk that's trying to take our house. I'm simply stating a fact."

"Well, I still don't see it, but I do know why he's talking the house down to that historical bunch. It's because his brother doesn't want us to one-up his place." He rolled his head slowly from shoulder to shoulder, making a mess of his brown wavy hair. "Hey, we can't help it that Johnny Roussel decided to buy the place next to ours. And we sure can't help it if he's worried we'll eventually get it restored completely, and no one will pay any attention whatsoever to that big old pond and stupid water fountain he put in his front yard. I'm telling you, if you ask me, it's his place that's an eyesore, not ours, and that pond is nothing but a mosquito magnet."

Nanette smiled. Dax never failed to cheer her up, even if she knew Johnny and Charles Roussel were determined to make her life—correction, all of their lives—miserable.

"Well, it doesn't look like we're getting any roofers today." She folded her arms as she examined the blue plastic product of Dax and Gage's handiwork. "You think the Roussels paid them not to come?"

Dax laughed throatily. "Hell, probably," he said, "but that tarp will hold. You wait and see."

"I'm counting on it," she said. "We need to eventually get started on the structural repairs, and we'll never get to it if we keep having to bail water out of the attic and patch the third floor's ceilings. The roof is definitely our first priority now. It's no fun going to sleep at night wondering if I'm going to get an impromptu shower."

She surveyed the edges of the plastic, tucked beneath the outer edge of the roof tiles. "You know, if Grandma Adeline hadn't decided that she *had* to have slate tiles on this roof, the Landmark Society in New Orleans would have tarped this thing for us."

"Yep," Dax agreed, then shrugged. "But she liked the tiles."

"I know," Nan said. "Obviously she didn't realize that the groups offering roof aid after Katrina would only provide help for soft roofs. Soft roofs. Why would you want plain old shingles when you can have slate tiles?"

"Sounds like you're agreeing with Grandma Adeline," Dax mused. "Even if she is causing us to have to fix our own roof."

"Yeah." Nan stole another glance at the aged gray tiles peeking from beneath the blue plastic. "They do add to the house's appeal, even if they didn't stand the test of the hurricane."

"It hit land at category four. Not much of anything stood that test, and we're getting things cleaned up." He stopped cutting his cane reed, an afternoon treat he'd snatched from their fields. "You want me to do something else tonight? I mean, it is my day off, so I probably shouldn't have called it quits on the roof so soon."

"Am I that bad?" She shook her head. "No, I don't want you to do anything else. You and Gage worked all day on that tarp. Gage didn't even get to rest before heading to the hospital, so no, I don't want you doing anything else but relaxing tonight. And I think you're right, anyway, the tarp will hold against a regular storm."

"Good, cause I really wasn't looking forward to getting back on that ladder in the dark," he said, chewing on the end of the sweet reed.

But his comment caused Nan to survey the sky, the churning gray clouds growing darker and more ominous by the minute. Where was Monique?

"Besides," Dax continued, "I'll probably get a personal note from Grandma Adeline tonight or tomorrow, judging from the kids I've heard today."

"You've heard children today?" Nan asked, interested in Dax's next assignment. She'd been two weeks without helping with a crossing and was probably due one herself, but she hadn't heard any thunder lately, other than the real rumbles currently joining blinding white flashes of lightning above the levee.

"I'm hearing girls," Dax said. "They're laughing and talking, but I can't tell what they're saying. I'm sure I'll figure it out after I get my letter. I checked the sitting room earlier, just in case, but there wasn't anything on the platter."

"Well, there is now," Nanette said, "And it's got Monique's name on it." A single raindrop plopped on her head, and she stepped back up on the porch to move beneath the shelter of its canopy. "I bet her skin has been burning all day, but has she come home? No indeed."

Dax merely shook his head. "She hasn't ever liked what we do, Nanette. And it isn't as though she had a choice in the matter. None of us did. We were simply born into it. I don't mind it, and neither do you, but helping the spirits really isn't her thing. I'd say she damn near hates it. If I were you, I'd cut my sister some slack. She told me she hasn't been with a man in six months, said Granny won't let her," he added, chuckling, "and that's a long time for Monique."

"I haven't been with one in two years," Nan argued, "and I'm doing okay."

"I'd say that depends on who's doing the judging." Dax's mouth curled in a knowing grin. "You seem rather stressed."

"I agree," Jenee said, slamming the screen door behind her as she entered the porch. She moved a black elastic band off her wrist and quickly pulled her long brown mane up in a high ponytail before plopping into the rocker next to Dax. The picture of a college student in the summer, Jenee wore a pale-pink T-shirt that showed a small section of tan midriff and a pair of tiny khaki shorts that showcased long Vicknair legs. No doubt about it, the family did okay in the genes arena, even if those genes did include an uncanny ability to communicate with ghosts. "You're always stressed, Nan," Jenee continued. "You really should lighten up."

Jenee, the absolute youngest of the bunch at twenty-one, was constantly on Nan about relaxing and had even bought her the largest gift set of stress relief aromatherapy that she could find last Christmas.

Nanette had not been amused.

"Listen, the entire reason I tried so hard to get Monique to move back in the house was so she'd actually show up when she received Grandma Adeline's call, but it doesn't matter. She still takes her sweet time, like always, even though I know her skin must be on fire. Granny doesn't take well to being put on hold. That time she needed me in the middle of giving my ninth graders their final exam, I heard more than mere thunder. A full-blown tornado took over my head, complete with hurled cars, uprooted trees and toppled houses." She shot another look at the driveway, as though she could magically force Monique's flaming-red convertible

Mustang to streak down the lane. "But if I can get home when Grandma Adeline calls, I do. Unlike Monique."

"At least she's living here now," Jenee said. "You have to admit she's gotten better about showing up since she gave up her New Orleans apartment and moved back."

"I actually think it'd be better if we all lived here, particularly while we're working to save the house," Nanette said. "The more Vicknair presence we show to the Historical Society, the better."

"You know Tristan can't live here." Jenee was quick to defend her brother's choice of living in nearby LaPlace. "He has to be near the fire station."

Resignedly, Nanette nodded. "I know, but there's no excuse for Gage not being here now, while we're trying to prove our case for saving the house."

"You think Gage, traipsing in and out with a different girl on his arm every night, would actually be an asset to the way the house is presented?" Dax asked. "Come on. He likes his freedom, and we'll all get more sleep around here if he's living in his bachelor pad. Besides, he's constantly getting called to the hospital, and he needs to be close enough to get there in an emergency. You've got four out of six of us. Seems that'd be enough to convince that demolition bunch that the Vicknairs are here to stay."

"Well, it sure hasn't convinced them yet," Nan mumbled. "And we only have two weeks before Charles Roussel sends them out here to re-evaluate the house and make sure it's not a hazard to the parish. I told them we'd have the roof fixed by then since we're supposed to do that anyway for the Historical Society, so we *have* to get it fixed. We can't let them tear this place down. This is where the spirits come for help. They need the house. They need us. And personally, I'd say it's a definite conflict of interest for the Parish President to be on the historical board, since he's also heading up the committee determining which houses are hazardous post-hurricane. It's a sad excuse for local government, if you ask me." She shot another despairing look down the drive. "You know what's really sad? Monique is the only one who currently has an assignment, and she's ignoring it."

"Don't worry," Dax said. "Like I said, I can feel one coming."

Jenee's rocker creaked as she propped her bare feet on the porch rail, closed her eyes and leaned back. Her neck rested on the highest wooden slat and her long ponytail draped over the back like a silky light-brown veil. "Not me," she said. "I haven't had a dream about spirits in nearly a month. I guess Granny hasn't needed me lately. If I had known, I would've headed to the beach for a long vacation during my summer break."

"As opposed to staying here and helping us get the house ready for inspection?" Nan asked.

Jenee's face reddened slightly. She eased one brown eye open and flashed an impish grin at Nan. "No, I wouldn't really have gone, but you have to admit, the timing would've been right, given I've had a month of no ghosts."

"Yeah," Dax agreed. "You've been a while. Maybe Grandma Adeline is giving you a chance to read that stack of psycho books in your room."

"They're psychology textbooks," Jenee said, opening both eyes to glare at him. "And I have read them."

"Learned anything yet?" he teased.

"As a matter of fact, my psychology classes are helping me learn more about why the spirits act the way they do, and they'll help me get a job in social services, too, wise guy."

"That sounds great, Jenee," Nanette said, smiling. Like Nan, Jenee had always known what career she'd pursue as an adult. She wanted to be a social worker; specifically she wanted to help troubled teens. Monique, on the other hand, had tried the waitress bit, then college at UNO and had finally found her niche in cosmetology school. She'd gone back to waitressing long enough to save money for a down payment for her shop, then opened Monique's Masterpieces and had flourished ever since. Monique's hair salon didn't have any correlation whatsoever to her spirit-helping nature, but then again, Monique didn't exactly enjoy helping the spirits, so it made sense that she'd selected a career that didn't help them, either. "Where is Monique?" Nanette hissed, squinting at the empty gravel drive.

"I'm sure she's on her way," Dax said, with a hint of laughter in the words. "Hey, I'd really like to go out to the field and snap off a couple more reeds before the storm hits so I'll have something to satisfy my midnight sweet tooth, but I can stay here and protect my sister from the storm of your wrath if need be." He smiled at Nanette, and her annoyance faded—slightly.

"Oh, I won't be too rough on her," she said, then added, "Bring me some, too, if you don't mind. I could use a dose of pure sugar."

"Don't mind at all." Dax nodded to Jenee. "Want to come? Or are you going to stay for the fireworks?"

"Are you kidding?" she asked, jumping from her rocker. It moved wildly back and forth as she ran to catch up with her cousin. "If we hear a Cajun cat fight, we'll be right back," she said to Nan.

"Oh, go on," Nan said, waving her away, as the telltale puff of smoke at the end of the darkened drive signalled that Monique Vicknair had finally decided to come home. "Well, it's about time."

2

THUNDER BOOMED and lightning cracked as Monique gunned the car down the drive to enter the stately sugar plantation that she'd called home for the majority of her life. Granted, it wasn't nearly as impressive as it had been before Katrina had mercilessly borne down on Louisiana, but even with the dingy porch columns and the blue tarp roof, it still commanded attention. It definitely commanded Monique's attention right now, because she had to get to the house, specifically to the second-floor sitting room, and open her grandmother's letter.

Big, fat drops of rain fell between overlapping magnolia branches to plunk on her head and cause her blond—or rather, sand—bangs to fall limp into her eyes. *Sand.* Had he really thought that was a compliment that would turn her on? No matter, Monique realized, since Grandma Adeline hadn't given any regard to whether Monique was in the process of being turned on, or off, at the time of her summons.

The rain grew harder, and she sped forward. Monique wished that she'd had the wherewithal to raise the convertible's top at the last stop sign. Now her leather seats were soaked, and tomorrow, the whole interior would have to be babied to the max to keep it from smelling like mildew. Just great. Not to mention the fact that tonight, she'd deal with a ghost, a ghost that had evidently been waiting for her arrival and was probably pissed. Nothing like an enraged specter to make an already lousy night complete.

She blinked through the water making small wet paths down her face and saw two shadows darting from the nearest cane field to the house. Dax and Jenee, she wagered, out snatching sugar cane for an evening snack. And she'd also wager that the shadow leaning against the porch post with folded arms, a cascade of pitch-black hair down her back and her shoulders held stern, was Nanette. And a none-too-happy Nanette at that. Well, fine. Monique never asked for this job, and she sure wasn't going to take any flack from Nanette for her almost-orgasm at Pierre's place.

After parking the car, she heard another sound, a ripping noise mingling with the thunder. A determined gust of wind brutally whipped at the plastic currently sheltering their roof. Lord, she hoped the thing held. She wasn't in the mood for climbing ladders and trying, once again, to make sure their dilapidated mansion stood yet another test of time. When were those historical folks going to give them the money they needed to keep the place standing?

Nanette stepped out into the rain and turned her attention from Monique to the noisy tarp.

Monique climbed out of the car and quickly worked to get the top up and cover her leather. Dax and Jenee joined in her effort.

"The tarp will hold, Nanette!" Dax yelled, gritting his teeth as he fought to clamp down one side of the Mustang's top. "Get on the porch and out of the rain." Then he turned toward Monique and Jenee, and in a tone that made it clear that he'd just declared himself the man in charge, he continued, "Go on. I've got this."

Monique's brows drew together, but she was hurting too

bad, burning too much, to argue. She did need to get inside, and get to that letter. When rain this hard actually felt good on her sizzling skin, it was high past time to answer the summons. Obviously, from the scowl on Nan's face, she was way, way past time.

"I know you felt it." Nan had to raise her voice to be heard over the rain pattering against the tarp-covered roof and splatting loudly on the stone steps leading to the house. Tiny channels in the grass-deprived yard were already sending streams of watery mud toward the edge of the house. "Why didn't you come when she called you?" she asked, frowning at Monique and then at the muddy ground.

Monique glared at her and silently dared her oldest cousin to spout any more accusatory remarks. "I was on the verge of great sex," she said, her skin burning more fiercely with every step. Even the thin fabric from her dress, rubbing against her rain-dampened skin, stung like a hot iron. She needed to get to that letter. Now.

"You can't ignore it anymore. You have to come when she calls," Nan said, as Monique struggled to cross the deep width of the porch. Breathing was difficult when her flesh burned so fiercely.

Jenee quickly moved to open the door for her, but Monique stopped walking.

"Don't," Monique managed, swallowing through her parchment-dry mouth. "Don't you dare start with me tonight, Nan. I'm here, aren't I?"

Nan blinked, then her jaw softened, and she frowned. "I'm sorry," she said. "It's the roof and the house and the mud and the Roussel brothers. Everything got me worked up, and then you didn't come."

"I'm here now, and I really have to get inside. I don't like this, Nan. You know I don't." Monique licked the rain from her lips to gather what moisture she could. "But I'm here."

"Yes," Nan agreed. "You are." She gave her a soft, apologetic smile, and Monique nodded her acceptance, then let Jenee guide her into the house, past the big sheets of plastic that closed off most of the first floor and up the stairs toward the sitting room.

Dax called, "No need to worry! The top's back on your car, sis."

"That's good," Monique said, removing her shoes at the top of the stairs. Her feet were aflame, and she wasn't going to be able to walk much further. Luckily, the sitting room was only a few more steps.

"You okay?" Jenee asked, as they crossed the threshold to the lovely rose-tinted room where Grandma Adeline had spent thousands of hours fine-tuning her knitting skills. It was the only room in the house that maintained the same lush appearance that the entire home had had prior to the hurricane. While the remainder of the house had suffered the full brunt of the storm, this room had remained unscathed, evidently protected by Adeline Vicknair, or some other powerful spirits.

Seeing the familiar lavender envelope, Monique entered the room, stumbled onto the red velvet settee and lifted her grandmother's summons from the shiny silver tray. Immediately, an icy waterfall of coolness quenched her sweltering flesh, washing over her like a blanket of comfort. The fiery burn was over—this time. Monique licked her lips, closed her eyes and smiled. "I'm okay now."

"I'll get you something to drink," Jenee said, turning to go, then stopping abruptly at the door. "Or is your ghost here already?"

Monique squinted one eye open and peered around the room. She hadn't even thought to look for her assigned specter when she entered, hadn't thought of anything beyond touching the letter and feeling at ease again. But now she did, and she saw no one. "No ghosts yet."

"Okay. I'll be right back with some lemonade." As Jenee quickly retreated, Dax and Nanette stuck their heads around the door.

"You made it in okay?"

"Feel better now?"

"You can come in. My ghost hasn't arrived yet," Monique said, chilled from the damp dress clinging against her skin. To think, she'd been feverish only seconds ago, but now that she held the letter, her flesh bristled with coolness.

She lifted the envelope marked with her name, then held it to her nose and inhaled her grandmother's favorite scent, magnolias. Monique wished this part of the whole spirit-helping business didn't excite her, but it did. Not that she'd ever admit that to Nan. She'd told Nanette the truth; she *didn't* like the way her medium status controlled her life. It was a pain—literally—when she had to stop what she was doing and heed the summons. Still, she'd be lying if she said this part of her family duty didn't excite her, wondering whose information was on the pages within and how she would influence their passage to the other side. However, Monique also knew that she was better off not caring too much about the individual. She'd complete her task then she'd move on. Getting attached to spirits wasn't part of her plan. Too much opportunity to get hurt, and Monique didn't plan on getting burned by a spirit. Burned by a spirit—a funny way of looking at it, given she burned every time one called.

"Here you go." Jenee wedged past Dax and Nanette to hand Monique a big glass of lemonade filled with ice and a round slice of lemon nestled in the middle.

"That looks wonderful," Monique said, accepting the

glass, while the wind beat in a maddening rush against the side of the house and the walls creaked in immediate response to the onslaught.

"You sure that tarp will hold?" Nan asked Dax.

"Man, I hope so," he answered. "But it probably wouldn't hurt for us to keep an eye on it."

"I agree," she said. "If we see it start to give, maybe we can climb up there and keep it tethered long enough for the storm to pass."

Jenee's nose wrinkled as she shook her head. "No way can I climb a ladder in the middle of a storm. I do good enough to stay on one that's stable, and in broad daylight." She grinned, then added, "But I'll hold it while you do."

Nan laughed. "Gee, thanks."

Dax turned toward Monique before the three of them left to witness how his tarp was weathering the storm. "You all set?"

"I'm fine," she said, waving them on. And she was. Now that the burning had stopped and she had the letter in hand, she was all set to take on this assignment, help some ghost find his or her way home, then return to her life in progress. And if she was lucky, return to Pierre Comeaux sometime in the not too distant future.

She ran her finger beneath the edge of the envelope and listened to the soft crack of the paper giving way as it opened. Then she withdrew three pages from inside. The first was her grandmother's letter on her usual pale purple stationery. Placing the two plain white sheets in her lap, Monique unfolded Adeline's request. A cut lace border created a scalloped edge around the page and instantly reminded Monique that this piece of paper had somehow traversed the boundary between the living and the dead and, in the process, provided her another chance to communicate with her feisty grandmother. "Hello, Granny," she whispered, then laughed when she saw the big blank space in the center of the page.

Adeline Vicknair had passed on when Monique was ten. During the decade when they'd both lived on this side, Monique had made it no secret that she wasn't enamored with the family duty of helping spirits. She'd told her grandmother on plenty of occasions that she'd do it if she had to, but she wouldn't like it, and she wanted to know as little as possible about the ghosts that she helped. Thankfully, Grandma Adeline had taken her granddaughter's comments to heart, as evidenced by the empty 'Reason for Death' section on the page. She knew Monique didn't want to know how the ghost died. She simply wanted to get the job done and get back to her life.

Taking a deep breath, Monique read the information at the top of the page.

Name of Deceased—Ryan Chappelle.

Monique had a female customer at her salon whose name was Ryan; she also had two male customers with the same name. She wondered whether this ghost was male, as she'd suspected earlier. Not that it mattered. She'd do her job, either way, and then she'd hope she wouldn't be summoned for, oh, a good year. In her dreams. She'd never gone more than three weeks without Grandma Adeline "doing her thing." Monique let her eyes roam to the remaining information, written in her grandmother's swirling script, at the bottom of the page.

Requirement for Passage—Learning to Love.

Monique blinked, squinted at the words, then frowned. Learning to love? What did that mean? Her previous assignments had been basically the same. They were all relationship problems and typically involved the same directive. Forgive spouse. Hug mother. Tell a child that he or she was loved. Tell a parent that he or she was loved. Something along those lines. But *learning* to love? And did that mean that the ghost Monique was about to be saddled with for however long it took for her to sort the problem out, usually a couple of days, was some kind of non-loving, uncaring weirdo?

"Come on, Granny, what were you thinking?" she asked, as a loose shutter flapped smartly against the side of the house. Monique turned to stare at the window generating the noise and wondered if her grandmother was able to do that from up there.

Probably.

"Okay," Monique said with a sigh, "I didn't say I wouldn't do it. I'm just a little surprised you sent this one my way."

Twisting back around on the settee, she flipped the purple page over, placed it on the armrest, then moved to the second sheet. As usual, it listed rules for dealing with the spirits. Monique could recite them by heart, but she was required to read the pages in their entirety before her assignment officially began.

She paused when she got to the no-touching rule. When had it been added? The first few guidelines seemed extremely professional, then the last one appeared to have been tacked on at some point over the years. She wondered which of her ancestors had caused the modification. Whoever it was, she'd bet that she'd inherited a good portion of those genes.

"I'm not the first rebel Vicknair."

A loud clatter caused her to jerk her head toward the window once more. That loose shutter had to be fixed, and soon. The thing was going to drive her over the edge. It was bad enough that she was wet and cold, not to mention starving, since she'd never got to taste the first bite of Pierre's crawfish étouffée, but now her nerves were frazzled too, courtesy of a rattling shutter.

When the thing finally banged its way back into place, she scanned the room once more and determined that her ghost was evidently taking his or her sweet time. If she had known, she'd have gotten in at least one encounter with Pierre. Then again, if she had waited any longer, her body would have flat-out burst into flames, no doubt about it. Nope, she'd returned home, like Adeline Vicknair wanted, so that damn ghost had better show up and let her get started.

Monique placed the sheet of rules on top of Grandma Adeline's letter so she could view the final page, the official document directing her grandmother to assign Ryan Chappelle to one of her grandchildren. It amazed Monique that the powers that be on the other side distributed their assignments as though sending a modern e-mail.

To: Adeline Vicknair, Grand Matriarch of Vicknair Mediums
From: Lionelle Dewberry, Gatekeeper First Class
Cc: Board of Directors, Realm Entrance Governing Squadron
Subject: Case # 19-01-6418—Ryan Chappelle
Current Status—Access Denied.
Required Rectification—Proof that claimant can achieve emotional love.
Time Allotted for Rectification—Nine days.

Monique's jaw dropped. Nine days? No way was she hanging out with a ghost for over a week. The longest assignment she'd ever had was three days. Nine. Days.

No way. Wasn't happening.

She'd simply waste no time taking care of business, which,

in Ryan Chappelle's case, was teaching him how to love, as if Monique knew the first thing about it.

"Damnation." She shook her head at the irony. She'd never been in love, and she was pretty pleased at making it to twenty-four without having it happen. Sure, lots of Vicknairs before her had managed to handle the emotion and their family obligations. But Monique had never quite gotten close enough to a guy to tell him that she happened to spend a large portion of her life communing with the dead. Somehow, it rarely came up in conversation.

Go figure.

Today was Friday, so nine days would have this ghost's deadline…a week from Sunday. Why so long? Was this spirit that big a challenge?

Super.

She bit her lower lip and concentrated on the task at hand. She could do it; she had to, because she was *not* going to live with a ghost as her shadow for nine days. She wasn't. She couldn't. Because that would obviously mean that she'd have to go another week without sex, and dammit, she'd waited long enough.

Speaking of which, she'd forgotten to buy a supply of batteries today at Wal-Mart, and from the look of the storm brewing outside her window, she wouldn't be able to swipe any from the flashlights without them being missed.

"Where are you, ghost? The quicker you get here, the quicker you leave." She squinted at the remaining information, the standard this-is-why-we-won't-let-them-in spiel, and recited aloud, "Regarding Case 19-01-6418, aka Ryan Chappelle, based on the unanimous recommendation of the Board of Directors, the aforementioned has been denied access beyond the realm due to his inability to achieve love throughout twenty-eight years of earth inhabitation."

Monique glared at the page, swallowed hard, and then continued, "While claimant has experienced his share (and then some) of physical bonding, he refused to open his heart to love. Thereby, the Board sees no reason to grant access to a spirit who cannot love. The Board has generously provided an adequate span of time for claimant to attempt to rectify the reason for denial. We believe this period, nine days, to be sufficient; however, if the assigned medium feels this calculation to be in error, a standard Form 489-074320-78X, *Request for Modification of Rectification Period*, may be submitted to the Medium Grievance Counsel for review. As with all assignments, should the claimant refuse or be unable to complete the assigned task within the rectification period, that individual's ability to gain access beyond the realm will be irrevocably denied."

Monique groaned toward the ceiling. "Granny, this would have been a great time to fill out one of those modification forms. Nine days is ridiculous." Her eyes moved to the center of the paragraph and she repeated, "While claimant has experienced his share (and then some) of physical bonding, he refused to open his heart to love."

His share. So, Ryan was male, and a male who had experienced a surplus of physical bonding. In other words, he liked sex. Well here was a newsflash for the powers that be—so did she. And to get this guy out of her life and conveniently placed on the other side, where he belonged, she had to teach him that there was more to a relationship than sex?

"How am I, Monique Vicknair, the woman who has been craving an honest-to-goodness, rock-my-world, curl-my-toes orgasm from something other than a vibrator for a good six months, supposed to convince this guy that there's more to life than just sex?" she spouted to the empty room.

Only the room wasn't empty anymore.

"Funny, that's exactly what I was going to ask," a deep, raspy and extremely Southern voice drawled from behind the settee.

Monique gasped, winced, then slowly—very, very slowly—turned to view the owner of the sexy voice. *Mon dieu*, he took her breath away. Definitely male. There was nothing at all feminine about this Ryan.

Nothing. At. All.

As with every other ghost she'd ever encountered, his appearance was like any living individual, except for a faint shimmering glow outlining his features. And mercy, what features they were. Dark hair, long on top, short on the sides, with sideburns that teased a strong jawline and accented a wide, smirking smile that made her stomach quiver. His eyes were jet-black within a forest of equally black-lashes, but then again, all ghosts had black eyes. That was one of the things Monique never asked the spirits—the color of their eyes—but this time, she couldn't stop from wondering whether his were green or brown or blue. Blue. She imagined a vivid baby-blue iris in the midst of that sea of black lashes.

Monique fought the impulse to ask the color. What was she doing, fantasizing over this guy's—correction, this ghost's—face? Besides, why would any woman in her right mind stop at the face, when the body was an equally mesmerizing tribute to the male gender?

Muscles on his muscles, that would be Jenee's description of the biceps bulging against the sleeves of his white T-shirt, the broad shoulders and sturdy chest that defined raw power and the chiseled abs, visible in spite of the soft cotton covering. Add slim hips and muscled thighs encased in blue denim and Monique could almost come from staring. Nine days looking at this and not having sex? Since when had Grandma Adeline gotten into torture?

"I see I'm underdressed for the occasion," he said, and that sexy Southern drawl rolled over her skin like hot cocoa butter. Where was this ghost from, anyway? Not that she wanted to know. That was personal information, and she didn't get into learning details about her spirits. But if she knew where he was from, maybe she could find out if there were any men of the living persuasion still hanging around town who happened to look like him, sound like him, and affect her libido like him.

"Underdressed?" she mumbled, her mouth suddenly very dry again.

"Compared to you." He indicated her red dress, stuck to her body like shrink wrap due to the rain. "I can remedy that," he said, and as Monique watched, his T-shirt and jeans slowly transformed to a black tuxedo, dashing and debonair and dangerous. "Better?" he asked, moving around the settee to casually sit on the other side, merely a plush pillow away from Monique.

Better? her mind questioned. *Better?* Heaven help her if she ever saw anything better than this. How did you top perfection? Monique didn't know, and she sure wasn't about to answer his question now. She might accidentally drool. If she'd had an orgasm with Pierre, maybe she wouldn't be so turned on by this semi-glowing male specter.

She blinked. Who was she kidding? She'd have to be dead not to be turned on right now. But even dead, she'd still find herself panting over Ryan Chappelle. No doubt about it.

"Then again," he said, "Were you dressed this way for my arrival, or was it for sex? Because from your statement when I entered, that you've been craving a real orgasm for six months, I bet that you've been pretty anxious to have a—" His eyes smoldered, and his voice lowered, easing each word out for emphasis. "—good, slow and easy—" His grin broadened. "—or hard, hot and heated tangle beneath the sheets."

Monique couldn't speak. If she didn't gather her bearings, she might forget to breathe. What could she say? Yes to all of the above? How many times, and when could they start? Monique could *feel* the fact that he wanted her, and she had no doubt that he could sense the same lust from her side of the fence. *Mon dieu*, the bonding rule was meant to help the medium connect with the spirit, to understand the ghost's needs for crossing, and to fulfill them. But she'd never sensed this type of need before. Pure, powerful desire. And she knew that wasn't the type of need she was supposed to fulfill. She couldn't touch a spirit, ever. That had always seemed a simple rule, until now.

What had she done for Grandma Adeline to do her this way? Giving her perfection in a beautiful male package—on a night she was horny as all get-out—and knowing she couldn't touch. Monique wanted to scream. Loudly.

"Did I mess that up for you tonight, Monique? Did I ruin your chance for an honest-to-goodness, rock-my-world—"

She held up her palms. "That's enough. I remember the rest." And hearing him say it out loud certainly wasn't going to help.

He smiled knowingly and placed his arm against the back of the couch so that it came close, very close, to where her back rested against the red velvet. "Because if I did ruin that for you tonight, I'm very sorry, and I promise to find some way to make it up to you," he continued, those black eyes drinking her in as though she was a shiny red apple and he was Adam, ready to take a big ol' bite.

Monique wanted to tell him that "making it up to her" wasn't necessary, that she was fine and could get her orgasm later, courtesy of the batteries that she was most certainly going to steal from the flashlights, whether the electricity went out or not. But the only words that wanted to slip from her lips were *Come on. Take a bite. Please.* Thank goodness for her limited self-control. Limited, because if she sat here by this devilishly handsome ghost for too long, she'd break every rule on that list and probably cause a few addendums for the next generation.

"Can I?" he asked. "Make it up to you?" That drawl reminded her of Harry Connick, Jr., and Monique so had a thing for Heavenly Harry. "I'd enjoy a little *taste*," he said.

No way. Their connection was happening fast—way too fast and way too damn strong—as if he'd read her thoughts. Had he? His smoldering black eyes said that if he hadn't, he'd at least known she was thinking *something*.

Monique had to get a grip on this situation, and she needed to get it fast. Move the conversation away from sex, move her mind away, not that he'd actually propositioned her or anything, but still…that's the way her brain, and most other parts of her anatomy, heard it, and she needed to get all of her two thousand parts focused on something else. Quick.

"How—how did you do that?" she asked.

"Do what?" His dark brows lifted with the question, and those intense eyes amazingly seemed to darken, so much that she couldn't tell where the iris ended and the pupil began.

"Change," she said, pointing to the tuxedo that had quickly taken his overall presentation from *Playgirl* centerfold to *GQ* cover in a span of seconds. Monique was a fan of both, so she really didn't care, but again, she had to get the conversation off anything sexual.

"When you've been living in the middle as long as I have, you learn how to make the most out of the perks," he explained, looking very out of place, all muscle and testosterone, claiming dominion over the predominantly pink and extremely girly sitting room. And over Monique.

Though it took some effort, she thought about his statement and realized part of it didn't make sense. Unfortunately, before she realized that asking the obvious question would provide too much insight into this ghost's past, she blurted it out loud.

"How long have you been in the middle?"

"Fourteen months," he answered automatically.

Fourteen—months? Monique hadn't even realized that was possible, and if he'd been there that long, why hadn't she already received him as an assignment? And what did a ghost do "in the middle" for over a year?

"Months?" she questioned, just to make sure she heard him right.

He nodded and gave her a sexy smile. "You see, I like it here, Monique. And I know Adeline expects you to convince me to make the transition, but I have no intention of crossing over. Ever. So, if you want to talk about something else, or if you want to do something else," he said, his black eyes glittering, "then I'm ready. But if you're wanting me to cross over, it isn't happening."

Monique could feel his determination, his flat-out resolve to stay on this side as long as he damn well pleased. She'd never sensed such sheer strength of will in a spirit, and she'd certainly never experienced the waves of barely harnessed desire, pulsing from his very soul with the intensity of a raging fire. And that inferno was spreading…to Monique.

What was Adeline Vicknair thinking?

3

If Ryan had known what was waiting at the end of his summons to meet with the assigned Vicknair medium, he wouldn't have put it off all afternoon. Little did he know a sassy hot fantasy in red was waiting to guide him to the other side. Regardless of the fact that he had no intention of going, he still wouldn't mind sharing a span of time with Monique Vicknair. Even better, she wanted the same thing.

Adeline Vicknair had told him that he would share a bond with his medium, as soon as that medium accepted Ryan's assignment. But he hadn't expected that tie to be so strong, so intense, so sexual.

He'd *felt* Monique the minute she opened the envelope, sensed her irritation at having her evening cut short, as well as her reluctance towards helping any spirits. But he'd also detected a hint of excitement, of a certain inner pride at her family's responsibility. True, she didn't like having to heed a spirit's call, but she reveled in the power to help in crossings. Whether she admitted it to the rest of the world or not, she couldn't deny it to Ryan. It was a powerful emotion. So powerful, in fact, that it almost seemed his own. Almost. This "bonding" that they shared was going to take some getting used to, particularly with Monique's emotions so exceptionally strong, so potent and mesmerizing.

And when he entered the room, he also recognized another powerful sensation emanating vigorously from the sexy female. Lust. Toward him.

Unfortunately, Adeline Vicknair had also told him about the rules for mediums.

Monique's arched blond brows drew together and her sweet little mouth opened and closed for the second time as she tried to determine how to respond to his declaration that he wouldn't cross over. This should be good. Obviously she hadn't met any ghosts who liked their in-between status; then again, she hadn't met him.

He liked his life the way it was, and if she thought she was going to change that, she'd better think again. He'd tried to explain things to Adeline, but the sweet older lady wouldn't take no for an answer, and she seemed to believe she had the "perfect grandchild" to help him out. Well, no doubt about it, Monique was perfect physically; however, if she expected to change his mind about heading toward the light, she was about to be disappointed. Sure, he might have stopped breathing fourteen months ago, but he hadn't stopped living, and he didn't plan to now.

He was having way too much fun.

"You don't want to cross over?" she finally asked, her eyes, like green-gold marbles, wide at the realization.

"No, ma'am," he said, laying on the accent that had charmed a throng of dreamers thicker than sorghum syrup. An audible gasp escaped her exquisite lips, and Ryan smiled. Monique Vicknair wasn't immune to Southern charm.

Good to know.

Her mouth quirked to the side as she seemed to process the facts. She took a deep breath. The action caused her already-tight dress to stretch even more across two beautifully high breasts, and from the firm little points pushing forward, she was either very cold or very excited—or, perhaps, both. Then she shivered, and Ryan's protective nature took over. You could take the guy out of the South, but you couldn't take the Southern manners out of the guy, or so his Aunt Elsa used to say.

"Obviously you were out in the rain," he said, reaching for a lush pink-and-sage throw folded neatly across a nearby chair. "How did you get so drenched? And why didn't you get out of your wet clothes?" He leaned toward her and draped the fuzzy cloth down the length of her body, cloaking those tempting nipples, that flat stomach and all that silky smooth skin.

Ryan's groin tightened. She really was exceptional.

Her hands gripped the top edge of the blanket, holding it against her chest while she hummed her contentment.

Ryan let the lower edge drop from his hands to rest against her legs. It was too short to cover her bare feet, and her red toenails and diamond toe ring stood out in stark contrast to the gleaming honey-toned floor. He frowned. "You didn't have shoes?"

"I was hot."

It'd have been so easy to ignore the innuendo behind the three little words, but Ryan wasn't into skipping out on fun. He moved his attention from her feet, and from wondering what it'd be like to kiss each of her toes, to her face. Then he scooted toward her on the settee and took quite a bit of pleasure in the way her throat pulsed in response. She may have been cold, but she was damn well excited, too. He could feel it so clearly, and that tantalizing knowledge brought his desire to near-combustible status.

"Trust me, Monique Vicknair, you're still hot," he said, and watched a red flush that nearly matched the bright hue of her dress tinge her cheeks.

"No," she said, visibly swallowing. "I meant that I was hot from my grandmother's summons, and my feet burned too much in my shoes." She looked at him as though waiting for a bounty of questions regarding her statement, but Ryan only had one.

"You were hot for me?" he asked, inching one brow up. "Ms. Vicknair, you hadn't even met me yet." He gave her an easy grin. "I knew I made a decent impression, but I had no idea I was that good."

She gave him an incredulous look that was downright adorable. "You have to be the cockiest ghost I've ever met, Mr. Chappelle," she said, matching his formal salutation and teasing his senses with the way that sweet mouth said his name.

"I prefer confident, ma'am," he said with a wink, "but cocky will do."

The tension in her body eased, and he could tell that Monique Vicknair was growing more and more accustomed to having him here, to having him near. Good, because he enjoyed being near Monique, and he planned on getting much, much nearer if she wanted. Judging from the way her body responded just to his suggestive teasing, and from her earlier proclamation that she really needed a good bout of sex, Ryan figured it was definitely what she wanted, even if she wasn't quite ready to take what she wanted…yet.

No problem. Ryan Chappelle was a patient man.

She laughed softly. "You realize that's the second time you've called me that."

"Called you what?" he asked.

"Ma'am. Around here, that's typically something kids call the elderly, or at least someone older than twenty-four. It's not something anyone's ever said to me before," she admitted.

"So, you're twenty-four," he said, nodding. "I'm twenty-eight, or four in dog years." Her responding laugh was exactly what he was hoping for. Monique Vicknair was becoming more relaxed around him, a ghost with a passion for pleasing women and an even stronger desire, at least for the moment, for learning what it took to please this particular female. "And for the record, where I come from, *ma'am* is a term of endearment." He edged forward and ran a finger down the cool curved handle of a silver teapot, placed to one side of an elegant tea service in the center of the coffee table. "So," he said, "are you going to ask me?"

"Ask you?"

"Where I'm from?"

A loud clap of thunder caused her to jump and reminded Ryan that the storm still churned outside, while another equally potent storm also raged within Monique. She wanted to know more about him, but she wasn't about to ask.

Monique doesn't want to know any details, Adeline had said. *She tries not to get too close to spirits, doesn't want to get attached,* the lady had explained, then she added, *It isn't anything personal.*

But it *was* personal, because Monique's determination to keep herself at a distance was exactly the kind of thing that had been missing in Ryan's current lifestyle, or deathstyle, as the case may be.

A challenge.

"I don't need to know where you're from," she said matter-of-factly. Then she scooted up on the settee, and the action made the papers balanced on the armrest fall to the floor. Monique dropped one edge of the blanket to reach for them, which exposed one breast, still very excited, from the look of things. His attention moved to the full globe pushing against the clingy red fabric of her dress. Was that hard little point pink? Blush? Cinnamon? And would he find out?

"I'll get them," he said, moving in front of her to gather the sheets of paper from the floor. When she reached for them, he didn't release his hold. Instead, he looked at Monique, saw the way her eyes smoldered and knew that, unless he was reading her totally wrong, he would definitely find out the color of those perfect points, maybe not tonight, but soon. Unfortunately, unless he was reading her totally wrong, he also saw more in her eyes. He saw hope. And he wasn't about to mislead Monique Vicknair.

"I'm not crossing over," he said, releasing the papers. "I don't want you to think that you can fix things for me, because in all honesty, nothing's broken. However, if you want to spend some time together, I'm more than interested."

She blinked, glanced at her grandmother's letter. "Why don't you want to cross? And why haven't you crossed already?" Shaking her head, she added, "I really don't understand."

"It isn't so bad in the middle. It's pretty damn good, in fact," he said, smiling. Truth was, he'd worked too hard to get the most out of life early on, to keep from making the same mistake as his parents made. But then…the accident. He swallowed, determined not to think about it. Now he was making the most of his current situation, enjoying the fact that he hadn't crossed over and enjoying even more the fact that he could still please women. Right now, he very much wanted to embrace that ability with Monique.

"So why are you here?" she asked.

Ryan had no choice but to give her the truth; ghosts couldn't lie. "Adeline. She's apparently made it her mission to get me through. She's the one who told me I couldn't cross because I'd never loved." He shrugged. "I told her—several times—that I made it through my rather short lifespan without losing my heart, and I sure didn't plan on breaking that streak just because I happened to stop breathing. Besides, if I lost my heart now, I'd cross over, and then all of this would end."

Monique placed the papers on the coffee table, then cuddled back into the soft blanket, eyeing Ryan suspiciously. "All of what would end? What have you been doing for the past fourteen months?"

Ryan had known she would ask, and he was prepared to answer. He just didn't know whether Monique Vicknair would believe the truth.

No time like the present to find out.

"I've been fulfilling fantasies," he said.

She didn't look convinced. "Fulfilling your fantasies? In the middle? How?"

"Do you ever dream, Monique?" he asked. "Dreams that are so vivid, so clear, that you wake up and try to determine whether it was imagined, or whether it was real?"

"Sure," she said, "Most everyone does. What has that got to do with your fantasies?"

"Not my fantasies, necessarily," he clarified, then cleared his throat and prepared to explain the bizarre twist his life had taken fourteen months ago. "Sometimes, when women have those dreams, the sexual ones about a mystery man who fulfills their every fantasy, the dreams where they wake up hot and heated and completely satisfied…" he said, watching the tender pulse throb softly in her throat as she listened.

"When women have those dreams…" she prompted.

"It isn't their imagination."

She sat silent, while the rain beat a steady cadence against the room's elongated windows. Then her teeth slowly grazed her lower lip, and she brought those green-gold eyes to meet his.

"You can do that?" she finally asked, the words husky and raw, as though she were forcing them to be spoken. "You can—invade a woman's dreams?" she asked again, and her tone wasn't so much intrigued as appalled.

Hell. "No," he said, attempting to move closer, and dismayed to see her trying to scoot further away. "I can't invade a woman's dreams. I can only be with a woman who lets me in, a woman who wants me there and essentially calls me to fulfill her fantasy."

"What was Granny thinking?" she whispered, clutching the blanket and pressing the gathered material against her throat. The action exposed the sweet curves of her calves. Ryan wanted to trace those curves, kiss them, lick them.

Monique's eyes abruptly widened, and she shifted the afghan to cover her legs. Had she sensed his thoughts?

"Women call you? How?"

Okay. At least her tone had converted from disgusted to curious. That was an improvement. And why should his ability to please women disgust her, anyway? He was only giving them what they wanted. And whom did it hurt that he enjoyed giving it? Besides, he didn't need Monique Vicknair's approval for the way he'd spent the past fourteen months, or for the way he'd spend the next fourteen, or the fourteen after that. But for some bizarre reason, he had to admit that he wanted her approval, very much. And he wanted to stroke those calves. The rules said she couldn't touch him; they said nothing whatsoever about him touching her, Ryan realized with extreme satisfaction *and* a strong desire to touch her. All over.

She gripped the blanket like a lifeline, and Ryan fought the urge to laugh. Obviously, she could sense his desire, but she needn't worry. Ryan would never force himself on any woman. No, he'd wait—until she asked.

"How do they call you?" she repeated. "What do you mean,

exactly? Do they know your name? And that you're the one in their dreams?"

"No," he said, taking a great deal of pleasure in this conversation. He hadn't had anyone to talk to about the way he spent his time in the middle. And knowing—sensing—that she was, in fact, now intrigued by it made the explanation even more fun. "They simply go to sleep wishing they had a dark, handsome stranger to take care of—things. If they really want me there, I can help their fantasies be as real as possible."

"You actually have sex with them?" she blurted.

"If you mean intercourse, the answer is no," he answered quickly, and was very pleased to see, and feel, her aggressiveness dissipate. "But if you mean do I help push them over the edge, bring them to orgasm with the right words or the right touch, then yes."

"Touch," she whispered, her eyes inadvertently moving to the pages on the table.

"Those rules are yours," he reminded her softly, "not mine."

"So you can touch," she said, her voice barely above a whisper, "and be touched?"

"Yes." He watched her mouth crook to the side. "Does that bother you?"

"That you don't have to follow the rules?" she asked, then answered, "No, not really. I'm just surprised."

"No," Ryan said. "Does it bother you that I've helped quite a few women achieve earth-shattering orgasms over the past fourteen months?"

Her shoulders lifted slightly. "I admit that the thought of a man, ghost or not, having sex with a woman while she sleeps doesn't exactly float my boat." She paused. "But the thought of a ghost who has no problems helping you get an earth-shattering orgasm in your dreams is rather, well, exciting." The corners of her mouth curved upward slightly, and her eyes grew heavy-lidded. She was thinking about it, thinking about him.

"Something you would want, Monique?" he asked, his manhood stiffening slightly at the possibility.

Her head seemed to shake on its own accord, as if she couldn't fathom saying yes. "No. And don't get me wrong," she quickly added. "I admit I'm tempted to ask you to show me exactly what you're talking about. You already know I haven't had sex in six months," she said bluntly.

The woman had no qualms talking sex, which was undeniably sexy. He envisioned her in bed telling him exactly what she liked, what she didn't. How fast. How slow. How hard.

"But even if those aren't your rules," she continued, "Like you said, they're still mine. And I don't even know what the consequences would be if I broke them."

Ryan considered telling her that the no-touching rule didn't say anything about the spirit touching the medium, but he decided to wait. She wasn't ready to give him permission to do it yet, and in any case, he didn't want to tell her what he could do. It'd be much more fun to show her.

The grandfather clock that centered the room's two heavily draped windows began to chime loudly.

"Midnight," she said, eyeing the clock. "I assume that counts as one day of your nine."

"I assume it does," Ryan agreed. "But it doesn't matter, I'm not in any hurry. Like I told you, I'm not crossing."

"Problem is," Monique said, standing up and draping the blanket around her shoulders like a fluffy shawl, "even though I may not like it, I told my grandmother that I'd help the spirits. She's counting on me to help you, and evidently, she believes you need to cross over."

She liked helping spirits more than she admitted. He noted the determined set of her jaw, the way her eyes focused on him as though he were Mount Everest, and she was getting set to reach the summit. This woman wasn't going to give up without a fight.

Ryan couldn't wait.

"You're destined to cross," she said, "And I'm destined to make it happen."

"Never thought much of destiny," he said, then couldn't hold back his grin at her glare. "And I never thought much of rules." She wouldn't think much of rules, either, if she realized he had the upper hand. He *could* touch.

She lifted her chin and said resolutely, "I've never thought much of rules, either, if I'm going to be honest about it. But my grandmother assigned you to me, so she must think I'm able to get you through to the other side. For some strange reason, she believes I can teach you how to love, and I really don't want to let her down."

"Because deep down, you don't hate this at all, do you?" Ryan asked. "You like helping the spirits, and you're excited about helping me. I know you do, Monique. I can feel it, that turmoil within you. You want to hate it all, being a medium, knowing that something has the power to control your very existence—because it does control you, doesn't it? You're called, and you have to come, and you hate being compelled. But at the same time, you get off on the thrill, on the power you have."

"Power?" she asked, as though his spiel hadn't caused her entire body to pulse with anxiety. He knew he was right. What was more, she couldn't deny it, because he could sense her emotions as though she were a part of him. And until he crossed over, which would never happen, she would be. Ryan could handle that.

"Yeah. The power of knowing that whether a spirit crosses over is totally up to you." He considered her for a moment, remembering the basic information Adeline Vicknair had supplied him in regard to the Vicknair family, and Monique's place in it. "You're not normally the one in control around here, are you?"

If her eyes could fire bullets, he'd be dead now. Too bad for her, he was already dead. "That's what bothers you, isn't it? You're not in complete control, and it pisses you off that on top of that, you actually enjoy what the powers that be make you do."

"I'm in control," she said, forcing her words through gritted teeth. "It's my decision whether I help you cross, and I've decided you will, whether you like it or not."

"That so?"

"That's so." She took a deep breath and held it, then let it out slowly. "Listen, I don't want to fight with you. I'm simply going to help you cross. I realize you have no qualms with your current existence, but whether you like staying in the middle or not, how would I live with myself if I was the reason that you never even had the option to cross? Look at that memo Grandma Adeline sent. You have nine days—eight now. That's one week from tomorrow. That's it."

When he made no effort to look at the papers, she huffed an exasperated breath and snatched them up herself. Monique recited the last line from the final page. "As with all assignments, should the claimant refuse or be unable to complete the assigned task within the rectification period, that individual's ability to gain access beyond the realm will be irrevocably denied." She dropped the pages on the settee. *"Irrevocably denied.* I'm not going to live with that on my conscience, whether you like your current in-between status or not," she proclaimed. "On or before the deadline, you're crossing. Preferably before."

"And who's making me?" Ryan asked, amused by this golden-haired, green-eyed and extremely spicy Cajun.

"I am," she said, "but I've had a hell of a day and I'm exhausted, and I'm going to bed to sleep on it."

"Want some company?" he asked. "I'm sure I could think of *something* to help you relax. You seem stressed. Are you planning to dream, Monique?"

Those beautiful eyes shot daggers through him again. "Don't even think about it," she warned.

"Oh, I'll think about it," he said, "And you will, too. If you change your mind, just say my name. I'll come. And so will you. I guar-an-tee." He tried to sound as Cajun as he could manage.

Her mouth quirked, fighting a grin. "Don't try it. You'll never pull off sounding local," she said. "And don't step one foot in my room. I don't need your help."

"That's right. There are plenty of flashlights around," he mused aloud, then relished her cheeks burning brighter. "And for the record, I'm from L.A."

Her jaw dropped. "I didn't want to know that, and don't tell me anything else." She took two steps toward the door then turned, frowning. "You don't sound like you're from Los Angeles."

"Lower Alabama." He grinned.

"God help me." She exited the room, giving Ryan a tantalizing view of her swaying hips along the way.

He laughed. If she planned on forcing him toward that light, or teaching him how to love, for that matter, she'd need all the help she could get. But he'd learned quite a bit tonight from his first interaction with Monique Vicknair. She was sexy, she was feisty, and she was more strong-willed than the spotted silver stallion he'd had in college. Six men had tried to break that horse, an Appaloosa with an attitude, and none had succeeded, until Ryan. He'd set the goal and achieved it, the story of his life, until fourteen months ago.

He swallowed past that particular memory and listened to the pipes within the plantation's walls creak and sputter as someone upstairs started a shower. Monique. She was probably peeling off that damp dress. Did she feel the cool fabric caress her skin and imagine Ryan's hands, touching every sweet curve, teasing every indention and swell? Or did she fling the cloth across the room while recalling his promise that he wouldn't give in to her attempts to make him cross?

He closed his eyes and sensed her aggravation, knew that the thin red dress was probably in mid-fling.

Strong-willed. She was a strong-willed woman with her will currently set on breaking Ryan Chappelle the way he'd broken that stallion. Slowly. Gradually. Thoroughly.

He grinned. What do you know, he'd finally found a woman who equally relished the one thing Ryan enjoyed more than anything else…

A challenge.

4

Monique punched her pillow with fervor, slammed her head against its soft middle and glared at the rain dripping down her bedroom window. She'd taken the coldest shower she could stand in an effort to get her mind off any form of heat, and off the prominent form of Ryan Chappelle.

It hadn't worked.

Then she'd put on the blue-mesh baby-doll nightie she'd bought at Victoria's Secret and quickly replaced the dead batteries in her favorite vibrator with the two she'd swiped from Nanette's flashlight. Usually, a new piece of sexy lingerie made her feel that much sexier and caused her orgasm to be that much harder. And after the night she'd had with Ryan, she needed hard. In fact, she *needed* more than a vibrator, but she'd take what she could get.

Ready for some simulated action, she'd held her breath, hit the switch…and the sucker didn't so much as quiver. Ditto for the other three male substitutes she yanked out of the drawer.

"Granny, if you have anything to do with *this,* I'll never forgive you," she spouted, punching the pillow again in an effort to fluff it up enough to smother her face. Maybe she'd accidentally suffocate and therefore be put out of her misery—and end the agonizing ache to break the rules, as well as the impossible quest to teach Ryan Chappelle to love.

To love? How could she ever discuss love with him, when all she could think about each and every time she looked at him was jumping his bones? And even if he were alive and kicking, she'd be damned if she let that desire take over. The guy was too dang cocky and needed to be brought down a notch or ten. The thing was, his cockiness was evidently well-deserved. She still could hear his words so clearly, delivered with that delicious Southern drawl.

Does it bother you that I've helped quite a few women achieve earth-shattering orgasms over the past fourteen months?

No, the fact that he'd helped other women didn't bother her. The fact that he hadn't helped *her* was another story. Why hadn't he? She could only imagine the words he whispered in the ears of those lucky females. All that intoxicating Southern charm bestowing comments that could probably make a woman's toes curl without so much as a touch of his finger.

But he touched, too; he said so.

She jerked her head to the other side to view the clock, declaring that 3:00 a.m. had now come and gone. Super. At least it was Saturday, and she didn't have to be at the salon until eleven. However, at this rate, she'd still be watching the water drip down the glass when it was time to get up. She envisioned Ryan's big, bold body, standing in the middle of the rain, with every droplet finding its way down extremely male planes and valleys…and a rod of steel.

Her core quaked. Who was she kidding? She wanted him, wanted what he'd given those other women, wanted to hear that sexy voice again.

"Lower Alabama," she whispered, then smiled into the darkness. "He's gorgeous, has a killer body and loves sex. Did he have to have a sense of humor, too?" If he were only breathing, he'd so go in Jenee's he's-a-keeper category.

Monique had never put anyone in that classification, but if she were going to, and if Ryan Chappelle dwelled in the land of the living full-time, he'd be there.

A big clap of thunder made her shudder, then a flash of lightning as bright as day split the sky and illuminated the expanse of her room.

Monique swallowed thickly. The rain and wind claimed dominion outside, but an entirely different kind of storm dominated her senses. A storm of lust and desire, an ache that covered her so completely she trembled with need. She needed him, wanted him to do the things to her that he'd done with those other women. And, Monique realized, she wanted him to do more, because she didn't want to be like the others. She wanted to stand out. She just wasn't sure how. One thing was certain though—she wanted Ryan Chappelle, right here, right now. And she knew exactly how to get what she wanted.

If you change your mind, just say my name. I'll come. And so will you.

Okay, so she wasn't going to bring him down a notch or ten, yet. But could she help it? She wanted to come, and right now, she didn't want to come with anyone but Ryan Chappelle.

She placed her hand between the mesh triangles covering her breasts, and the mad beating of her heart pulsed against her fingertips. Could she really do this? With a ghost? And could she do it without breaking any rules? She swallowed, licked her lips and decided to find out.

"Ryan."

Monique waited a heartbeat, then two. She listened for his voice, focused on the shadows in her room in an effort to see his body materialize, but she heard nothing, saw nothing.

"Ryan?" she repeated.

Had he lied? No, ghosts couldn't lie. One rule that worked

to her favor. But she also knew that ghosts had the ability to come and go from one location to the next at will.

What was taking him so long?

"Oh, no," she whispered. It had been over three hours since he'd left, and he'd definitely been sexually charged at the time. No doubt a guy who could fulfill women's dreams would waste no time finding a woman totally willing to take advantage of his talents.

She flipped over in the bed, pounded both fists against the pillow and wished this damn night would end. Ryan Chappelle was pleasing a female right now, and it wasn't her. Why hadn't she called him sooner?

Frustrated beyond measure, she flung her hand toward the top drawer of her nightstand and yanked it open. Then she withdrew the vibrator that typically "got her there" and grasped it tightly within her hand.

"I know these batteries are good. This thing better work." She hissed the words toward the ceiling, just in case Adeline Vicknair had taken part in making Monique's night even worse. Why was her grandmother picking on her, anyway? "Come on, baby." Monique flipped the switch then nearly cheered when it buzzed to life.

"Come on, baby?" Ryan repeated, stepping from the shadows. "Baby?"

Lightning spilled through the window and placed his massive body in silhouette. The watery glass behind him gave him an eerie aura, making his ghostly glow blur around the edges. He looked, in a word, magnificent.

Magnificent…and wet.

"Where have you been?" she asked, edging up in the bed to examine the small puddle generating on the floor around his dripping tuxedo. And to think, she'd been imagining him all wet all night, and here he was. She switched off the buzzing vibrator. No need for imitations; she had the real thing.

Tall, dark and dripping.

"How did you get so wet?"

"I was about to leave, then I heard your tarp rip. Sounded like thunder, but with more punch." He shrugged. "So I decided to stick around a while and fix it. Damn nearly fell off the roof. I have to be careful, you know. Wouldn't want to kill myself." He chuckled low, then pushed his hand up his forehead to smooth back damp, dark waves.

Monique wanted to touch those curls, wanted to know if they were soft and silky, or coarse and springy. Would her fingers pass through the thick bounty easily, or would it twine around her knuckles and tickle her palms? Monique desperately wanted to touch those waves—and everything else. If she could only push the rules out of her head. Was there really a way to be with him without breaking them? And if there was, would he be willing to try?

"It's a good thing the wind died down, or that tarp would have ripped completely in two before I had a chance to tack it back down," he said, reminding her where he'd been when she whispered his name. He'd faced that nasty storm head-on, by himself, in order to save their roof and help her family. Why?

"Is it okay now?" she asked. "Will it hold through this storm?"

"You care about this house, don't you? More than you want anyone else to know, right?" he asked.

She swallowed, knowing she did care, but also knowing that she'd never admitted it out loud before. Admitting she cared about the house meant admitting she cared about the spirits.

"It's okay," he said. "I know the answer, Monique. In fact, I know how you feel about lots of things. All part of our bonding, I guess. So tell me, do all spirits connect with you the way I do?"

Monique hesitated, refusing to tell him the truth, that no spirit had ever made her feel like *this* before, like she wanted anything and everything he could give her. But what *could* he give her if they couldn't touch? She saw him smirk and knew that he'd sensed her thoughts. "Stop it."

"Stop what?" he asked innocently.

"Reading my mind."

He had the nerve to laugh. "I can't read your mind, Monique. I can simply discern your thoughts, your emotions. And I won't stop. I like *feeling* you. Besides, I don't think I could stop if I tried. It's not as though I'm trying to connect with you. It simply happens."

"Just tell me about the tarp. Will it hold through the storm?"

"I believe so. I did the best I could," he answered, stepping toward the bed. "I always do my best. At everything. Is that why you called me here, Monique? Are you wanting to see me at my best?"

He looked so sure of himself, and ready, willing and able to show her he had good reason for that belief. Goodness knows Monique wanted him to give her a taste of the best. The best orgasm of her life, she imagined. But there was that pesky matter of those rules. What happened if they were broken? Would she burst into flames? Would the Vicknair plantation fall to the ground? Would every family member who'd passed on and those in the present and the future curse her soul for letting them down and discarding the family heritage because she needed a good lay?

His cocky look turned into a questioning one, then he frowned and shook his head. "You *didn't* call me here to talk about crossing over, did you? Because—and I mean this—I have no intention of even visiting the other side, and I have no desire to be called to a sexy woman's room merely to talk. You wanted me when you called. I felt it then, but now you aren't so sure." He stepped away from the bed. "Call me when you want me, Monique."

"I do."

Ryan's retreat stopped in mid-stride. White teeth gleamed as he turned and smiled. Straight, white teeth. Gorgeous, sexy smile. Monique examined the mesmerizing male. It was easy to look him over, since that faint ghostly illumination show-cased the entire, intriguing package...and unfortunately reminded Monique that he was a spirit.

"I mean, I did call you because I want you," she said.

"That's all I needed to hear." His footsteps squished on the hardwood as he stepped toward the bed, removed his wet tie and dropped it to the floor.

"But—" Monique started, then wanted to kick herself for halting his progression.

"But?"

"But I want to ask you a few questions first."

He frowned. "About crossing over?"

"No," she said, "Well, not directly. Don't you want to get out of those wet clothes?"

"I thought that was why you called me here, to get me out of these wet clothes, and to get you out of that sexy nightie." He gave her an easy smile, then sighed loudly when she made no immediate comment. "But if you want to ask me some questions first, I'll oblige. However, I would like dry clothes."

Monique suddenly realized that she still clutched the vibrator for all she was worth. She dropped it like a hot iron, and it rolled across the mattress to nudge her hip. She barely noticed; she was too busy watching Ryan's wet tuxedo do a swift conversion to the white T-shirt and jeans he'd had on earlier. His hair instantly dried, too. He looked amazing, but there was no way this guy wouldn't look good. Wet. Dry. In a tuxedo. Or a T-shirt and jeans.

Or nothing at all.

He casually sat in the large wingback chair Monique kept by the bed for when Jenee had dreams about spirits and wanted to talk. The shiny cream fabric with the white swirling print emphasized his luminescent glow. This was no ordinary man. This was a ghost, a ghost that specialized in fulfilling fantasies. If he fulfilled hers, what were the consequences? And was she willing to risk it? Moreover, was she willing to send him away, when she wanted him so badly it hurt?

"You said you have some questions," he said, stretching his long legs out and crossing them at the ankles, as though he was ready to discuss anything she wanted, for as long as she wanted, and would then be available to give her…everything she wanted. "If we're not talking about crossing over, then we must be talking about living in the middle. Is that it?"

Monique nodded. That was it. This whole situation was so abnormal from her usual dealings with spirits that she didn't know how to handle it, didn't know how to handle him. Or their bonding. She'd always bonded well with her assigned spirits, enough to understand why they'd been given a certain requirement for crossing and to know what they needed to cross over. But with Ryan, it was more than a mere bonding. It was as though they were actually joined somehow, a real part of each other. She knew he'd fixed that tarp because he'd realized that she would have wanted it fixed. He knew—truly knew—her secret desires. And that made her, quite simply, wonder if he knew all of her desires, particularly the fact that right now she wanted him more than her next breath.

What did a medium do when she wanted to break every rule on that list and allow herself the pleasure she'd missed for the past six months? Shoot, who was she kidding? She'd bet Ryan Chappelle could give her the kind of pleasure she'd missed her entire lifetime.

"What do you want to know, ma'am?"

Mon dieu. That accent would be her undoing. If she only realized how entrancing it was, she'd have visited Alabama years ago. But none of the Vicknair mediums traveled too far from home. There was too strong a chance they'd be away when they received a summons. Come to think of it, she'd never been assigned a spirit from Alabama. She'd also never been assigned a spirit who didn't want to cross over. In fact, she'd never had a spirit who was willing to answer questions.

Most spirits didn't want to chat, let alone answer the niggling little questions that had teased her senses during every crossover, they wanted to remedy the problems that kept them from crossing and move along. However, with Ryan hanging out in the central realm for over a year, and with his declaration that he wasn't ready to head toward the light, he obviously was in no rush to complete his task.

How much would he tell?

"Go on, Monique," he coaxed. "Ask."

"How do some spirits see the living from the other side? I know my grandmother sees me, hears me. But not all spirits can see me, can they?" Monique had asked Nanette this very question. She'd even asked her grandmother before she died, but neither had known.

Ryan placed his elbows on the worn armrests of the chair, steepled his fingers in front of his chest and regarded her thoughtfully. "To view a living soul from the other side, or from the middle, a spirit must have a strong affection for the breathing person or a fervent desire to see that individual."

"Have you seen me?" She asked the question on impulse and immediately wished she could retract the four words, but she couldn't deny that she wanted to know. Had he seen her from the other side?

She glanced down at the mesh nightie. The thin fabric didn't leave much, if anything, to his imagination. If Ryan Chappelle had been able to see her from—wherever he was, had he seen all of her? An incessant prickle of anxiety burned Monique's cheeks as she awaited his answer.

"Yes," he said. One corner of his mouth curled upward when he heard Monique's sharp intake of breath. "And no."

"Are you going to explain that?" She didn't attempt to hide her irritation with his smug behavior. How could he invade her privacy that way? And why would Adeline Vicknair have sent him here if she knew he'd been playing Peeping Tom?

Monique pulled the comforter up to her neck then wondered if he could see through the downy fabric. "Can—"

"No," he said. "I can't see through things. I'm a ghost, not the Man of Steel."

Monique fought the urge to laugh. He'd said he could see her from the middle realm. Actually, he'd said "yes and no." What did that mean?

Undeterred by her annoyance, he stood and moved toward the bed, looking at her intensely.

Monique tightened her grip on the edge of the comforter. "What?"

"You called me here for something. Remember?" He sat on the bed then leaned toward her, his rugged face merely inches from hers. Close enough to kiss. The king-sized bed seemed tiny with his massive presence. What had she been thinking, calling him—a bona fide ghost—here? And wanting him to give her an orgasm, no less. She'd definitely been way too long without sex, or she'd never have considered something so outrageous. Surely she wouldn't have. Then she looked at Ryan Chappelle, the intriguing glow defining his body, the mysterious black eyes, the mouth that promised to please…

Oh, she knew exactly what she'd been thinking, and she was thinking it again. She wanted this ghost. Bad.

"I never tried to see you from the middle, Monique. However, if I had known how captivating you were, I promise you I would have."

Her mind seemed to clear from the thick fog of lust, and she remembered why she'd been mad. "Ghosts shouldn't be able to see everything. It isn't right."

"You didn't let me finish," Ryan said, scooting up on the bed, so that his hip grazed her leg and sent a shiver straight to her uterus. Good thing the thick comforter was between them.

"If I had tried to see you, I could have, but never nude. Ghosts can't see through clothing, and they can't view nudity unless it is expressly allowed by the individual. Even now, in this room, I can only see you clothed. I cannot see all of you, unless you allow it. That's a rule I can't control. However, even if I could see every woman in the world completely naked, I wouldn't. I'm from the South, Monique, and we tend to lean toward the gentlemanly side of things. Therefore, the only women I've seen without their clothes are the ones who wanted me to see them that way."

Good to know, Monique mused. "Another question," she said, curious about this new insight into the spirit realm.

"Go ahead."

"Say I called you here and I wasn't wearing anything, nothing at all, and then you came because you were called."

He nodded as she paused. "If you can't see me unclothed, what exactly do you see?"

Ryan's luscious mouth twitched. For a moment, she thought he wouldn't elaborate about the specifics, what he could see and what he couldn't, but then his husky voice commanded her undivided attention. "A privacy veil. Sheer and golden, the veil illuminates your body, but protects you from my view, or any other spirit's view. No spirit can see you unless you want to be seen. I promise."

Before she had a chance to change her mind, Monique crawled out from under the covers. Easing off the bed, she walked around the end, her feet chilled slightly from the cool hardwood floor, and turned so she stood directly in front of him. Then she crossed her arms in front of her chest and ran her fingers under the tiny straps of the nightie. "And a spirit cannot tell a lie," she said.

"That's right." Ryan's voice faded, losing its steely edge. His hands fisted around the fabric of the comforter as he studied her fingers, toying with the top of her nightie.

Monique's eyes never left his as she slowly shifted a strap down one shoulder, then the other, and let the soft fabric caress her body as the material puddled to the floor.

A blue mesh thong. She stood in front of a spirit wearing nothing but a blue mesh thong.

"What do you see now?" Her voice was shakier than she would have liked. She wanted him to view her as strong and brazen, as a woman who would remove her clothes within an arm's length of a virtual stranger.

Within an arm's length. Ryan's muscles rippled against the soft cotton of his shirt. His hands, long-fingered and strong, could easily reach forward and brush against her skin, against her breasts and lower. He'd been so cocky that she wanted to torture him a little before letting him have what he wanted, and what she wanted as well. But the torture was twofold. She wanted him to see beyond that privacy veil, and at the moment, she wanted him to touch.

Ryan shifted on the bed, his eyes grazing her body sensually from head to toe. Monique wondered if she had been wrong. She speculated whether he could actually see her, all of her, now. Maybe she didn't have to verbally give him permission. Maybe, since she really wanted to be naked with him, he could already see her in her entirety and this was one big joke to the gorgeous ghost. But she *hadn't* given him permission, even in her mind.

"Do you really want to know what I see?" he asked, and her momentary embarrassment at her spontaneity escalated.

She swallowed, nodded.

"I see golden hair shining in the moonlight, flowing down a slender back. I see green-gold eyes searching for answers, longing to know more about the man who is tempting her sensual, baser needs. I see a heart-shaped mouth, nervously bitten by a woman who is apprehensive and anxious and curious and sexy and intrigued. A delicate face with high cheekbones, straight nose and exotic arched brows. And I see a body that is hidden beneath a curtain of gold shimmer, only feeding my vivid imagination of what lies beneath."

A bold blaze of lightning invaded the room and illuminated those dark, dark eyes, examining her with riveting intensity.

"Ryan," she whispered, finding it difficult to speak in her extremely aroused state.

"Yes?"

"Close your eyes."

"Yes, ma'am," he said, and obeyed her command.

Monique's breath caught in her throat as she slid the thong

down her legs and let it fall to the floor. She swallowed thickly, made her decision, then put all her attention on one thought.

"Open your eyes," she directed, then watched him drink her in. "Now what do you see?"

He moistened his lips, swallowed visibly. "I see perfection. Beautiful and bold, curved and silky, tantalizing and tempting perfection. I see you, Monique, all of you, and you're as exquisite as I'd thought," he said. "More."

Her pulse skittered, her skin tingled with delicious desire. "I want you—" She paused.

"Damn, it sounds like there's a 'but' coming," he said, crooking one corner of his mouth. "Monique, you're not going to stand there and show me—everything—then tell me no, are you?"

Pierre's words from earlier, his reference to her being a tease, found their way back into her mind. But she wasn't a tease, and she wasn't trying to tease Ryan Chappelle now. She wanted him, wanted him more than anything she could remember in a very long time, but—the rules.

"We can't touch," she said, "And I don't know how we would…"

His brows lifted, mouth curved upward. "Hell, is that all that's bothering you?" He stood then tilted his head toward the bed. "Get back in, Monique, and let me show you what I think of that rule."

Taken aback, she stepped past him and eased into bed, then pulled the cool sheet over her naked flesh. "I do want you, Ryan, but I don't want the whole family to pay for it."

"We're not going to break those Vicknair rules," he assured her. "Trust me."

Trust him. She barely knew him, and all he had to do was touch her, and she'd be throwing the whole family heritage right out the window, she guessed. No one had ever said for sure what would happen, but she didn't want to risk it, even for a round of wild and wicked with the hottest man—make that ghost—on the planet. But she wanted to trust him, really she did. She wanted to trust him and let him do anything he wanted. As much as he wanted. She just had no idea how he'd pull that off without touching her.

"You won't need that sheet." He slowly pulled the soft fabric down her body, studying and apparently appreciating every exposed inch along the way.

Monique realized with sudden clarity that she was completely naked, completely displayed for his thorough perusal, and he was still clothed. "I want to see you," she said.

"You will," he promised, "But not this time. This time is for you." Careful not to touch her skin, he ran his hand down the outer edge of the bed then leaned over her to scan the other side, squinting his eyes as he searched the mattress.

"What are you looking for?" she asked.

"There it is," he said. "I believe you had a name for it, didn't you? Baby. Wasn't that it?" He lifted the shiny silver vibrator from where it had fallen to the floor and held it up so it caught the moonlight and gleamed.

Monique's eyes widened. She rose up on her elbows and peered at the handsome specter, currently eyeing her favorite vibrator. "What have you got in mind?"

"Lean back, Monique, and close your eyes. I promise, *I* won't touch."

Okay. This was going to be awkward, she knew, but she had a feeling she knew exactly what he had in mind, and she didn't do *that*. However, the only way he'd know was if she told him. Unfortunately, she didn't plan on telling him in the middle of sex, which meant she had to tell him now, since she assumed the middle of sex would get there pretty dang quick. "Ryan?"

"Why aren't you leaning back?" he asked, that sexy drawl making her nipples harden, then he hissed out a ragged breath. "Monique, I can feel you—saying no."

"It's just that…"

"What?" he asked, his jaw clenched tight as he held his desire at bay.

"I use that, and it works, but I don't…"

"Don't what?"

"I don't put it inside. I know it's strange, but I guess if something is inside of me, becoming a part of me, I don't want it to be an inanimate object. I want it to be a man. So I don't want you putting that inside of me." She rattled the statement off as quickly as possible to get it over with. She'd looked away from him midway through, and now she squinted and turned toward him to see his reaction.

He wasn't smiling. He was merely staring. Not saying a word, not making a move, just looking at her.

"Still want to try it without touching?" she asked, wanting to cry in defeat. It could be done, she knew. She did it all the time. Closed her eyes, put the tip of the pulsing wonder against her clitoris and let her imagination take over, her body lose control. It worked very well, in fact. But maybe Ryan Chappelle wouldn't be satisfied with this process unless there was actually some form of penetration. And Monique couldn't do that. She just couldn't.

"I'm sorry," she said, realizing that calling him here had been a huge mistake.

"I'm not," he said. "I'm intrigued. And for the record, your rules say that you can't touch a spirit. They don't say one word about a spirit touching you."

5

RYAN CHAPPELLE hadn't been so captivated, so mesmerized, in a very long time. More than fourteen months. She'd been stunning in the see-through nightie, her rose-tinted nipples pressing against the mesh. In truth, when she'd stood before him in the cock-teasing lingerie, she'd been so close to naked that Ryan had thought the real thing couldn't possibly be more fascinating.

He'd been wrong.

When she'd given him permission to see everything, and that veil had been removed, Ryan had been spellbound, his entire body burning with a desire to touch those excited nipples, trace his fingertips down the sweet curves of her breasts, along her side, down the soft indention of her waist to that beautiful feminine core, where he had no doubt she was wet from desire. She hadn't had sex for over half a year, and she hadn't used her vibrator that way, either. In other words, though she'd experienced orgasms in that time period, she hadn't been touched deep inside, where her body undoubtedly yearned to be sated. Monique hadn't felt the penetration, the exquisite pleasure of joining completely with a man.

And she wanted that pleasure. Her green-gold eyes, heavy-lidded and looking at him with unquenched desire, told him she wanted that complete pleasure that would fill her soul. *He* wanted to give her that, wanted to kiss her there, wanted to touch her everywhere.

"You're allowed to touch me, but I can't touch you," she said, her bewilderment evident. "That can't be right. You can't touch me." Her nudity provided an awe-inspiring embellishment to the four-poster bed, white satin comforter and pale-pink satin throw pillows. She was surrounded by beauty, but surpassed it all.

Hell. He wanted to touch, wanted to press the tip of his throbbing cock against that tight center and hold it there, whisper in her ear what he was going to do to her, then do it, slowly, entering her, filling her, claiming her completely with his touch. But he couldn't.

Unless she asked.

"Can you?" she repeated. "Touch me?"

"If you let me," he said, then he leaned above her. "Is that what you want, Monique?"

She did want him to, Ryan knew. He could feel her yearning for him to touch her everywhere, to fill her completely until she couldn't tell where her body ended and his began. But he also sensed her fear, and he knew even before she spoke that the fear was winning her inner battle.

"I can't let you," she finally said. "If you touch me, I won't be able to stop you from, well, anything. I know I won't," she admitted.

"And this is a problem—why?" he asked.

"You said you hadn't been with a woman completely while you've been in the middle."

"I haven't."

"But you're wanting to, right now, with me. I know you do. I can feel it," she said, her voice quivering.

"I won't deny it," he said, grinning. "And you want me, too."

"I know."

He moved closer, so close that her words feathered against his lips.

"Why me?" she continued. "Why didn't you do that with other women, yet you will with me?"

"You're different," he said honestly. "I *feel* you, Monique. And I want you."

"Which is exactly why I can't let it go that far. I can't give myself to you that way, Ryan, without losing part of me along the way. You're right. Our relationship is *different* because of the bonding. And if I'm with you that way, then I won't be able to handle it when you cross."

"I'm not crossing," he said adamantly.

"You are," she said with equal resolve.

With a near growl, he moved his face away from hers. She still wanted him—he knew that—and dammit, he wanted her too. And she'd been willing to give herself to him, when she thought he couldn't touch. "Fine," he said firmly. "I won't touch. Will that work for you?"

She hesitated a moment, then softly asked, "You still want to?" Her eyes glistened in the moonlight. "Without touching?"

"Yes, I still want to," he said, determined. "And I'm still waiting for you to lean back and close your eyes." He could do this, surely he could, because this beautiful woman was counting on him to give her what she needed, and he wasn't about to let Monique Vicknair down.

She settled her head on the pillow, her blond waves cascading over the expanse of white satin, and looked at him with eager anticipation.

"Monique." He leaned over her, careful not to touch her silky skin, those firm breasts rising and falling with her quickening breath, or the enticing center between her legs. "You haven't closed your eyes."

It was a good thing he was already dead, because if he hadn't been, this would definitely do him in. Yet amazingly, Monique had the power to make things worse with a single request.

"I don't want to close my eyes. I can't. I've never done anything like this with a spirit before, and I want to see. I want to see you. All of you." Her mouth trembled before she added in a soft whisper, "Please. Let me see you."

He'd had every intention of getting naked with her earlier, when he thought they were going full speed ahead, letting him please her completely, letting him have her completely, the way he hadn't had a woman in fourteen months. Hell, he wasn't certain that he *could* have intercourse with a woman while he was in the middle. He hadn't tried, because it hadn't felt right to join with a woman while she dreamed. But with Monique, everything felt right. She *was* different from the others; she knew he was a spirit and could tell him that she wanted him, Ryan Chappelle, filling her, coming inside and enjoying that blissful union of the souls. But she didn't want to go that far.

He could have done—or at least tried—everything with Monique, if she'd said yes. But she hadn't, and Ryan thought he could handle a non-touching bout of sex with Monique only if he were fully clothed. Naked, he'd be so *there*. It would be so easy to push against her, to push into her, become one with her, if only for a moment in time.

"Please," she repeated. "I need to see you. I've never seen a spirit like that, and—" She chewed her lower lip.

"And?" Ryan asked, the single syllable a near growl.

"And more than that, I've never seen you," she said. "I'm burning again," she admitted. "I'm burning as much as I did when the letter came, but this time, I'm burning to see you. I'm letting you see me. Let me see all of you."

"Do you know how hard that would be?" he said, rising from the bed, knowing he was doomed to give her exactly what she wanted, no matter how difficult. For some reason, the thought of saying no to Monique Vicknair didn't seem a possibility, not feasible at all.

"How hard what would be?" she asked.

He pulled his shirt up his body, over his head and tossed it to the floor. "Not touching you," he said, unfastening his jeans and guiding the zipper down, "if I'm completely nude, completely aroused and as close to you as a guy can get without intercourse. Do you have any idea how hard this is going to be, Monique?"

Her eyes widened as he removed his shoes, his socks, and then his jeans.

"You weren't wearing anything under your jeans," she said, stating the obvious, while her eyes focused on his hard cock, aching with a need that she wouldn't sate, not tonight. Have mercy, it was a good thing he was Southern, and a gentleman. For his own sanity, he'd better keep reminding himself of both facts. Because his baser needs clawed at his soul, telling him she wanted him, wanted him to stroke her long and deep and hard until her body clenched tight, until he lost himself within the hot depths of her core. "You're so…beautiful," she said on a breathy sigh.

Taken aback, Ryan laughed; he couldn't help it. *Beautiful?* Not exactly the most masculine description in the book. "Beautiful?" he questioned, glad that she'd managed to remove a fraction of the tension in the room, even if his cock had only stood up straighter at her choice of words.

"You are," she repeated, slowly moving her gaze from the straining part of his anatomy to his face. "I don't know if we can do it without touching." She gave him a soft smile. "I

wanted to make you hurt, because you seemed so damn sure
of yourself, but this is going to hurt me more than you. I'm
aching to touch you, Ryan."

Her honesty ripped at his senses and nearly broke his
control. Nearly. Touching him might be what she wanted
physically, but he was beginning to realize that if she broke
that rule, she'd never forgive herself, and he couldn't—
wouldn't—have Monique Vicknair regretting anything that
happened tonight. "But you don't want to break the rules," he
said, reminding her of her earlier words. "And you're not
willing to let me touch you, either."

Pained. That was the only way to describe her expression
as she slowly nodded in agreement, in spite of the yearning
he knew burned her from the inside out. He knew, because he
burned as well…for Monique.

"I can't break the rules," she said. "I don't want to ruin it
for everyone else. I can't. And if I let you, I'm afraid that…"

"That what?" he asked.

She bit her lower lip, frowned. "I don't know," she whispered.

"Yes, you do," he said, so in tune with her emotions that
he didn't even question the intense sensation. "You're afraid,
Monique. Afraid that if you let me touch you, you'll never
want to let me go. And as much as you try to act like you don't
care about family duty or spirits in general, you do. You don't
want to let the Vicknairs down, even if it means giving up
something you want very much."

"You?" she questioned softly.

He grinned. "Yeah. Me. But you don't have to worry about
what will happen if I touch you, Monique."

"Why not?" she asked, her eyes widening.

"Because I promise not to touch." He spoke the words and
prayed they were true. Then again, they had to be, didn't they?

As a spirit, he was "physically incapable" of telling a lie. And he'd just promised not to touch a marvelously naked Monique.

This would be the death of him. Scratch that. He was already dead. But if he could have died like this, pleasing Monique, he'd have died a very happy man.

She took a slow breath, let it out and moistened her lips. "How?"

Have mercy, he hoped he could please Monique, thoroughly, without his erection getting the better of his senses. He could almost come just looking at her, but he wouldn't. This time, as he'd told her earlier, was for her. It was all about her. And it would happen without a single touch.

No pressure.

"Here," he said, taking a large, overstuffed pink satin throw pillow and holding it toward her. "Lean back against the white pillows, then slide this one under your hips."

She did, and a brief flash of lightning illuminated the room and displayed Monique Vicknair, her body at an angle, head down and bottom high, resting on the pillow.

"Now spread your legs for me." He picked up the silver vibrator from where he'd placed it on the nightstand as another surge of lightning displayed her sweet, wet center, opened before him and, oh, so ready.

Ryan's cock was so hard, so hot, that he had to grit his teeth to control the maddening desire that made him want to lick, suck and nibble on the beautiful feast before him, then plunge into her with everything it took to quench her need—and his.

He turned on the vibrator, listened to the soft buzzing join the thunder in the distance, and heard her sharp inhalation as she watched and waited. He let her hear the noise then lifted the silver bullet-shaped object for her to view. "Is this what you need?"

She licked her lips. "Yes."

He knew this would make his own aches worse, but he wanted to—had to—make the most of her pleasure. "Not yet," he said, moving to one side of the bed.

"Not yet?" she questioned, her voice an urgent plea.

"That's right. Just in case this is the only time, I'm damn well going to do it right."

She opened her mouth as though she were going to argue, then took a resigned breath and whispered, "Okay."

Ryan sincerely hoped this wasn't the only time he'd ever have Monique Vicknair, but he wasn't about to pull a quickie, then regret it later. Besides, even though he couldn't enter her, he still wanted her to know what it'd be like if the two of them could ever join completely, touching and all. If she ever agreed to let him. After tonight, he prayed she would want more, and that she'd want it enough to put her fears aside and let him do everything he was about to describe.

"This is my mouth," he said, taking the vibrator to the soft flesh behind her right ear and placing the trembling tip against her lobe, "nibbling on your ear." He eased it slowly across her neck, dipping down to graze her collarbone before moving it to the other lobe and doing the same.

"Oh," she gasped, then smiled. "That's—very nice." She rolled her head to the opposite side, flipping her hair out of the way and exposing her neck for him to have better access at the sensitive skin.

Good. She enjoyed this game. And he was only getting started.

He rolled the pulsing vibrator down her sternum, then up the curving inner swell of her left breast. It was hard to manipulate the apparatus without touching her, but he was doing it. And doing a damn fine job of making her squirm in the process. He held the tip over her nipple, while she fisted her hands in the sheet and bit her lower lip.

"I want to touch you," she moaned. "It's killing me, I want to so much."

He wanted it too, wanted her to touch him, and even more, wanted to touch her. She had no idea how much. But he'd made a promise, and he'd keep it.

Ryan moved the vibrator to her other nipple, while she twisted to view his penis, hard and heavy against the side of the bed. His stance was awkward, his feet firmly on the floor, while he leaned over her body supporting his weight with one arm. With the other, he teased her into excruciating desire. She wanted him. He wanted her. But she'd have to settle for what was allowed by her rules, and he'd have to settle for what was allowed by Monique. Thank goodness there weren't any rules banning a spirit's use of vibrators.

He smirked. Vibrators were banned in some states, weren't they? What about Louisiana? Obviously, if they were, Monique didn't care. She thoroughly enjoyed the silver wonder moving down her belly toward the apex of her legs.

Digging her heels into the bed, she lifted her hips, opening wide in anticipation of the pulsing sensation against her clitoris. Ryan wanted to build that anticipation, deepen the climax, and he knew how. He stood and moved to the foot of the bed and viewed Monique, her body practically writhing now with the need to come.

"Ryan, please."

The end of his cock ached with desire. What he wouldn't give to drive into her, deep into her center, where she wanted him. He placed the vibrator against her inner thigh, then moved it slowly around the outer edge of her nether lips, swollen and exposed and enticing. Her stomach dipped in, and she held her breath, while Ryan inhaled her intoxicating feminine scent.

Forcing his cock to stay put, he set his sights on intensifying her orgasm. "I'm nibbling you here, Monique," he said, easing the throbbing vibrator up her lips and toward her clit. "Nibbling and biting and licking and sucking, and moving to that spot that's burning, swollen and pink and ready for me to take."

She moved her legs wider, pressed her hips higher. "Yes, Ryan, please."

He held the vibrator directly above her clitoris, while he watched her sex quiver and flex, ready for penetration. He couldn't give her that, couldn't give himself that, either.

But he could give her this.

"I'm licking my way closer, ready to touch you, smelling your delicious fragrance, wanting you so much that my cock is nearly ready to explode," he said, and slid the vibrator to that sweet spot, exactly where she wanted it, needed it. "This is me, Monique, my mouth clamping down and sucking you until you can't take it any more. Sucking and nibbling and biting, until you can't hold on, until you have to let go and set that spiraling, burning, maddening tension free—"

Her scream pierced the night at the same moment that the most vivid flash of lightning Ryan had ever seen illuminated the room, and Monique, in a dramatic white-gold radiance, creating an image that would forever be tattooed on his mind. Monique Vicknair in the heat of climax, her eyes glazed from the powerful release, her mouth parted, nipples hard and taut and high, stomach quivering, vagina pulsing. In that moment, she exposed her soul, showing him a beautiful woman in complete abandon, a woman letting go and losing herself to delicious, heated desire.

Losing herself to *him*.

Ryan could only imagine being inside her during the onslaught of climax. He could only imagine her feminine muscles flexing and pulsing around him. He could only imagine…until she said yes.

"Damn." It was the only thing he could say.

Breathing hard in the aftermath of her climax, she shimmied up the bed and stared as he moved away, picking up his clothes from the floor.

"Ryan," she whispered, as he stepped into his jeans then fought to pull his zipper past his erection.

"I'm sorry, Monique." He shook his head. "Not sorry that this happened, but sorry that I can't do it again. This is—too much. You're too much. I want you more than I've wanted anything in a very long time, and if I can't touch you, it's not enough." He wasn't trying to force her into giving him permission next time, if there was a next time; he was merely stating the truth. No way could he do this again without touching. "Hell, I don't even know if I could stop at touching, Monique. I want inside you, deep inside you."

"You said you never did—everything—with the others," she said.

"I didn't. And I'm not completely certain it's even possible. But with them, touching was as far as I wanted to go. This is different."

"How?"

How? He honestly didn't know. Because it was Monique? Because she knew who he was, what he was, and still wanted him? Maybe. Or maybe there was even more to it than that, more than he cared to put his finger on right now. Maybe, just maybe, it was because this woman had the power to get him through to the other side, and he damn well didn't want to go. Maybe he was afraid of getting this close to her again, afraid it might help her accomplish her goal.

"It's just different," he said.

"Well, it isn't fair." She pulled the white satin sheet up her body as she spoke. "And I'm the one that's sorry. I wasn't thinking when I asked you to take off your clothes. It obviously made things worse on you," she said, staring at the bulge in his jeans. "And I can't make that better without touching you, can I?"

"No, you can't. But I'll take care of it," he said. He always did. Each and every time. God help him, he wanted inside a woman. No, not "a woman"; he wanted inside Monique.

"I really am sorry," she said. "More sorry than you can imagine, because I want to touch you as much as you want me to." She tucked the sheet beneath her arms and leaned forward to slide the throw pillow from beneath her legs. Then she inhaled audibly and tilted her head, as though having a profound idea.

"You know, I may not be able to help you that way, but I could help you another way," she said.

"How's that?" he wondered, knowing good and well a vibrator wasn't going to do it for him.

"Spirits never hurt when they cross over completely. And they have everything they need, everything they want. Have you thought about that, Ryan? It would be good, crossing over, living there, having everything your heart desires. I could help you find that. I haven't worked out how yet, but I can help you learn to love. I know I can. I wouldn't have gotten your assignment if I couldn't. You would never ache for more. And you're hurting because of me. I'm supposed to make things better for you, not worse."

She sounded so sure of her abilities that he hated letting her down, but he wasn't going toward that damn light. Should he tell her why? That the guy who'd lived so recklessly when he was on this side, the man who'd dared death to take him on at every opportunity when he was breathing, was actually terrified of calling the game over. He'd been so determined to get all he could out of life that he'd gone too far and ended up losing it all too soon. Twenty-eight was way too young to die. And he was way too young to complete the process by walking toward that despicable light. It wasn't time for him yet. He didn't know why he believed that so strongly, but he did, and he wasn't going to cut his time short now, simply because Monique Vicknair wanted to accomplish her task. Sure, he was taken with her, but not enough to lose his senses completely.

"I don't want to talk about crossing, Monique." He paused, then said what had to be said. "And I don't want you calling me again. You're going to try to get me to cross over, and I don't want to go. Or you're going to let me please you, which is a wonderful thing, but I don't think I could restrain myself next time. I wanted to come inside you so badly that it still hurts. This time, I didn't. But even a Southern guy has his limits, and I think if I try to do this again, I won't be able to hold back."

"I'll have to call you again, Ryan. I have to try to help you cross, and you will have to see me again, for the next eight days, unless you cross before the deadline. We're bonded, remember? Connected. You have to see me again."

"Not like this," he said. Then before Monique had a chance to say another word, he turned and walked into his home, his destiny, his night.

6

DAZZLING SUNSHINE woke Monique bright and early, in spite of her late-night activities with the compelling ghost. She stretched in the bed, looked at the clock and was amazed that it was barely past seven. She would have sworn she'd slept for hours. She was so relaxed, so deliciously sated, that she'd slept like a baby. Unfortunately, a genuine sensation of emptiness began to make her feel rather melancholy. Emptiness from knowing that she hadn't done a thing for Ryan's desire, and from knowing how desperately she wanted to.

Last night shouldn't have happened. She knew that now; she'd known it then. She'd wanted to be with him, any way she could, and that had hurt him so much that he hadn't wanted to see her again. How could she have let things go so far? More than that, how would she keep them from going that far again when she saw him? And she would see him. She had to, because she had to help him cross. There was no way she could live with herself if Ryan Chappelle was stuck in the middle forever because she didn't do her job.

Like most spirits, he was afraid of the unknown. Monique had sensed that fear last night when she'd mentioned crossing over. He saw the transition to the other side as giving up, as failure, and Ryan wasn't the type of guy to give up on anything. She sensed that too, probably more than anything else she *felt* through their bond. And that fact told her a couple of things. One, she had to convince the captivating spirit that the other side was actually better, not worse, than his current existence. And two, if Ryan Chappelle was determined to touch her, she was in for the fight of her life. Because Ryan *had* stated the truth last night, when he guessed her reason for telling him no. If he touched her, truly touched her, Monique would never want to let him go.

Mon dieu, Granny, why did you send him to me? You must have known I'd want him. And I can't. We can't.

Naked and miserable, she crawled from bed, picked up her discarded nightie and thong, then moved toward the bathroom to shower. While the stream of hot water pelted her body, Monique remembered the image of Ryan Chappelle standing in front of the rain-drenched window, with that luminescent glow defining the most beautiful image, the most beautiful man, she'd ever seen. And the only man she'd ever wanted more than her next breath. The only man she couldn't have completely, and would never have in any way again, since she couldn't fulfill his needs.

If I try to do this again, I won't hold back.

She stepped out of the shower and toweled off with an intensity that rubbed her skin almost raw, but right now, she welcomed the pain. She wanted to feel Ryan, and she couldn't. More than that, she couldn't remove the image of him, standing at the end of her bed and looking so…unfulfilled. And now, he didn't want to come back and didn't want to cross.

But he had to. She couldn't merely let him be, could she? If she didn't help him through to the other side within the specified time, he'd be miserable forever. He'd already said that he wouldn't go beyond bringing a woman to orgasm when he visited her dreams. He'd also said that he wouldn't do more with Monique, because she didn't say yes. So, what was he doing in the middle, exactly? Pleasing women while receiving no pleasure in return? Surely that wasn't the kind of eternity he wanted. And even if it was, Monique couldn't let it happen, not after he'd given to her so freely, after he'd shown her how unselfish he truly was—the kind of man, of spirit, who would give everything he could give and expect nothing in return. Because of that, she wanted to make sure Ryan got everything he deserved. The love of his life could be on the other side, *if* he'd just cross.

Monique grimaced. Did she really believe that, or did she want him to cross for another reason entirely? If she didn't get him to cross in the next eight days, he'd be in the middle eternally. Which meant he'd be accessible to Monique, forever. Not a good thing. Because after last night, she realized that compared to Ryan Chappelle, all living men were nothing. He could—would—ruin sex for her. Even the thought of Pierre Comeaux didn't do a thing for her now, not when compared to the wickedly handsome spirit that hadn't even laid a finger on her yet.

Monique blinked. *Yet?* What was she thinking? She could not let him touch her that way, couldn't let him do anything to her that way. Ryan Chappelle was a spirit. She wasn't. Case closed. And she'd do good if her mind remembered that fact, instead of letting her libido take over the reins.

He simply had to cross. That was all there was to it. And Monique had to find a way to make that happen.

Hearing a car door slam, she wrapped the towel around her and moved to the window. Gage stood beside his pickup and rolled his head from shoulder to shoulder, then stretched his arms and yawned broadly. No doubt her older brother had been up most of the night in the E.R. at Ochsner Hospital, and he'd probably spent the early hours of the morning in a female's bed. A lack of sleep didn't appear to affect his sexual appetite at all, yet he never seemed quite satisfied.

As if sensing her presence, Gage turned his attention from assessing the storm damage to the window where his sister stood. He grinned and gave her a friendly nod, before turning toward Tristan, hauling a tree limb the size of a small car toward the burn pile by the sugar cane. Shaking his head, Gage moved to join Tristan, the oldest male cousin of the lot, currently using every one of his firefighter skills to teach that big hunk of oak who was boss.

Monique smiled. Gage probably had had E.R. patients most of the night, and Tristan had undoubtedly battled a fire during the same time period, yet both of them were here, bright and early, ready to help with cleanup. Though they might not live in the family plantation, the two oldest Vicknair males definitely did their part to keep the place running. And speaking of Vicknair males...

Where was Dax? True, he usually visited a couple of the doctors on his pharmaceutical route on Saturdays, but never this early.

Monique scanned the yard, covered in leaves and limbs that had been hurled from the string of magnolias and huge oaks during the storm. The yard was a muddy mess, plain and simple, and would require all of them working together to remove the debris. Good thing she'd woken up early; she could help for an hour or two before work. However, it was also Saturday morning, which meant Nanette would expect all of them to gather, at least for a brief period of time, to discuss restoring the house. Another fun day in the Vicknair neighborhood.

At least Monique had one positive thing on her mind to

keep her going. Ryan Chappelle. Have mercy, he'd given her the best orgasm of her life last night, and have mercy, she was determined to give him what he deserved, too. A trip to the other side and to happiness. She just had to figure out how. But first, she had to help the family.

She entered the kitchen to find Nanette, sitting at the ancient mahogany table that had enhanced the center of the room for as long as Monique could remember. Eight people could sit comfortably around its perimeter, though Vicknair reunions often found many more huddled around it enjoying platefuls of jambalaya, étouffée and boudin. Today, however, Nan was the only Vicknair around and there were no plates at all on the table, just a big stack of papers and notes, and a single steaming mug of coffee.

"Morning." Monique crossed the room toward the coffee-pot, already half-empty. Either Tristan had enjoyed a cup or two before heading out, or Nan was working on a serious caffeine fix.

Monique guessed the latter.

"Dax brought beignets before he left," Nan said, indicating a brown-and-white bag by the stove. She took another sip of coffee, then stood and crossed the kitchen to rummage through the cabinet by the sink.

The kitchen cabinets were a deep mahogany that matched the table perfectly and contrasted starkly with the white-tiled floor. Unfortunately, most of the cabinets were scuffed and scratched, with a few lacking essential pieces of hardware, like the one Nan had opened with her fingernails since the handle was missing in action. The floor tiles had plenty of cracks and crevices too and needed a good dose of TLC. However, next to her bedroom, the kitchen was still Monique's favorite room in the house, and she had the sudden desire to show it to Ryan before he crossed over.

"Someone named Pierre called last night after you went to bed," Nan said, jerking Monique's thoughts out of this kitchen and into Pierre's, where she remembered his promise of doing her on his center island before the night ended. When she'd left him, she'd been miserable that it hadn't happened; now, she was elated that it hadn't. Pierre would have been a quick fix to her sexual needs, but he wouldn't have affected her the way Ryan had. She swallowed. Ryan hadn't touched her, not physically, but he had *touched* her, emotionally.

She had to get him to cross.

"Do you want the number?" Nan asked, finding the industrial-sized bottle of ibuprofen in the cabinet and bringing it back to the table.

"Number?" Monique asked.

"Pierre's number. He left it for you to call." Nan grimaced as she pushed on the cap. "It's on the notepad by the phone."

"No," Monique said. She didn't want to call Pierre, didn't want anything to do with Pierre, which was surprising, given she hadn't had more than an orgasm with Ryan. Logically, she should still want full-fledged sex, but she didn't. Not with Pierre, anyway. In fact, she realized with a tinge of disbelief, she didn't want full-fledged sex with anyone right now, except Ryan. "Oh, my," she whispered. She really needed him to leave, before he completely ruined any chance of her having a normal relationship with a man again. Normal. As if she even remembered the meaning of the word. Nothing about the Vicknair family was anywhere near normal. Even so, she didn't plan on adding "full-fledged sex with ghost" to her ever-growing list of abnormal qualities.

"What?" Nan asked, still working on getting the bottle open, her forehead wrinkled in obvious discomfort. She wore a black tank top and khaki shorts, quite a difference from the conservative attire she chose during the school year, and black onyx studs were in her ears.

Monique stared at the dark, sparkling earrings, intense and round, like Ryan's glittering eyes. Her breathing hitched as she recalled the way they had darkened even more when he was aroused.

"What?" Nan repeated, her irritation palpable.

"Nothing." Monique placed her cup of coffee on the table, then reached for the medicine bottle. "Let me help."

Sighing heavily, Nan handed it over, then smiled gratefully when Monique twisted off the cap. "Advil and Community Coffee, the breakfast of champions."

Monique laughed softly, then took a sip of her own coffee and wondered if she needed a few Advil, too, to help ease the tension caused by Ryan. Sexual tension. Emotional tension. All-out tension. What if she never wanted another man again? What if no one else would do?

With her mind on that agonizing possibility, she took a way-too-big gulp of coffee then coughed her way through the scalding liquid passing down her throat.

"Easy now," Nan said. "Something wrong?"

"You're the one popping Advil with your coffee," Monique pointed out between coughs, not willing to share her own personal dilemma. Heaven knew that Nanette was worried enough about saving the plantation; Monique didn't need to add the fact that she wanted to do a ghost to Nan's current troubles.

"Tristan brought some information on the Godchaux-Reserve house, that plantation further down River Road that was approved for the National Register of Historic Places. He thought we could look at what they did to get added to that list and follow their example. Right now, we're just trying to get restoration money from the local Historical Society, but if that place got national status and national funding, we might have a chance at that, too."

"Sounds like a good idea."

Nan flipped through the pages and took another sip of coffee. "Why couldn't the Vicknair family have gotten into selling coffee like the Saurage folks in Baton Rouge? With their Community Coffee—" She took another sip from her mug. "—and the fabulous way they blend the chicory just right, they're set for life. We, on the other hand, are still dealing with sugar cane and surviving year-to-year. You never know what the cane is going to bring in, and with all of these hurricanes and not enough flood insurance, it's never enough."

"But this is a sugar cane plantation," Monique reminded her.

"I know, and so is this Godchaux-Reserve house," Nan said, holding up a page and frowning.

"Then why don't we do what Tristan said and follow their example?" Monique asked, thinking he might have actually found a way to end all of their post-hurricane troubles. For nearly two years, they'd been trying to bring the house back to the way it was before Katrina, yet even with all six of them working constantly to follow the instructions Nan had regarding full restoration, they had too little time and way too little money to do the job right.

"The thing is," Nan said, getting up to pour another cup, "the way that plantation got approved to receive money from the River Road Historical Society was to turn the place into something like a museum. You know, a place where people walk through and learn the history of a sugar cane plantation, that kind of thing." She paused to savor the first hot sip from the new cup. "Based on the information in those papers, the federal government would even give us a tax credit if we restored the house, but only if it's income-producing, such as a museum, like the Godchaux-Reserve place, or a bed and breakfast."

"We could do that." Monique brightened at the thought. "And we could probably make enough off the tours to supplement the cane income, too." Monique couldn't fathom why Nanette wasn't outside hugging Tristan's neck for finding the answer to their prayers.

"Hello," Nan said sarcastically, "Think about it. A nice little group of folks decides to take a nice little tour through our big ol' house and just happen to cross the sitting room when a pale purple envelope materializes on the tea service."

"Oh," Monique said softly.

"Oh," Nan repeated, again sarcastically. Obviously, she'd woken up this morning in nowhere near the sated, blissful state as Monique. Maybe Nan needed a talented ghost to visit her bed at night.

Monique kept that thought to herself.

"Or perhaps they would be sitting on the front porch drinking coffee and eating beignets, then you zoom up the driveway in your Mustang and jump out, frantic to get inside because your skin is on fire and you have to get to that letter," Nan continued. "The way you did last night."

"Right, that definitely wouldn't be good," Monique agreed, grinning.

"This isn't funny," Nan warned.

"I know. But you have to admit, the entire picture does sound rather humorous."

Nan's eyes widened as if she suddenly remembered something. "Did your ghost show? I'm assuming so, since you obviously aren't burning now and you seem so, I don't know, satisfied?"

Monique nearly choked on her coffee. *Satisfied.* What

made Nan choose that word? "Yes, he came," Monique said, and this time fought the impulse to wince. In truth, Ryan hadn't come; she had. With gusto.

"He crossed last night then?" Nan asked, apparently expecting Monique's usual response, *Yes, without any problems.* But Monique couldn't provide the answer Nan wanted.

"No, he didn't. In fact, he doesn't have any intention of crossing—ever," Monique said, as Dax entered through the swinging door that separated the kitchen from what used to be a formal dining room, before the cracks in the ceiling, holes in the walls and water stains on the threadbare carpet. "He's apparently been in the central realm for fourteen months and enjoys it there."

"Your ghost didn't cross over immediately?" Dax asked, grabbing a beignet out of the bag then heading toward the coffee. He wore his favorite LSU baseball cap, a T-shirt that had seen better days, and faded jeans with a hole in one thigh.

"I thought you left," Nan said. "Didn't you have to work things out with the girl's parents? Convince them to take that trip?"

"Whose parents?" Monique asked.

"My ghost's parents. Actually, I had two ghosts visit this time," Dax answered, between bites of beignet. "A six-year-old named Chloe that I'm supposed to help cross, as well as a young woman, Celeste, who evidently stayed behind to help Chloe through. Both girls were in the same bus accident. Anyway, I was going to visit Chloe's parents today, but Celeste said they still aren't ready. Evidently, the community where they live is having a memorial service for their daughter this afternoon, so they won't even consider leaving until that's over." He looked toward Monique. "You said your ghost didn't cross right after he died? That's strange, because

Celeste and Chloe didn't cross immediately, either. That's the first time I've had that happen. They died three weeks ago, but they didn't come see me until last night."

"Why not?" Nan asked, her brows furrowing at this new glimpse into the realm beyond the living. As Monique suspected, the family hadn't heard of ghosts who deliberately chose not to cross. Then again, Gage dealt all the time with spirits that refused to believe they were dead; maybe this was no different. But it had never happened to her before, and it obviously had never happened to Nan or Dax, either.

"It's this trip to the beach." Dax finished off his beignet, grabbed a plate from the cabinet and loaded it with more of the square, sugar-coated doughnuts before carrying the mini tower to the table. He held them toward Nan and Monique. "Want some?"

"No thanks," Monique said, amazed at the consumption level of her younger brother. He was twenty-three now, but still ate the same volume as when he was seventeen and playing football at St. Charles High.

"What about the trip to the beach?" Nan ignored the beignets Dax was waving under her nose. "I thought you told me last night that your assigned ghost stayed to tell her parents goodbye, and the older girl wanted to make sure the little one found the light."

"That's what I thought last night," Dax said. "But after talking to them again this morning, I learned there's more to it than that. If it were that simple, Chloe would have crossed with Celeste right after the accident, but they stayed for Chloe to go on this beach trip."

"What beach trip?" Monique asked.

"Chloe never saw the beach when she was living. Her parents had planned to take her next week, but then they had

the bus accident on the Fourth of July and the parents, naturally, canceled the trip. The girls were headed to a summer
camp. Chloe was attending the camp; Celeste was a counse-
lor." He shrugged. "Anyway, Chloe doesn't want to cross over
until she has seen the beach with her parents, but the trip has
been canceled."

"So what are you going to do?" Monique inquired.

"After the memorial service, I'll meet Chloe's parents and
convince them that their daughter needs their help to cross
over," he said matter-of-factly.

"You received that information with your letter? You know
where her parents live?"

"Yeah, I did, so I'm supposed to go see them," Dax said,
not containing his excitement. During most crossings, the
assigned medium simply talked to the ghost, encouraged him
or her to visit the loved one, then waited for that overpower-
ing sense of relief when the spirit completed the goal and
found the light. Monique had never received information on
where a ghost had lived. The only way she'd find out is if a
ghost told her, which none had ever done, until last night.

Lower Alabama.

She smiled at the memory.

"What's that about?" Nan asked, raising her dark brows at
Monique's grin.

"It's just funny that after all this time helping the spirits,
Dax and I are both trying to help ghosts that aren't quite ready
to cross." True, that wasn't why she had smiled, but it was an
odd occurrence and worth mentioning.

"I'll tell you what's funny," Tristan said, entering the
kitchen and letting the screen door bounce hard against the
frame behind him. He was tall and tan and athletic, the type
of fireman who would typically grace the Louisiana Firemen

calendar, an annual production that unquestionably show-cased the fact that firemen worked out regularly. Tristan, however, wasn't into that kind of blatant look-at-me mentality.

Gage followed Tristan into the kitchen and Monique couldn't help but smile at her older brother. On the other hand, if Louisiana ever started a hunky doctors calendar, Gage would qualify as cover material and would be thrilled at all the attention. He grinned back at Monique, his white teeth gleaming in the midst of his rugged tan face.

Nan cocked a brow at Tristan.

"Watch it," Gage warned, "he's fuming."

"You're just lucky you were helping," Tristan said, turning on the water faucet and scrubbing the brown gunk off his forearms, before moving down to his hands. "Which is more than I can say for the rest of you. Eating beignets and drinking coffee while we're dragging limbs the size of small tractors across that yard. And we could use a tractor, by the way."

"Well, when we run across a boatload of money, we'll buy one," Nan said, scowling.

"Hmph." Tristan continued scrubbing. "At least Jenee has an excuse. I met her heading down River Road this morning. Today's her day to volunteer at the homeless shelter?"

"Yes," Monique said, winking at Gage as she added, "And we didn't know you needed help, Tristan."

"Shit." Tristan moved away from the sink so Gage could follow suit, then dried his hands while eyeing Dax's plate of beignets on the table. "You know, I'd give you a good talking-to for hogging so many beignets, if I didn't know you fixed that tarp last night. Damn saved the roof." Tristan smiled. "Good job."

Dax's questioning gaze darted from Tristan to Gage to Monique and Nanette. "I spent most of the night right here," he pointed to the table, "drinking coffee while I talked with Chloe and Celeste, the ghosts who came last night. What happened to the tarp?"

Gage's head tilted, and he shot a what-the-hell look at Tristan before answering. "It ripped nearly in two. Someone pulled the sides together in spite of that whipping wind and managed to nail the pieces down to protect the roof. We'd have lost all of the remaining tiles, I imagine, if it hadn't been fixed. As it was, we lost barely a handful. If you didn't fix it, who did?"

"Ryan Chappelle," Monique answered, instantly remembering him dripping wet when he entered her bedroom.

"Who?" Nan asked.

"My current ghost. The one who's been in the middle for fourteen months."

"He hasn't crossed?" Tristan asked. "In fourteen *months?*"

Other than the low hum of the coffeemaker, the kitchen grew intensely quiet, with her siblings and cousins all waiting for an explanation. Unfortunately, telling them that Ryan kept a death grip on the land of the living in order to fulfill women's fantasies seemed an intrusion of his privacy. Plus, Monique suspected that wasn't entirely true. Ryan had enjoyed fulfilling fantasies, but he also hadn't crossed because he'd never loved, and he was afraid of the unknown. And if she told them about the women's fantasy thing, it'd also make them wonder whether Monique had received any of his, um, fulfillment. No way would she be able to face them if they knew she'd had an orgasm courtesy of her ghost. They might actually see that as breaking the rules, which would force her to explain that she hadn't touched him and, in fact, he hadn't touched her. Then, naturally, they'd want to know how she and Ryan accomplished that feat, and Monique was *not* going there, particularly with Gage and Dax, her bookend brothers, leaning forward in their chairs and waiting for her response.

"Well?" Gage finally said. "Why hasn't he crossed?"

"He has his reasons, and I can't tell you." She gave them what she hoped was an apologetic smile. "Sorry."

"But he's the one who fixed the tarp?" Tristan asked. "You're sure?"

"Yeah, he told me he heard it rip, so he decided to stick around and fix it."

"Why?" Tristan shot a skeptical gaze at Nan. "Why would he do that?"

"Maybe he likes a challenge," Dax offered. "Maybe he's the daredevil type." He ran the corner of a beignet through the surplus of powdered sugar on his plate, then popped it in his mouth and swallowed. "Is that how he died, Monique? Doing some daredevil stunt? Cause getting on that roof last night in that storm was damn near crazy."

"I don't know how he died. I don't find out how spirits die, remember?" Monique said. "And I think he fixed it because he wanted to help us. I guess if you're already dead, you don't really have the same fear of dying anymore, don't you think?"

Gage laughed. "No, I guess you don't. Wonder if he'd be willing to come back and help us haul debris to the burn pile."

Tristan snatched a beignet from Dax's plate and tossed the whole thing in his mouth before his cousin could protest. Merely a year younger than Nanette, he relished his role as oldest male cousin and occasionally took advantage. "Well, we wouldn't need his help cleaning up outside, *if* we could get the entire family to pitch in."

Monique took her coffee mug to the sink and rinsed it. "I can give you two hours. I've got a perm scheduled at eleven."

"I can give you three," Dax offered, "then I've got to pay

a visit to a doctor on my route. After that, I've got to head toward Houma to visit my ghost's parents."

"I'll take your three, Dax," Tristan said, then turned toward Monique. "And I'll take your two hours and raise you two more after you get off." When Monique's jaw dropped, he continued, "Hey, I know you're done by five. It doesn't even get dark until nine, so I'm leaving two hours for whatever else you want to do. We need you, Monique." He scanned the table. "Hell, we need everyone."

"We're coming," Nan said. "I would've been out there earlier, but I was trying to get a handle on what those folks did at Godchaux-Reserve to see if it would be suitable for saving this place."

"And?" Tristan asked.

"No can do," she said emphatically, stacking the papers then shuffling them into place against the table. "They open their home for public viewing, like a museum. How are we supposed to do that when we never know when one of Grandma Adeline's letters is going to arrive? Or when a ghost will happen to show up at the house?"

"Hey, voodoo and ghosts are a part of Louisiana culture," Gage said. "Hell, we might be able to charge more on the off chance that one shows up while they're touring."

"They wouldn't be able to see it," Monique reminded.

"No, but they could sure enough know that it was here," Gage countered. "Your guy fixed the roof last night, didn't he? If someone would've been around during that feat, they'd sure have seen the tarp getting nailed down. Don't you think they might have suspected a little ghostly interaction?" He grinned at Tristan. "I think it might work."

"No." Nan firmly vetoed the idea.

"You'd rather they bulldoze the house before you let them

in on our secret?" Tristan asked incredulously. "You know, we're not the only people near New Orleans who have specters in our closets. Shoot, we're merely going to blend."

"Can you imagine what I'd have to deal with at school if my students found out I live in a haunted house?"

"Technically," Dax said, leaving the table to check out the bag of beignets and frowning to find Gage and Tristan had emptied it, "it isn't a haunted house. To be haunted, ghosts have to inhabit the place. Ours is merely a speck on their roadmap to crossing over. None of them hang around for long." He shot a look at Monique. "Well, none of them did, until your guy came along. If he's been in the middle fourteen months, he might be around for a nice little visit. Hey, maybe we can make him a honey-do list, tailored for ghosts. He's already fixed the roof. What else can he do? He wasn't a carpenter when he was living, was he, Monique?"

"I didn't ask his profession," Monique snapped, as though she couldn't care less. Problem was, now she wondered. What had he done when he was living? And thanks to Dax's daredevil query, she also wondered how Ryan had died. She'd never wanted to know how previous ghosts had died. Not once had she even been tempted to ask. But with Ryan, she wanted to know, and she prayed it wasn't painful.

Her stomach quivered as she remembered him, naked and glorious, leaning over her bed in a determined effort not to touch her while he brought her to climax. Another proof of how deeply this ghost cared. He hadn't had to abide by the Vicknair rules, but he had. For her. He hadn't had to weather that storm to fix their tarp, but he had. For the family? Or for her? And again, why? Though she knew. Because of their bonding, he knew that she cared more about the plantation and her familial duty than she admitted. No matter how much she disliked the lack of control her medium status bestowed, she still relished the uniqueness, the individuality, of what their family did for so many spirits. And she truly cared about this home, so much that working on it every spare minute she had didn't bother her at all. She wanted it to shine again, to be the place that Grandma Adeline had cherished so much, and many Vicknairs before her. Ryan knew how she felt, and he'd reacted to her desire by helping them save the home. How could she ever repay him?

"Hey, instead of standing there staring out that window, you could come get in a couple of hours with us, like you said you would, Miss Priss," Tristan said. He only used his personal nickname for her when he wanted to rile her feathers. So she was a bit prissy and undeniably girly. So were Nan and Jenee, though he didn't give them nearly as hard a time. Then again, Nanette was older than Tristan and, as oldest cousin, typically the family decision-maker, whether Tristan liked it or not. Jenee was his baby sister, so she rarely got the brunt of his teasing. Which meant Monique was prime for the picking. It didn't mean, however, that she had to take it without a bit of sass of her own.

"Listen here, I'll get more done in my two hours than you'll accomplish all day."

"Doubtful, since you haven't stepped foot out of the house yet," Tristan countered, while Gage chuckled.

"Sis, he's baiting you," he warned.

"Don't I know it," Monique said. "But I'm going to do my part." She moved out of the kitchen into a small mudroom that her grandmother had used for rooting poinsettias, which grew as big as trees along the sides of the house and took Monique's breath away when they bloomed at Christmas.

"And if you want to get into particulars, it was my ghost who took care of that tarp last night," Monique reminded.

"Since Ryan isn't on the family tree, I'm going to chalk up his contribution to my branch."

"Gotta admit," Gage said, as he and Tristan followed Monique outside, "she's got ya there." He laughed, and it quickly escalated into a yawn.

Monique pivoted. "You work all night at the hospital?"

"I got off at two," he said, then gave her that wry smile that had melted many a Cajun female's heart.

"Yet you still haven't slept, have you?" she questioned, knowing the answer.

"I will, as soon as I'm done here." The pale-blond streaks in his hair glistened among the darker brown locks, making him look every bit the bona fide playboy that he was.

Monique yanked on the yellow gloves she'd confiscated from the mudroom, found a rake resting against a tree and swiped at the leaf-covered earth to gather her first addition for the burn pile. "So did you know her, or was this another one of the damsels in distress that find their way into the Ochsner E.R., and always when you're on duty?"

It was no secret that the women of LaPlace, many of whom went to Monique's salon to get their hair and nails done, would drive past closer hospitals to visit the Ochsner E.R. at the mildest onset of a cold in the hopes that Dr. Gage Vicknair would have to touch them in some way.

Whatever charisma her brother held for women, he had it in spades. Every woman wanted him, and once they got him, they simply wanted him again. Rough life for a playboy. Or so you'd think. To Monique, he always seemed distant under that playboy facade, but he hid it well, very well. So well, in fact, that she'd never mentioned her suspicion that her notorious brother really longed to settle down. Why did she wonder if Ryan was the same?

"I did know her," he said. "But I'm not one to kiss and tell."

"Since when? And more importantly than whether you knew her, do I know her? As in, am I going to see her for regular visits to my shop now that she's slept with my brother?" Monique kept swiping with the rake, while Gage gathered up the slate tiles that hadn't hung on during the storm.

"God help us, are we talking about his sex life again? It really gets old," Tristan declared.

"Nah, it doesn't," Gage said, winking at Monique. Then he turned his attention toward the tiles he'd gathered. "What do you think?" he asked Tristan. "We've got less than two weeks before the roof inspection. How're we going to get more tiles?"

"Hell if I know," Tristan said. "There's no bank around willing to give us credit on this place, but I'm not ready to give up yet. We'll get these tiles back on today and try to determine exactly how many more we need. Good thing Monique's ghost stepped in last night to help, or we'd probably have lost them all."

Thinking how grateful she was for Ryan "stepping in," Monique watched her family work sprucing up the place. Nan grumbled about coming up with a mission statement for saving the house, while Tristan fussed in general, primarily because he was tired from fighting a fire all night. Dax climbed a ladder and began peeling back the tarp so they could replace tiles, and Gage, working beside Monique, vocally defended his lifestyle of pleasing women and being pleased by them, without commitment, from Tristan's teasing.

Her movements with the rake faltered as she thought about Gage's standard of living compared with Ryan's. They were both playboys, neither having learned how to love emotionally, both dwelling on the physical aspects of relationships instead. However, Monique believed that her older brother wanted more, maybe not right that instant, but eventually.

Did Ryan want more, too? And how could she get him to consider the possibility? To consider the potential of loving someone, really loving someone, enough that he'd cross over. Ryan didn't even get the good end of the physical deal, since he didn't receive pleasure from the women he visited.

Monique ached for him, for his inability to have the kind of pleasure he'd so freely given her, teasing her with words as that buzzing vibrator touched her everywhere. While the silver battery-operated object may have actually touched her skin, in Monique's mind, she'd felt exactly what he described.

His mouth, nibbling her ear. His teeth, grazing her nipples. His tongue, dampening her flesh in a sexy trail from between her breasts to between her legs. And Ryan, licking, sucking, nibbling and biting that part of her that made her scream with satisfaction.

She wanted to help *him* feel that gratified. In truth *she* wanted to be the one to touch him, kiss him, hold him, suck him, adore him, the way he'd adored her last night.

But she couldn't.

"Damn rule," she muttered, then realized she'd raked the earth so hard a blister had formed on her inner palm in spite of the gloves. No way that wouldn't burn when she worked with shampoo and color. Today's work would be loads of fun.

"What?" Gage asked, cocking his head and looking at her as though he knew what she'd been thinking.

Thank God he didn't.

"I said 'damn fool,'" she said, shaking her head. "I was a fool to think these gloves would keep me from getting blisters." She peeled off the yellow fabric and showed him the circular welt.

Frowning, he looked at his watch. "You've only got an hour before you go to work. Why don't you head on inside and shower?"

"It's ten already?" Had she actually been out here for two hours? Scanning the ground around her, she saw five big piles of debris that she'd generated during her raking frenzy while thinking about her brother's playboy status…and Ryan's. She shot a glance at the roof, where Dax carefully rolled back the area of the tarp where a huge, elongated rip was centered at the steepest peak. How had Ryan stayed up there and tacked those pieces down in the middle of that horrific storm?

Gage moved to stand beside her. "Your ghost knows a thing or two about roofing. He did a good job, and did us a huge favor in the process," he said. "Must be a nice guy."

Monique smiled. "He reminds me of you."

"Well, he just keeps sounding better and better." Gage gave her his trademark wink before shoving her playfully in the arm. "Now go on and get your shower. I'll take up the flak if Tristan says anything about you leaving. And I'll move these piles over to be burned. Then we'll get started on those tiles. No sweat."

She kissed his cheek. He might portray a playboy-without-a-care for the rest of the world, but she knew better. Dr. Gage Vicknair had a heart of gold.

Turning toward the house, she took another peek at the roof, where Dax studied the area beneath Ryan's handiwork.

"I tell you, we owe that ghost of yours," Dax called. "He really saved our hides."

That ghost of yours.

He isn't mine, Monique thought inwardly, though she smiled and nodded at her brother. Then, she silently added, *But, oh, how I wish he were.*

She walked mechanically through the house, entered her room and selected her clothes for the day. After tossing them on the bed, she paused and moved a hand to her mouth, suddenly very tingly, very warm.

"I wonder," a deep voice said near her right ear, "Do you bond this closely to all spirits, feeling everything they want you to feel, like the fact that I just thought about kissing those delightful lips? That is what made you touch your mouth, Monique, isn't it?"

Monique swiveled so quickly she nearly lost her balance. Instinctively she reached for the massive male, but remembering the rule, she jerked her hands back in the nick of time. "Ryan, you scared me to death!" she yelled.

"No, I didn't do that," he corrected. "You're definitely still in the land of the living, ma'am." His mouth crooked up on one side, displaying straight white teeth and a sexy confidence that made her quiver all over. "And if you want to get right down to it, I didn't scare you as much as I excited you. Isn't that right?" He focused on her lips, and immediately they began to tingle.

She slapped her hand over her mouth and mumbled against her palm. "Stop it."

He tilted his head as though wondering whether she meant the request.

"I mean it," she said emphatically.

Shrugging, he backed away from her then sat casually in the same wingbacked chair he'd occupied briefly last night.

Monique eased her hand away and cautiously grazed her lower lip with her teeth to try to make the tingling subside. "You said you wouldn't do anything to a woman that she didn't want."

"That's true," he said easily.

"So why did you do that?" she asked, pointing to her mouth. "And how did you even know that you could?"

"I assumed I could when I went through your every emotion this morning. I knew when you woke, felt your guilt for leaving me unsatisfied last night—"

"What?" she interjected, shocked to her toes.

He ignored the interruption. "Knew when you saw Gage and sensed your intense worry over him, over his lack of commitment and his playboy status."

"This isn't fair," she declared, but he continued.

"Felt the sincerity in your heart about saving this house, your admiration toward Nanette for her determination to restore the plantation, and the fact that you love this place and everything it represents just as much, or more, than the remainder of your family. Even if you choose to hide that fact to the rest of the world."

"But—"

He held up a hand. "And I felt your reaction when your brothers referred to me as *your ghost*." He settled in the chair, crossed his feet at the ankles and eyed her with unhidden interest. "So, do all ghosts bond this intimately with you, or am I special?"

"No ghost has ever prolonged their crossing," she said, her irritation building. How dare he hone in on her thoughts, on her desires? "Most ghosts know their role and do their part obligingly, without fuss and without wasting time. They do whatever it takes to cross, and then they leave. Case closed."

Ryan smiled smugly. "So I *am* special." He focused on her face, then let his eyes slide down to her neck, which immediately started feeling very…nice. Warm. Seductive. Erotic.

Monique's eyes closed slowly as she embraced the powerful sensation. She couldn't help it. She moaned. Then she jerked her eyes open and shook her head. "No," she protested, taking small steps away from Ryan and hoping she was heading in the general direction of her bathroom. Everything seemed rather fuzzy. "You can't do that."

"I can," he countered.

She swallowed hard. "Okay. Okay, you can. But you shouldn't. You said you wouldn't do anything a woman didn't want."

"And I'm keeping my word. I haven't done a thing that you don't want. Remember, I can sense your desires. I know what you want, Monique. And I'd wager I can also feel exactly what you like, and what you don't. You wouldn't even have to tell me. I can figure it out all on my own."

Boy, if that didn't sound appealing. But she couldn't. They couldn't.

"I wouldn't have to lay a finger on you," he said. "The way I see it, we can do any- and everything we want by merely thinking it." His smile hitched back up toward his cheeks. "Granted, I'm kind of hoping you'll see that it's so good that you'll want to move on to the real deal, but I don't mind this as a starter."

"We're not going to do that," she snapped. "I'm supposed to help you move on, not help you—"

"Get off?"

"Exactly," she said, but her heart was racing, and her panties were wet. That sensation on her neck had felt so real, as if he was actually nuzzling her there, nibbling and sucking. Monique wondered if this worked two ways. She looked at his wide, corded neck.

Ryan's hand slowly moved to that very spot. "I guess it does, doesn't it?" he asked.

"What does?"

"This thing between us. It works both ways."

Mon dieu. Now what was she going to do? "I have to get you to cross. You said you know how I feel about this house, about the family and what we do. Well, you're right. I might complain about it, but helping spirits cross is what makes us unique; it's what makes us who we are. And I'm supposed to help you, not play sex games with you."

"Who says you can't do both?" he asked, those black eyes glittering with mischief.

"What?"

"Why don't we compromise, Monique?" Ryan asked. "I don't want to cross, but you're determined to get me to anyway. You don't want to play sex games—or rather, you do, but you don't want to admit it—but I'm determined that you will…anyway. Why don't we both give a little, so that we can both have what we want?"

Her throat was suddenly very dry. "Care to explain that?" she asked hoarsely, as she continued edging toward the bathroom door, as far away from the handsome spirit as possible.

"You're about to go to work, right?"

She nodded, glad that he seemed ready to talk about something reasonable.

"So tonight, when your work day is done, why don't the two of us see exactly what's possible with this whole bonding deal, only going as far as you want to. I mean, technically, we aren't touching, but it's pretty damn close."

"That's what *you* want," she said.

"Right. I know you want it too, but we'll call that my reward from our little compromise."

"And my reward?" she asked.

"If you let us explore this whole bonding thing, then I'll explore the possibility of crossing over."

"What do you mean by *explore* it?"

"I'll let you come up with a plan of action, however you think will best move me on past that light, and I'll give it a shot."

"You'll try to learn to love?" she asked. "To cross over before the deadline?"

"I said I'd give it a shot. That doesn't mean I think you'll be successful. It simply means I won't fight you every step of the way."

Monique thought about that. She really did need his cooperation. And she couldn't deny that she was wondering how far this whole phantom touching thing could go. Could she satisfy him by merely thinking about what she'd do?

"My bet's on yes," he said, flashing a deep dimple in his left cheek.

"You *can* read my mind," she said, aghast.

"No, ma'am," Ryan corrected. "I can't. But I can sense your emotions, and that one right there had 'Can I do everything I wanna do to him?' written all over it."

"You're terrible."

"Yeah," he said, "I am. But you're thinking it, too, aren't you?"

"Thinking what?"

"That you're intrigued by the idea of having mental sex with me."

"Well, I mean…" she stammered.

"Go on, admit it," he coaxed.

"Okay. Maybe I am," she conceded, realizing he already knew the truth. He knew her every thought, which was scarily disarming. Even so, she wasn't about to let him have the entire upper hand. "But we're going to discuss a way to get you to cross, too. That's *my* part of this deal."

"Sure we will," Ryan said. "Right after your toes curl."

7

"YOU STILL take walk-ins, don't ya?" Dax's voice carried above the sound of water splashing in Monique's shampoo bowl.

She looked up from rinsing Evette Cambre's new curls to see her brother removing his LSU cap to display overly long, chestnut waves that barely allowed his hazel eyes to peek through.

"You visited a doctor with that mop on your head?" she asked, smiling. She'd been smiling all day, ever since she'd seen—and felt—Ryan Chappelle this morning.

"Hey, I can control it with that gel stuff you gave me, but I'm heading to the beach tomorrow, remember? When this gets wet, I won't have a chance of viewing the—" He paused, then grinned. "—beach scenes."

"Beach scenes, my behind," Monique said. "You're talking bikinis."

Evette giggled. She was a new mom at thirty-one and had, as her doctor had instructed, foregone hair color during her pregnancy. In lieu of a traditional baby gift, Monique had presented a soft pink blanket to her darling baby girl and a color, cut and highlights to the new mom.

"I'm going to deep-condition you under the dryer before we style it, okay?" Monique squeezed the excess water from Evette's hair, then guided her to a chair where a preheated pink dome-shaped dryer waited to surround her damp head.

"Thanks," Evette said, then smiled broadly at Dax. "And have fun at the beach."

Dax reciprocated the gesture and assured her, "Oh, I will." Then he nodded toward the vacant table in the nail-sculpting area of the salon. "Where's Inez?"

"She took the day off to be with her grandkids," Monique said of her sole employee, a nail sculptor with a penchant for voodoo. Although she'd previously employed up to three stylists and two nail sculptors, during the past year she'd learned that less was more when it came to salons. In other words, the fewer stylists on board, the more clients she had exclusively. It wouldn't have been a huge factor before Katrina hit Louisiana, but once the Vicknair family had to pour every spare dime into restoring the plantation, Monique had simply needed more dimes to spare. The two stylists she had let go had been offered other jobs at salons in Metairie and didn't mind her honest request that they let her have the bulk of business here for a while.

In fact, whenever she took a rare day off, she gave her former stylists free rein of her shop to service their local customers. It had worked out well for all of them, and they'd managed to maintain their friendships.

Monique double-checked the temperature of the air beneath the dome. "All right. Twenty-five minutes," she told Evette, before moving back to her station where Dax stood nearby. A home away from home, her personal area at the shop was complete with a black leather chair, pink styling tools and a large oval mirror. It suited the retro theme she'd used when decorating the salon, with black-and-whites of Elvis and Marilyn strategically spaced along the walls, shiny chrome trim on her styling tools, and black-and-white tiles adorning the floor. She loved her shop, and she loved it when her family came by to visit, particularly when the visitors were Gage or Dax.

She motioned Dax to her chair, snapped a black cape around him, then used the foot pump to lower the chair's height and put his head at arm level.

"I didn't realize you were going to the beach with them," she said softly, fairly certain Evette couldn't hear them, but not wanting to take any chances.

"I could use a trip to the beach, and since my assigned ghost will be with me, I shouldn't piss off our grandmother by leaving town. It's tough to take a real vacation when you may have to get back pronto," he said. "You know. You live it, too. This is a can't-miss opportunity, and I'm not gonna miss it."

"I can't remember the last time I left town. Did you get off work?"

"Taking a week's vacation," he said. "And Nan even told me to go. Said I'd probably work harder around the house after I rested up for a week."

"That's Nanette, always trying to figure out how she can get more work out of you," Monique said. "So, how do you plan to get Chloe's parents to believe that you've talked to their daughter?"

Dax grinned. "I asked Chloe what I could tell them that would let them know I had talked to her. She couldn't think of anything, so Celeste chatted with her to try to figure something out. I mean, she's only six," he said, shrugging. "It was a tough question for a six-year-old. But Celeste got her to talking and found out about the special way Chloe sucked her fingers when she was a baby. She said her parents still laughed about it often. She didn't suck her thumb; she sucked her middle two fingers, so it looked like the hook-'em-horns symbol for the University of Texas, except the bent fingers were in her mouth."

"You think that'll do it?" Monique asked, spraying his hair with water then parting it.

"It should get them considering the possibility, but just in case it isn't enough, I also asked Chloe if she has a favorite toy. She does, a pink stuffed rabbit named Stinky."

"Stinky?"

"She said she spilled milk on it once, and Stinky hasn't smelled the same since, even after several washings."

"I see." Monique snipped away the excess baggage on Dax's head while she listened.

"Chloe wants me to come to the beach so she'll be able to communicate with her parents. And I get a beach vacation and more time with Chloe and Celeste before they cross."

Monique's scissors stopped momentarily, and she eyed her brother in the mirror above her counter. "You like them, don't you?"

Dax's brows dropped a notch, as though he were about to frown, but he caught it and converted it to a small smile. "Why wouldn't I like them? Chloe's a little doll, and I admire the fact that Celeste saw the light and could have gone on over to the other side but chose to stay and help Chloe."

"What do they look like?" Monique asked.

"Celeste and Chloe?"

"Yeah. I'm curious." Monique was more than curious, but she didn't want to let Dax in on her thoughts entirely, not yet. Could it be that their grandmother expected the two of them to work together to fix Ryan's problem with crossing? And would Dax be interested in trying?

"Chloe is tiny, with big eyes, a full mouth and a cute little dimple that creases her left cheek when she grins real big."

He smiled, evidently thinking of the little girl, then he took a deep breath, let it out slowly, and added, "Celeste is tall and thin, with long blond hair that falls in spirals to her waist and eyes that are dark and round and inquisitive. She's got the same type of full mouth, except on a grown woman, it's more—sensual—I guess you'd say." His face colored a bit as he spoke, but Monique pretended not to notice. "Hell, Monique, she's the most beautiful woman I've ever met in my life. She's stunning, inside and out, and she's a ghost." He shrugged. "If she were living, I'd ask her out in a heartbeat, but she's not. Sucks, but that's the way it is."

Monique kept cutting, and wondered if Celeste might be meant for Ryan. "I guess it was nice to find out so much about Celeste and Chloe, when you visited with them," she said. "I don't know that much about Ryan."

"You never want to know anything about them," Dax reminded her. "Or you never have before," he corrected himself.

Her eyes inadvertently darted to the computer by her cash register. She kept records for all of her customers, their cuts, colors, makeup and so on in a database on that computer. But she wasn't thinking about any of that now. She was thinking about her high-speed Internet access, where she could potentially find almost anything she wanted to know about Ryan Chappelle with the mere click of a few keys.

"Uh-uh, sis," Dax warned, "Don't even think about it." He'd obviously followed her eyes to her monitor and keyboard.

"Think about what?" she questioned, trying to play dumb and failing.

"If we try to find out their pasts in order to help them, that's one thing, but if we're doing it out of curiosity, that's another. Don't you remember what happened when Jenee tried finding information on her very first assignment, before she realized that was off limits? Her computer blew up. It didn't merely crash, or even lose the hard drive—the sucker was annihilated. Tiny little pieces everywhere. I know you remember."

"I do," she said, hating the rules more than ever. And that rule wasn't even on the list. They'd simply learned it through trial and error…and lots of computer parts.

"The only reason I learned more about Celeste and Chloe was because they told me," he said.

Exasperated, Monique rolled her neck to one side and popped it loudly, then slowly worked it the other way and did the same.

"That's a bad habit," Dax said.

"It isn't a habit," she contradicted, ready to argue with someone, and he was the nearest one around. "In order for something to be a habit, you have to do it for twenty-seven days straight. I've never popped my neck twenty-seven days in a row."

He looked at her as though she'd sprouted a second head. "Where did you hear that?"

Monique frowned. She couldn't remember. Here she was with an interesting little bit of trivia, and no clue whether it was fact or fiction. "Oh, forget it," she said, ignoring his laughter. This whole thing with Ryan was throwing her world off-kilter. She decided to get back on subject. "Was Celeste married when she was living, or engaged or anything?"

"She wasn't married, and she hasn't said anything about a boyfriend or fiancé. She died at twenty-two, had finished college in the spring, so she was basically just getting started at living." Dax tilted his head to cast a suspicious look at his sister. "What are you getting at, Monique?"

She used her palms to move his head upright. "Don't lean. You want a good cut, don't you?"

"Yeah," he agreed, "but more than that, I want to know what you're up to."

"My ghost can't cross until he learns how to love. I've been trying to figure out how I'm supposed to teach him." She didn't add *and trying to figure out how to make him cross when I really want him to stay.* "And I can't help thinking that it's odd that both of us get ghosts that didn't cross over immediately."

"I'm not following," Dax was saying when Evette edged her head out of the dryer.

"Am I done, Monique?" she called, waving her *People* magazine beneath her face in an attempt to cool off from the heat.

Monique glanced at the timer by her station. "Ten more minutes, Evette. If you can stand it that long, your ends really will look better after the coloring."

"I can do it," she said, popping her head back under, then proceeding to fan the magazine beneath her face like there was no tomorrow.

Monique grinned, looked at Dax's cut in the mirror and nodded approvingly. "You're going to have a blast at the beach." She reached around him to grab a can of mousse, dispensing a huge white blob in her palm. She rubbed her hands together then smoothed the foamy substance through his waves. "Perfect."

Dax leaned forward to withdraw his wallet from his back pocket, but Monique shook her head.

"Like I'd take your money."

He obviously knew she wouldn't, because the end of his wallet hadn't even cleared the top of his jeans before he tucked the leather rectangle back in.

"Thanks," he said, then folded his arms. "By the way, I'm not leaving this chair until you tell me what you've got up your sleeve."

"I want Ryan to meet Celeste," she said, before her brain had a chance to stop her mouth. The truth was she *didn't* want Ryan to meet Celeste, or any other woman. Unfortunately, the truth hurt. She shouldn't care whether Ryan Chappelle fell in love with someone, particularly if that someone was another spirit. That was what she was supposed to accomplish. But if Ryan did meet Celeste and did fall in love, then he would cross over, thereby eliminating any chance whatsoever for Monique to see him again on this side.

The thought of never seeing him again didn't merely hurt; it stung, and Monique couldn't quite figure out why. It wasn't as though they'd shared a whole lot of time. She'd spent less than a day with the striking ghost, but in that day, she'd given herself to him, as much of herself as she could. Yet Monique yearned to give him more. She wanted to give him everything.

But she wouldn't. Couldn't. And nothing was going to change that reality. However, if she didn't do everything in her power to help him cross before his allotted time expired, she'd never forgive herself. Surely Ryan didn't plan to stay in the middle forever, or if he did, it was merely because he didn't realize how good things would be on the other side of the light. Everything was better over there, right? That's what she told the ghosts she helped, and none of them had returned to tell her any differently.

"You want him to meet Celeste?" Dax's voice rose in surprise. "Why?"

"Ryan can't cross until he learns how to love. Celeste is in the middle, too. She's a sweet, gorgeous ghost; he's a sweet, hunky ghost. What's there to figure out?" Monique acted as though the idea didn't stab her heart like a knife. It was the perfect solution, playing matchmaker between her ghost and Dax's, but that didn't mean she didn't want to scream, even as she looked at Dax's reflection in the mirror and forced a smile.

He gave a resigned sigh and unsnapped the black cape, wadded it and tossed it in the chrome bin for dirty garments. Then he closed his eyes and shook his head.

"You know what?" he asked.

"What?"

"I'm afraid you're right. I almost hate saying it, because, hell, I can't deny that I've been feeling *something* toward Celeste. I mean, I've tried my best to act as though this is merely another assignment, and it should be, but it's not. I was glad when Chloe asked me to come with them to the beach house this week," he admitted. "I was absolutely ecstatic, because that gave me more time with Celeste. But…"

"But?" Monique questioned.

"But she told me that her biggest regret about dying so young was that she never had the chance to love. Shoot, I thought maybe she meant that she never had the chance to love me." Dax flashed Monique a grin. "Kind of big-headed of me, wasn't it?"

"Not at all," she answered, running her fingers through his hair to make it ripple into place. "It's sweet, and honest." She took a deep breath, heard the timer buzz, then whispered in his ear. "I want Ryan, too," she admitted. "But I believe he's meant for her."

Dax nodded regrettably. "So you gonna send him to the beach to meet her this week?"

"I'd better, but I'm not sure I know how. We're supposed to get together tonight and discuss his crossing," she said, thinking it best not to tell her younger brother what else they planned to do. Telepathic sex. Would he even believe her?

"How long until he has to cross?"

"A week from tomorrow," she said. "Seven more days." That was it, all the time she had with Ryan, if she got him to cross. And she would. She had to.

"You can make him cross by then," Dax said, then winked. "You haven't lost one yet, and what guy wouldn't want Celeste?" He paused. "You think she'll be attracted to him, then?"

"She'd have to be dead not to be," Monique said, then laughed when he gave her an incredulous I-can't-believe-you-said-that look. "That was bad."

"Yeah, it was," he agreed. "But at least I know she won't mind his appearance."

"That's an understatement," Monique enlightened her brother. "He's absolutely the best-looking—"

Dax held up a hand. "I get it. And that's enough," he said, standing up from the chair. "Well, if it's any consolation, I bet she's the equivalent in female form. Absolutely gorgeous."

Monique swallowed. "That's—good. He's nice, too," she added.

"So is she."

"Then all they have to do is meet and see if sparks fly." She tried to sound positive.

"Monique?" Dax questioned, looking very uncomfortable with whatever he was about to say.

"Yeah?"

"I don't want her hurt," he said honestly. "She really is incredible, and I don't want to see her hurt."

Monique's chest clenched tight. Dax obviously felt more for Celeste than he was admitting, maybe even more than he realized, and she knew exactly how he felt. "I know you don't," she said, "And for the record, I don't want him hurt, either."

Dax wrapped an arm around her and gently squeezed her against him as he kissed her cheek. "We'll be all right, sis."

"Sure we will," she said, blinking past the sudden impulse to cry. Then she leaned away from him and grinned. "We always are."

"Hey, can I get out now?" Evette yelled, her voice a squeal over the low drumming of the dryer.

Giggling, Monique hugged Dax and watched him leave. Tomorrow, he'd head to the beach. Then she had one week left with Ryan. *No,* she mentally corrected. Not one week with Ryan, one week for Ryan to learn how to love…with Celeste.

A gentle pressure squeezed her shoulders, her arms, her heart. It gave her a heady feeling, as though she were held in an intense embrace, a lover's embrace. Then her neck tingled briefly beneath her right ear.

Ryan.

The low roar of the dryer dissipated with a loud click, as Evette, sweating and red-cheeked, climbed out. "I'm done," she said, shaking her head. "I can't take any more conditioning. You ready for me?"

Monique swallowed, nodded. "Yes," she said. "I am." She *was* ready for Evette, but was she ready for the sexy ghost who'd just given her a hug and a kiss that had left her weak-kneed and starry-eyed?

Probably not.

But even so, Monique couldn't wait.

8

MOST DAYS passed fairly quickly in the middle. Ryan could honestly say that some weeks seemed like mere hours, minutes even. But today crept along with the speed of thick sorghum syrup in the middle of winter. Slow. Excruciatingly slow for a guy who loved sex and who vividly sensed Monique's willingness to give him exactly what he wanted. Sex…with her.

Unconventional as it'd be, since this would be an entirely mental joining, Ryan was turned on by the idea of doing something so new, so different, so unique.

So *Monique*.

From the remainder of the world, even her brothers and cousins, she guarded her emotions, her passion for life, death and spirits. But the truth was she lived for it. She didn't *want* to enjoy helping spirits, didn't want it to be so important, but she couldn't help it, and that scared her. Ryan knew why, sensed why. She was afraid of getting too attached, then watching whomever she cared about move on. Right now, she was terrified of that happening with Ryan, but she still wanted him while he was here, which was a good thing. Because Ryan definitely wasn't crossing over until he spent more time, more intimate time, with Monique. They had a connection that went beyond the bond formed between medium and spirit, and he was certain she felt it, too.

If he'd only met her when he was on this side, maybe she would have been "the one" his friends always warned him about, the girl who would match his enthusiasm for life and get him to settle for one female—her. Monique Vicknair was that kind of woman, the kind who made you lose your senses and forget everything else. He'd sure forgotten everything else today.

And Ryan had been on her mind all day, too. He knew it, observed it, absorbed it. A couple of times he'd touched her with his thoughts and had even recognized the precise moment that she acknowledged him holding her, kissing her in his mind.

The entire scenario was intoxicatingly erotic, and he could only imagine how much better it'd be tonight. Now. He'd given her time to come home, work on the house with the family, eat, visit with Nan and Jenee, then prepare for him.

She was sitting on the edge of her bed with her back facing him and her hair pulled up in a sexy twist with long wisps brushing her neck. While he watched, she lifted an antique perfume bottle from the bedside table and sprayed the fragrance beneath each ear, on the inner side of each wrist, and then turned the bottle to face her chest and sprayed some more, leaning her head back as the tingling mist met her breasts.

Ryan's cock hardened at once.

"I know you're here," she murmured, without turning around. "I feel you."

"I'm here," he acknowledged. "And I feel you, too."

"Do you like pink?" she asked, tilting her head to the side and lifting one shoulder as she indicated her hot-pink nightie, its crisscrossing straps beautifully showcasing her back.

Hot pink. No traditional black or red in Monique's bedroom ensembles. Last night, she'd worn the palest blue, and tonight the most vivid pink. He loved it that she never failed to surprise him. And he definitely loved tonight's hue. "I like pink."

She stood from the bed, turned to face him and smiled. "I chose it for you this afternoon. Were you watching me when I tried it on? Or did you feel me then? Because I thought I felt you." Her hand moved to the very spot that he had nuzzled when he'd sensed her preparing for their evening together.

"I didn't watch," he said. "But I felt your excitement, and knew you were thinking about me."

Her fingertips gently stroked the valley between her breasts.

"And I touched you then," he said. "Right there." He nodded toward her fingers.

"I know." Her smile confirmed that she hadn't minded him touching at all. "*I'm* going to touch *you* tonight, Ryan."

"I'm counting on it, ma'am," he said, then raised his brows when she laughed.

Monique shook her head, as though trying to force a rational thought into the sexually charged atmosphere. She visibly swallowed, cleared her throat. "And after we've done *that,* then…"

"Then we'll talk about this female you want me to meet."

Her head lifted, eyes open wide. "You know?"

"I sensed," he corrected. "And I told you we'd talk about your plan for me to cross tonight, but with all due respect, I'd really rather not talk about it until I get my end of the deal." He boldly eyed her body in the shiny pink satin. Two spaghetti straps dropped to small triangles that barely contained her breasts. Wide strips of the pink fabric crossed at the center of her chest to form a bow that appeared to hold the entire thing together, particularly since the lower portions of the nightie didn't make any attempt whatsoever to meet in the middle.

The Harlequin Reader Service® — Here's how it works:

Accepting your 2 free books and 2 free mystery gifts places you under no obligation to buy anything. You may keep the books and gifts and return the shipping statement marked "cancel". If you do not cancel, about a month later we'll send you 6 additional books and bill you just $3.99 each in the U.S. or $4.47 each in Canada, plus 25¢ shipping & handling per book and applicable taxes if any.* That's the complete price and — compared to cover prices of $4.75 each in the U.S. and $5.75 each in Canada — it's quite a bargain! You may cancel at any time, but if you choose to continue, every month we'll send you 6 more books, which you may either purchase at the discount price or return to us and cancel your subscription.

*Terms and prices subject to change without notice. Sales tax applicable in N.Y. Canadian residents will be charged applicable provincial taxes and GST. All orders subject to approval. Credit or debit balances in a customer's account(s) may be offset by any other outstanding balance owed by or to the customer. Please allow 4 to 6 weeks for delivery.

If offer card is missing write to: Harlequin Reader Service, 3010 Walden Ave., P.O. Box 1867, Buffalo NY 14240-1867

NO POSTAGE
NECESSARY
IF MAILED
IN THE
UNITED STATES

BUSINESS REPLY MAIL
FIRST-CLASS MAIL   PERMIT NO. 717   BUFFALO, NY

POSTAGE WILL BE PAID BY ADDRESSEE

HARLEQUIN READER SERVICE
3010 WALDEN AVE
PO BOX 1867
BUFFALO NY 14240-9952

GET FREE BOOKS and FREE GIFTS WHEN YOU PLAY THE...

SLOT MACHINE GAME!

Just scratch off the silver box with a coin. Then check below to see the gifts you get!

351 HDL ELXA   **151 HDL EL4X**

FIRST NAME		LAST NAME

ADDRESS

APT.#	CITY

STATE/PROV.   ZIP/POSTAL CODE

7	7	7	**Worth TWO FREE BOOKS plus 2 BONUS Mystery Gifts!**
🍒	🍒	🍒	**Worth TWO FREE BOOKS!**
♣	♣	♣	**Worth ONE FREE BOOK!**
🔔	🔔	🍒	**TRY AGAIN!**

www.eHarlequin.com

(H-B-05/07)

DETACH AND MAIL CARD TODAY!

© 2009 HARLEQUIN ENTERPRISES LTD.
® and TM are trademarks owned and used by the trademark owner and/or its licensee.

On the contrary, the two sides flared out, displaying a flat abdomen, an adorable bellybutton and a miniscule matching satin thong.

Ryan couldn't speak.

"It's called a flyaway baby doll," Monique said, her voice raspy as her fingers toyed with one edge of the nightie. "I figured it's one step better than the privacy veil."

"It's a hell of a lot more steps better than one," he said.

Her smile broadened.

"And the other good thing about it is this feature." She moved her hand up to pull at one of the ties forming the bow. As soon as the two ends slid apart, the pink satin fluttered to the floor, leaving Monique Vicknair in a shiny pink thong and nothing else. A beautiful vision, Ryan knew, even though he couldn't see it at the moment.

He groaned aloud.

"What?" she asked in mock innocence, batting her lashes for effect. "Something wrong?"

"You better be thankful I'm a man of my word," he said, staring at Monique, completely covered by the golden privacy veil and smiling at him like the devil. "I said I wouldn't physically touch you if you didn't want me to, and obviously, you don't. But if I could, I'd grab you and make you let me see beneath that veil, ma'am."

"I love it when you call me ma'am," she whispered. Then she sighed softly. "And since you put it that way…" Her lashes lowered as she evidently concentrated on letting Ryan see.

The veil disappeared, and the mouthwatering thong was, as Ryan had known, the only scrap of clothing left on her perfect body.

"Take it off," he said.

"Say please."

"Now."

She slid a finger beneath the tiny strap at her right hip, then another beneath the matching one on the left. Then slowly, very, very slowly, she pushed the fabric away. "How's that?" she asked.

"Perfect."

Raising a hand to the back of her head, she removed the clip that held her blond locks captive, and her hair obligingly tumbled past her shoulders, with the tips of it resting above the swell of her breasts. "How are we going to do this?" she asked. "And when are you getting naked?"

"You get on the bed," he said. He'd thought about how they would "do this" all day and was ready to get started. While Monique crawled seductively across the pink and white satin on her bed, Ryan removed his clothes.

"You're beautiful," she said, eyeing his nudity with unhidden fascination.

Ryan smirked. "You really need to come up with a better word. *Beautiful* isn't quite what a guy has in mind when he undresses."

"Sorry," she apologized, though obviously she wasn't. "But you are." Her attention moved to the chair beside her bed. "Why don't you sit there?"

Ryan thought standing on the other side of the room would be the best place for him. That chair was very close to the bed, and he was very close to losing his reserve. What if, when the two of them started letting their sexual imaginations soar, he got completely lost in the moment and climbed on top of her in the bed? "I don't know, Monique."

"Don't trust yourself?" she challenged.

"Actually, I'm not sure that I do," he admitted. "I want in you, Monique, but I'll take what you're offering."

"Telepathic sex?" she said with a sneaky grin.

"I didn't realize it had a name."

She laughed. "I thought of it today. And come on. Sit down close to me. Surely you can control yourself if I do my part."

"Your part?" Ryan questioned, moving toward the chair a bit awkwardly, due to his raging hard-on.

"To satisfy you," she said matter-of-factly.

He dropped into the chair. His throat was dry, his mind was nearly dizzy with the possibilities, with the desire. "Monique, no woman has 'satisfied me' since I've been in the middle. I've satisfied them, but when it came to me…"

"Yeah, I know. You took care of things," she said, then let her eyes linger on the "thing" he took care of. "But tonight, I don't plan on that happening. If I can touch you in my mind, I should be able to touch all of you, right?"

"Damn, I hope so."

She eased back on the overstuffed pillows, situating her hips to spread her legs slightly and give him a tempting view of her center. "Ryan," she whispered.

"Yeah?"

"Prepare to be satisfied." She closed her eyes, licked her lips, then breathed deeply, her breasts rising and falling with the action. Then, to Ryan's absolute astonishment—and undeniable delight—he felt her warmth against the tip of his penis.

"Close your eyes," she instructed, and damn if he didn't feel the heat of her breath against his erection.

He couldn't formulate words, so he didn't argue. He closed his eyes. And growled his enthusiasm as soft, fluttering kisses moved down his length. It had been a long time, a very long time. Hell, he wasn't going to last long. This was definitely going to be a fight on his part.

"Ryan," she moaned, as those kisses edged back up his

penis, and they weren't as soft now. Each sensation was getting hotter, and he definitely felt more pressure as she moved back toward the tip, not kissing anymore, but sucking. He knew it, even before he opened his eyes and saw Monique on the bed.

He nearly came just looking at her. Her eyes were closed, head tilted back and her mouth open, as he sensed her taking him inside, her tongue swirling around the end before she drew him further in. Her hands gripped the comforter, and her hips undulated steadily, in perfect harmony with his own hips, pushing forward, each wave of exquisite desire building toward a climax that he'd wanted…for over a year.

The thought of what she was doing, of what Monique was giving him—what no other woman had done in over fourteen months—brought him to the edge. As if sensing just how close he was, Monique dug her heels into the mattress, raised her hips and moaned as the pressure around his penis tightened, and Ryan felt Monique claiming him, taking every inch of him.

His release came fast and furious and was nearly painful in its sheer force. It went on and on, violently and deliciously, until he thought his body would simply fall out of the chair. The growl that raged from his chest during his massive orgasm caused the woman giving him this ecstasy to open her eyes and take it all in. Now, she continued to watch as the waves of passion subsided, her tongue moistening her lips and her eyes glistening with lust.

"You're beautiful," she said, watching his hips, his cock, the final thrusts.

Ryan managed to smirk. "I'm too spent to argue with you," he said. Then he inhaled deeply, capturing the moment, the complete satisfaction. He looked at her, this exquisite woman who had given him the best orgasm of his life—without touching him at all—and realized...

"I didn't touch you. Even in my mind." Then he shook his head. "I could barely think, but I promise to get that right...in a few minutes."

She laughed, then shook her head. "No, you won't. Not tonight. Last night, you pleased me, and yet you got nothing in return. Tonight was all for you."

Her words took him by surprise. "I *want* to touch you, Monique."

She smiled again, then her grin quickly turned into a yawn. "Not tonight, even if that's what I want, too. Because you promised we'd talk about you crossing, and you already know that I want to talk to you about Celeste." She twisted on the bed to scoop up the pink nightie from the floor, then quickly put it on. It didn't cover her completely, of course, so she flipped back the sheets and climbed beneath them. Then another soft yawn escaped her pretty lips. "But I worked on the house this morning, and again tonight, and I did three perms and a color in between, so I won't be able to hold my eyes open much longer. And I do want you to meet Celeste. Tomorrow. I only have seven more days to help you cross."

Ryan was floored. She'd given him the best sex of his life, then moved right into a speech about how she wanted to fix him up with another woman, so he could cross over and leave her forever. When he'd been in the land of the living, this would have been a dream come true. Sex with a woman who didn't want you for the long haul. Now, however, it annoyed him. He opened his mouth to let her know, but before he said anything, her attention moved from his face...to his cock. And stayed there.

"Ryan? You didn't come?"

Talk about a one-two punch. Monique Vicknair certainly wasn't into cuddling after sex, or talking about what had happened, which would have been fine when he was breathing, but now he was pissed. He wanted this—expected this—to mean more to her. In the back of his mind, he'd essentially believed that if they had great sex, she'd forget her ludicrous attempt to hook him up with another woman so he could learn to love and then cross over. Had she been thinking about hooking him up the whole time she'd given him that orgasm?

No. She hadn't. Because Ryan had sensed the passion behind those kissing sensations. Problem was, he couldn't feel it now. Right now, he sensed that she wanted to discuss this other woman…and his inability to come. Monique Vicknair had given him the sexual high of his life in the middle, then had effectively shot it down in one—make that two—blows.

"I've got a newsflash for you," he said, standing and putting his clothes on the normal way, so she'd have to watch. "I don't bleed, either."

"But you did have an orgasm."

He suddenly wanted to snarl, but he held it in check. "Yeah." He buttoned his jeans. "I did. You see, there's not exactly a need for procreation in the middle. Guess the powers that be don't feel I need that particular part of the scenario. But trust me, I still feel it just the same."

He sat back in the chair, stretched his legs out in front of him and attempted to look casual. No way would he let her know that she'd managed to do what no other woman had ever done. Make Ryan Chappelle want to throttle her. She wanted to do more; he could sense it. But she didn't want it enough to let it happen. In other words, she really was determined to fix him up. Fine. He'd meet this Celeste, but he still had no intention of heading into that light. He simply hadn't "lived" enough yet, and he wasn't calling in his chips early if he could help it. That was what had happened to his folks. He wanted more. Ryan ignored the fact that wanting more was what had ended his life in the first place.

Monique tilted her head as though she were following his train of thought. Then again, maybe she was, because she didn't ask any additional questions about his inability to ejaculate and moved right on to the next item on her agenda.

"I haven't seen her, but Celeste is beautiful, according to Dax. And she's got a good heart. She stayed in the middle to help a young girl cross over. The little girl is Dax's current assignment," Monique explained.

Ryan blinked. For some reason, he'd thought Monique planned to teach him how to love with a breathing woman. Celeste was a spirit? But her being a spirit would make sense, due to the fact that breathing women only pictured Ryan in their minds, and only when they were asleep. Yeah, a spirit was better. "I haven't seen her in the middle."

Monique tucked the comforter beneath her arms and shimmied up in the bed. "I never thought of that. Do you usually see ghosts that are in the middle?" she asked with undeniable curiosity.

Ryan took a deep breath, then let it out. She really was trying to help him, even if it meant sending him away before he got everything he wanted tonight. Plus she had given him his first orgasm in fourteen months that wasn't self-induced. Hard to stay mad at her after that. "I've seen a couple," he said. "Not many. Most aren't in the middle long, if at all. Evidently, most spirits see the light right off the bat and head on over."

"But you haven't met a ghost named Celeste?" Monique asked.

"No. I guess you're wanting me to change that, though, right?"

"I know you don't want to cross," she said softly, "But I don't think you've really thought about the alternative. If you don't cross by next Sunday, you'll be in the middle forever, like it or not. And it would be my fault." She shook her head. "I'd never be able to live with myself if I didn't help you."

"And you think you can teach me how to love—in a week—a woman I've never even met before?"

Her lower lip trembled slightly before she answered. "I have to try. But in all honesty, I'm not sure I can, either. I don't know how to teach someone to love, Ryan. I've never been in love. I've dated lots, but I've never told a guy those three words, never even felt the desire to. Sex is great, but love seems scary."

Then she grinned, and he wanted to kiss her. So he let his thoughts wander...

Monique emitted a soft moan and put her fingertips to her mouth. "Ryan."

"Yes."

"I don't think we should do anything else tonight."

"But you liked it," he said confidently.

She laughed. "Yes, but I'm serious. We need to talk about you meeting Celeste."

Well, at least she admitted she liked it, wanted it. That was a start. "Okay. But I don't see how meeting her will automatically put me in the 'falling in love with her' category. It's highly unlikely, given no other female ever put me there." He smiled. "I kind of prided myself on the fact, when I was breathing."

"Love-'em-and-leave-'em kind of guy, huh?" she teased.

"At least I left them happy."

Monique's laugh was more robust this time, rolling from her stomach and echoing off the ceiling. "You're too much, Ryan Chappelle."

"Thank you, ma'am," he said and winked. "Now, go ahead and tell me how to find this Celeste spirit, and I'll go meet her. But that's as much as I'm promising tonight."

"She's in Pensacola. Do you need an address?"

He smirked. "Nope, I just need a general direction. Spirits tend to stand out to fellow spirits. I'll sense her location, go and have a meet-and-greet. That work for you?"

"For starters. I'd like to talk to you again tomorrow night, about how your 'meet-and-greet' went and what to do next," she said, as though teaching a class and assigning homework.

"What to do next? You mean to fall in love with this woman I haven't met?"

"Yes."

Ryan knew his chances of meeting this spirit and falling head over heels were slim to nil, given that he'd never lost his heart before, and all the other parts of his anatomy were zeroed in on the sexy woman in the pink nightie, but he didn't want to argue. And he had told Monique he'd do his part. "Okay. I'll come back tomorrow night and discuss the potential of learning to love the spirit lady. But only on one condition."

Monique cleared her throat, cheeks flushed slightly. She knew what he'd ask, but she wasn't about to admit it. "What condition?"

"That tomorrow night, we do this touching thing again, but as a joint participation."

"But—" she started.

"Take it or leave it."

"Fine. But if I'm willing to do that, then you've got to be willing to follow through with the next step for learning to love."

"The next step? Do you even have a next step?" he asked.

Her cheeks grew even redder. "Not yet. But I will by tomorrow night."

Ryan laughed. Damn, she was cute. "Fine. I'll go see Celeste, then tomorrow night we'll have our touching session, and then I'll learn about this as-of-yet nonexistent next step. It's a deal, ma'am." Then, before she could protest, he mentally kissed her lips, taking great effort to heat her up thoroughly before he left. Her soft gasp when the kiss ended told him everything he needed to know. Tonight, Monique Vicknair would dream of him. And tomorrow night, she'd have him.

9

NAN'S BACK HURT with every movement, her neck had a crick in it that she didn't think came from sleeping wrong and pains radiated from muscles she hadn't known existed. She'd slept late, which wasn't good, since the family had planned to spend the majority of Sunday working on the roof, but she simply hadn't been able to crawl out of bed when her alarm went off at six. Heaven help her, she'd nearly be thankful when she had to go back to teaching in a couple of weeks. Even trying to interest ninth graders in the Second World War would be a welcome reprieve from her daily worrying over saving the house. And maybe if she stopped worrying, things would fall into place. The Parish President would call off his attempt to destroy their home, the family would miraculously find a way to make all of the improvements that Nan had promised the Historical Society, and then said Historical Society would grant them the funds they needed for full restoration, without requiring them to turn her beloved plantation into some kind of modern freak museum, complete with Grandma Adeline's spirit, six mediums and a revolving door for ghosts.

She finally made it to the bottom of the stairs, and amazingly learned that the sorest muscles on her body were the ones composing her butt. Great. Edging toward the kitchen, she prayed that she hadn't taken *all* of the ibuprofen yesterday and silently cursed herself for not programming the coffeemaker to start automatically. Lord knew she needed a cup, or twelve, pronto.

Pushing the swinging wooden door, she entered the kitchen and smelled heaven, in the form of chicory and caffeine. Then she saw the source of her salvation and managed a smile. "Monique. Thank you for making coffee."

Her cousin had been so focused on the notepad in front of her that she hadn't heard Nan enter. Now she raised her head, took one look at Nan and gasped. "Nanette, you look like hell."

"And good morning to you, too," Nan said.

Within fifteen seconds, she was sitting beside Monique at the table with a hot cup of coffee in one hand and the Advil bottle in the other. Remembering yesterday's battle with the bottle, she extended it toward Monique.

Monique put her pen down, took the bottle and twisted off the cap. "Think you may have overdone it a bit yesterday?" she asked, handing Nan the pills.

Nanette chased two with a hot swallow of coffee. She squinted as the scalding liquid made its way to her stomach, then took another breath and another much-needed sip. "We have one more weekend to get that roof fixed. I go back to school in a couple of weeks. Dax has gone to the beach. Gage and Tristan are both scheduled to work the next six days straight, and you're asking me if I overdid it yesterday? Shoot, I didn't do enough."

Monique sighed loudly. "I'm off work tomorrow, so I can help all day then. And I plan to help today as well, but nobody has shown up yet."

"That's because it's just you and me. The homeless shelter called Jenee last night to see if she could come help today, since they were shorthanded again." Nan took a big gulp of coffee. "She offered to stay, but really, until we get more tiles, there isn't a whole lot we can do, and Jenee can't climb up on the roof anyway without getting squeamish."

"Well, I'm here for the day," Monique said. "What do you want to do?"

"As soon as I've got enough coffee in me," Nan said, "and that's liable to take a pot or two, then I say we gather the tiles that we salvaged during the last couple of storms and see how many more we need to complete the job."

"I thought we put those on yesterday," Monique said.

"Not all of them. There are some in the shed out back that weren't in the best shape, but I'm thinking that they're better than nothing, even if we have to overlap them generously to cover the broken spots."

"Then what are we going to do? We'll have to get more tiles somewhere, and they're really pricey."

"Gage said he was working on it and to give him until next Saturday, so I'm going to let him worry about that for a while." Nan leaned toward Monique and eyed the yellow ruled paper. "What's that?" She read the single line on the page. "Learn to love?"

"I've got to come up with a game plan for getting my ghost to cross," Monique said. "But so far, I can't even define the first step."

"First step?" Nan questioned, finishing off her coffee then rising to pour another cup.

"The first step in learning how to love," Monique explained.

"I didn't realize there were steps involved," Nan said, grinning. "And *that's* what he has to accomplish to cross? Learn to love?"

"Pretty amazing, isn't it?" Monique asked, now doodling

flowers and hearts at the top right corner of the page. "Me, trying to teach someone how to love. I've never been in love, but if I don't figure out how to make it happen for Ryan, in merely seven days, no less, then he'll be stuck in the middle forever."

"And you're wanting to list the steps because…"

"Because we're going to talk about it again tonight, after he spends the day with Celeste."

"Celeste," Nan repeated, trying to remember where she'd heard that name.

"The ghost who stayed behind to help Dax's spirit cross," Monique said.

Nan nodded, remembering. Then she put her cup on the table. "You're playing matchmaker to two ghosts?"

Monique lifted her bright-yellow mug, emblazoned with a smiley face, peered inside and frowned. "I don't even remember drinking it," she mumbled, standing to pour more coffee in her cup. "And yes, I'm playing matchmaker. He has to learn to love before next Sunday. Can you think of a better way for me to get that to happen?" She walked slowly back to the table.

Nan thought about that. She'd never been assigned a ghost who had to learn how to love, so she didn't know how she'd handle it. "I guess introducing him to another spirit would be as good a way as any, if the two of them hit it off. Have they met yet?"

"By now, they probably have. I'll find out if they clicked when he comes back tonight. But even if they did, I'd like to give him a game plan for making sure it all happens by next Sunday."

"Isn't this the ghost who didn't want to cross?" Nan asked.

"Yeah, but he made a compromise with me. He's going to at least try whatever I come up with."

"A compromise?" Nan asked, focusing on the oddest part

of this scenario. "What kind of compromise exactly?" To Nan's surprise, Monique's cheeks turned pink. "Monique?"

"I'd really rather not say."

Then Nan thought back to last night. She'd slept soundly for most of the night, but there had been that one time that she could have sworn she heard something. "You know, I thought I dreamed it."

"Dreamed what?" Monique asked.

"In my dreams, I heard a man," Nan said.

"A man?" Monique questioned, but she looked guilty. Very guilty. "What was he doing—uh—saying?"

"He didn't say anything," Nan affirmed. "But I think he was doing something. No, I know he was doing something. He was yelling, or rather, growling, through what seemed to be a colossal orgasm." While Monique paid rapt attention to the flowers and hearts, which now tripped all the way across the top of the page and down the side, Nan pressed on. "Tell me I imagined it, Monique. Tell me that your ghost wasn't somehow having an orgasm with you in your room. And for goodness sakes, tell me that isn't possible. It shouldn't be, if you're keeping to the rules, because you cannot touch a spirit. You know that." Nan preached in full teacher mode.

"We didn't touch," Monique whispered. "Not physically."

"What does that mean?" Nan asked, horrified at the possibilities. What had her wildest cousin done? And how would Monique's recklessness affect the family business?

"Apparently, because of the bonding with the spirits, we *can* touch, in a way. We can do it in our minds."

Flabbergasted, Nan pressed her palms against her warm mug and drank as she contemplated what Monique had said. Do it in their minds? What the hell?

"He was in the chair; I was in the bed," Monique continued.

"Yet he came?" Nan asked, her bewilderment evident.

"Oh yeah." This time, Monique set a smile free. "Powerfully."

Nan didn't want to touch that one. "And he's coming back tonight so you can teach him how to love someone else, and in the meantime, the two of you can have another go at this— brain sex."

"Brain sex. I like that," Monique said. "I called it telepathic sex, but brain sex would work."

"What exactly did you do? What *can* you do?"

"You really want to know?" Monique asked, her eyes wide with surprise.

"No," Nan blurted, making that decision rather easily. She did not want to know the details of what went on in Monique's bedroom last night. Sex with a spirit, no less. And she'd thought Monique couldn't get any wilder.

She'd obviously thought wrong.

"Okay, okay." Nan tried to come to grips with this situation. She'd had a hell of a week, and was about to have another one unless somebody happened to drop off a truckload of free slate tiles at their front door, but she didn't need to make it worse by trying to decipher why in the world her cousin had gotten involved with a ghost. A ghost that she had to teach to love, in seven days! "Let's don't talk about the no-touching sex right now," Nan decided aloud. "I'm going to have to think about that a little more first. But you're right. You do need a plan of action for teaching him how to love. At least you've got a prospect in mind for the female."

"From what Dax says about Celeste, she's beautiful, smart and sweet. He said any guy would fall for her, and to be honest, I think he's fallen for her a bit, too," Monique said.

"Super. I have two cousins making it with ghosts. Nothing like making our family even more outrageous. And I thought being mediums was enough." Nan shrugged. "Who knew? We can 'do' ghosts."

"This isn't funny," Monique said.

"You're right," Nan agreed. "It isn't." She looked at the pad. "Okay, I'd say number one is for two people to meet, and they should accomplish that today, right?"

Monique wrote it down and nodded. "That's a good start. Number two should be attraction. They have to be attracted to each other."

"So you told me Dax said Celeste was beautiful. Is your ghost good-looking?" Nan asked.

Monique closed her eyes and sighed.

"Fine," Nan said. "So an attraction shouldn't be too big of a problem. Then they need to get along. Chat, get to know each other. Then spend time together, you know, talking about the big stuff—their pasts, where they see themselves in the future. And then, if things progress right, the natural next step will be…"

Monique's eyes popped back open. "Nanette?"

Nan snapped to attention. "Yeah?"

"You sound like you're talking from experience." Monique scribbled furiously, apparently trying to remember everything her oldest cousin had said and recap it on the page.

Unfortunately, Nan couldn't stop the stinging sensation that told her her face was flushing. "We're not talking about me."

"Want to?" Monique questioned.

"No." Nan pulled the pad from Monique and read the list aloud. "One, meet. Two, attraction. Three, chat. Four, talk about past, present and future. Five, intimacy." She nodded. "That's a pretty cut-and-dried version, but that's basically it, from how I envision it."

Monique eyed her speculatively, but didn't say anything else, which was good, since Nanette had no intention of talking about her personal history with love with Monique, or anyone else. Besides, she didn't have time for the emotion. And the two of them didn't have time for this conversation, truth be told.

"Ready to start on those tiles?" She finished off her coffee as she moved across the kitchen, then placed the cup in the sink.

"This is it?" Monique asked, looking at the skimpy list.

"Those things are a lot harder to accomplish than they are to write down. Trust me, that's plenty."

"I'll give him one thing at a time," Monique said. "Basically, he's already done one and two. And if they got to visit today, he may have accomplished number three as well."

"I'd say that number three and number four will take more than a day," Nan said. "Both of them died. That alone should warrant quite a bit of conversation."

"Yeah, you're right. But I've only got six days after today. You think they'll get all that done by Wednesday?"

Nan laughed. "Nothing like putting a deadline on love. I have no idea if they'll have all of it done by Wednesday. I'm saying that it should take more than a day. But you're probably right. They'd need that to happen by Wednesday so they can have a little time to get to the intimacy phase before he has to cross."

Nan could tell by the pained expression on Monique's face that she hadn't liked that response. "You okay?"

"Yeah," Monique said, snapping the notepad against the table before standing. "But honestly, I'm afraid I'm not going to get him to cross in time, that he'll be stuck in the middle forever and it'll be my fault."

"You wouldn't have received an assignment that wasn't possible to accomplish," Nan reminded her. "What would be the point?"

"But what if it is possible, but I still don't pull it off?"

Nan leaned against the kitchen cabinets and studied Monique. There was more to this than she was letting on, and Nan suspected she knew exactly what it was. "You're afraid you won't accomplish your assignment because deep down, you don't want him to cross, do you?"

Monique's head shook slowly.

"Honey, I'm sorry." Nan wrapped an arm around Monique's trembling shoulders. "I wish I could tell you that you should let him stay, but I can't. He *has* to go. If he doesn't, like you said, he'll be stuck in the middle. And eventually, you're going to cross to the other side. Then what? He'll be in the middle, and you'll be over there for eternity. Not exactly what you've got in mind if you're wanting to be with him, is it?"

Monique dropped her head on Nan's shoulder. "No, it isn't. And don't worry. I can do it. It's just going to be hard."

"Still planning to have brain sex with him tonight?" As she'd intended, the question made Monique laugh.

"I could say no, but I'd be lying," Monique answered.

"You think he'll be able to fall for someone else when he's having sex every night with you, whether you're touching or not?" Nan asked.

"It's just sex," Monique clarified. "Why would that keep him from doing everything on that list with Celeste? It isn't like we're falling in love, or anything like that."

"Okay," Nan said, though she wondered if that weren't exactly what it was like. "Then let's stop talking about it and go start on those tiles."

10

Monique was extremely tired, emotionally and physically. If this were a normal night, she'd have fallen into bed and dropped off to sleep instantly. But this wasn't a normal night, and she was examining the short list of Learn to Love requirements when Ryan appeared in the chair beside the bed.

"How was your day?" he asked, as though he were a husband talking to his wife after a long day at the office.

The image scared her, more than she cared to admit.

"It was only a question, Monique," he said, grinning. "No need to get spooked."

She forced a smile. "Sometimes that bonding thing isn't so hot."

"Yeah, but other times, it's very hot. Scalding, even." He eyed her burnt-orange gown. One of her favorite pieces of lingerie, it was satin with sheer panels down each side and made her feel extremely feminine.

"You like it?" she asked.

"Nice color. Suits my mood," he said.

"Your mood?" she questioned.

"Fiery. Tonight isn't going to be a one-way deal, Monique."

She cleared her throat and blessed the fact that the orange gown, with its smooth satin flowing to her ankles, covered her more than practically every other piece of lingerie she owned, even with the sheer panels. She wanted to be covered, at least to start with, because they had to talk about her plan. And tonight, she was determined to talk first, then play, *if* she could convince Ryan to go along.

He brought a long-fingered hand to his brow, then gently pinched the bridge of his nose as if he had a sudden headache.

"You okay?" she asked.

"Sure I am. I'm dying to have sex with you, and you're going to make me talk about that piece of paper in your hand first, and about crossing over."

"That is my part of our deal," she reminded him.

"How could I forget?" he replied smoothly, moving his fingers away from his head and sitting back in the chair. He folded his hands together at his abdomen and stretched his long legs in front of him, as though settling in for a heart-to-heart. "Okay, I'm ready. Fire away. What do you want to know about my day with Celeste?"

"First I want to ask you something," she said.

"Okay."

"I didn't feel you today. I mean, I thought I did this morning when I was with Nan, but it wasn't very strong, and then the rest of the day, well, nothing. Why? Was it because you were with Celeste and the two of you were hitting it off?" She tried her best to act as though she wanted him to say it was.

"You're right," he said easily. "You felt me this morning, but only long enough for me to sense that you were doing your damnedest to get me to that light." He straightened a little in the chair. "After that, I didn't want to stick around."

Monique didn't want to touch that, so she asked, "What did you think of Celeste?"

He cleared his throat. "Well, your brother was right. She is a very attractive lady. And she has a good heart. Truthfully,

I didn't get to talk to her much because she was helping Chloe stay calm upon seeing her parents, but I could tell she's as beautiful on the inside as she is on the outside."

"That's what Dax said." Monique stared at the notepad to keep from looking at those intense dark eyes. Ryan thought Celeste was attractive, and that was good, right? Right. She just had to keep telling herself that. "So, if you go back to Pensacola tomorrow, do you think you might get more chances to talk to her, maybe chat a bit, and then move on to talking about more personal things?"

Ryan peeked at the list. "You've got an agenda for me on how to love?"

"Sort of."

"Well, hand it over." He reached for the notepad and they paused for a moment, her hand on one side, his on the other. Monique felt the intense heat of him extend through the paper barrier.

"You want me." The three words were more of a declaration than a question.

"Yeah."

He gave the page a gentle tug and took it from her grasp. "And yet you want to kick me over to the other side."

"I have to," Monique defended herself.

"So you say." He scanned the list. "Looks like we can check one and two off. I met her, and there was an attraction."

"There was?" Monique asked, not sure how she really felt about this revelation. He'd already admitted that he found her attractive, but somehow "there was an attraction" stung more.

"She's an attractive woman, so my side of that equation was fulfilled. And my looks, as far as I know, have never repulsed any female."

He smiled, and Monique melted. No, Ryan Chappelle was

far, very far, from repulsive. She studied the way his white T-shirt molded the broad flat planes of his chest, the way his biceps pushed against the sleeves, the way the denim of his jeans cradled slim hips. And she knew exactly what was hidden beneath those jeans, could almost *taste* it.

Ryan shifted in his seat, and Monique was fairly certain that portion of his jeans grew. He knew her thoughts, so she had better damn well control them until they finished discussing the list.

"Okay, so the first two are taken care of," she agreed.

"As far as number three goes, I wouldn't say we 'chatted' exactly today, since most of her time was spent with Chloe. If I go back tomorrow, I suppose that's what we'll do—before we hit the discussing past, present and future deal. That seems to be the plan here."

"It's a lot to do in a week, isn't it?" Monique asked, dismayed. What if she couldn't get Ryan to love? What if she couldn't get him to cross? And if she didn't, would she spend the rest of her life blaming herself for not making it happen? How would she know that she tried her hardest, when deep down, she didn't want him to leave?

"You know what might help me accomplish these?" he asked, tapping the notepad.

"What?"

"Practice." His black eyes examined her intensely.

"Practice?" Monique repeated, her throat tightening.

"You do want me to accomplish everything on that list this week, right? With Celeste?"

"Yes," she said, and hoped he didn't recognize the semi-lie. She wanted him to accomplish everything, to cross over, but the thought of him getting to step five, intimacy, with Celeste didn't sit very well. At all.

"Okay. Then you won't mind helping me practice a bit."

"I guess not," Monique said.

"Well, let's see, you and I have accomplished number one and number two. We've met, and there is obviously an attraction."

"I'll say."

His low laughter rumbled in the air and rippled down her skin.

"We've chatted," he continued.

"Yeah, we have," she agreed.

"So I guess we're to the step where we talk about past, present and future. If I'm going to do that with Celeste, I could probably use a bit of practice. Do you want to go first?"

She swallowed. Practice learning to love. With Ryan. All kinds of alarms were going off in her head, but none of them were strong enough to make her say no. "What do you want to know?"

"When did you learn you were destined to be a medium?" he asked, surprising her with the speed with which he formulated the question. How long had he been wondering about her past?

Monique remembered the day she'd learned about the Vicknair heritage. "I was six when Grandma Adeline called me into her sitting room and showed me one of the assignment letters on the tray. At that time, the spirit sending the assignments was her grandfather, Jean-Claude Vicknair. Like Grandma Adeline, he didn't take kindly to mediums who kept him waiting. I remember once when my father didn't respond quickly enough, he made Daddy's skin burn so badly that he had tiny blisters on his hands by the time he got to that envelope."

"Sounds painful."

She shrugged. "Daddy was testing the waters, and he learned who was boss. I'm just glad Grandma Adeline doesn't take it that far with me."

"You test the waters, too?" Ryan asked.

"Like father, like daughter, I suppose," Monique said with a smile.

"When your grandmother told you, is that when you actually started intervening with ghosts that needed help?"

"No. It doesn't work that way," Monique explained. "When I was a child, my father served as medium for our branch of the family. The gift doesn't kick in until you're eighteen, so Dax, Gage and I watched and learned, the same way our cousins watched and learned from their parents. We all knew what was coming, but we had a little time to prepare, which was nice. That'd be a pretty intense burden to drop on a six-year-old."

"That's how old Chloe is," Ryan said, reminding her that he'd spent his day with Dax's current spirit. "I can't imagine giving a little girl that age the responsibility of getting spirits to cross, particularly a stubborn spirit like me."

Monique grinned. "Hey, I'm twenty-four, and I still don't know if I'm ready for a stubborn spirit like you."

"You're ready for me, Monique," he replied, his voice changing to that husky version she'd heard last night, when he was aroused.

"Obviously I am, or they wouldn't have given me the assignment," she said, trying to tamp down the sexual tension until they finished talking about his crossing. "Anything else you want to know?"

"Why have you never been in love?"

The question surprised her, but she surprised herself even more when she answered. Sharing herself with Ryan simply seemed the thing to do. Besides, in a week, he'd be gone. Unfortunately. "I haven't felt close enough to any man to tell him about what I do, helping the spirits. And I can't give myself completely to someone who doesn't really know me. If he doesn't know about me helping spirits, he doesn't know me."

She was amazed at the relief flowing through her with this admission. Internally, she'd always known why she held back, giving her body to men, but refusing to hand over her heart. Now that she'd said it out loud though, she felt intensely relieved, and intensely vulnerable.

"I know about you."

A simple statement, but it said plenty. Ryan did know about her, about how she felt regarding the spirits, the family, and about him.

Monique needed to change the subject. "Now you have to reciprocate," she said, trying to sound as though she was still merely talking about the method of falling in love, instead of actually sensing *something* happen within her very soul. "After Celeste opens up and talks to you about her past, then you talk to her about yours."

"Okay," he said. "The biggest part of my past, the way I see it, is how I died."

Monique jerked her hand up to stop him. "No, Ryan. Please. I don't want to hear how you died."

"But Celeste and I have both stopped living. Don't you think we should discuss how we both ended up in the middle?"

"Yes. Yes, I do. I believe the two of you should discuss it, but you don't have to practice that part with me. I don't like to learn how spirits die. I don't want to know. It hurts." She didn't add, *and it'd hurt way too much to think of you dying.*

"Then what do you want me to tell you?"

"Tell me about your parents," she said, thinking that would be safe ground.

He looked pained for a moment. "They died young, very young, in a car accident. Dad was forty-four, Mom was forty. They spent their entire lives living for the future, planning for retirement and never taking advantage of the here-and-now.

No vacations. They'd take them later, when they had more time and money. No spontaneous purchases. That would happen when it better suited their lifestyle. So they lived, they worked and they died."

Realization dawned. "You didn't want to live that way. You were determined to try—everything."

Ryan nodded. "Yeah, but I guess I went overboard. I decided there was nothing I would miss out on, no matter what. If there was something I wanted to try, I tried it. If there was something I wanted to buy, I bought it. I liked to live on the edge, and I particularly liked things that typically scare people, like being high. And I'm not talking about high on drugs, or anything like that. I mean literally being high, thousands of feet above the ground, in the clouds. I liked that exhilaration, feeling you were on top of the world, and I planned to feel it as much as possible. And that, in a sense, cost me my life."

What had he done? Monique fought the incredible urge to ask. She didn't want to know. Really. She couldn't let herself get *that* close, not to Ryan Chappelle nor to any other spirit. She wouldn't.

"Ryan."

"Yeah?"

"I think you'll do fine sharing your history with Celeste. But right now…"

"You want me," he completed.

"I do."

"Darlin'," he said, emphasizing that silky Southern accent, "I thought you'd never ask." And then he stood and pulled the T-shirt over his head to display a beautiful set of ripped abs with a tantalizing thin trail of dark hair down the center leading to the top of his jeans, which he unbuttoned. Next came black boots, and they hit the floor with two loud thuds as he tossed them aside. He moved back to the top of the jeans and eased the zipper down. "Come on, darlin'," Ryan encouraged. "You don't have any reason to wait. Tonight's for both of us, remember?"

Never taking her eyes from his, Monique stood on the opposite side of the bed and shifted her shoulders so one orange strap fluttered to her elbow. Then she did the same with the other. The fabric, held up by the thick straps now resting at her elbows, pooled at her waist. His attention focused on her breasts.

"You see me, don't you?" she asked.

He finished with the zipper and removed his jeans. As usual, he wore nothing underneath. Her center quivered at the beautiful vision, this incredible man in all his naked wonder. "Yeah, I see you," Ryan said. "But I want to see everything."

She let the straps fall, felt the smooth silk shimmy down her legs…and focused on willing the privacy veil away. From the stormy lust in those black eyes, she thought it had worked. "Still see me? All of me?"

"Every exquisite inch."

She tried to gather her courage. She wanted to try something, something to let the two of them experience even more together, but wasn't sure if he'd be willing.

"Tell me," he instructed.

"Tell you what?" she asked, edging toward the bed and crawling up on her side. Monique knew he liked the way she looked on this bed, in the sea of pink and white, so she let him look. Balancing on her side, she propped her head on her hand and gently moved her top leg over the lower one, creating a subtle friction at the juncture between her thighs, and thinking about how good it would feel to have him there. Right there.

"Tell me what you're wanting to do tonight," he said. "I

can sense you want something *different,* but I have no idea what. He moved toward the bed, his thick erection at Monique's eye-level, and she boldly examined it.

"I want you," she said. "Here." She patted the opposite side of the bed.

Ryan's surprise was obvious. He looked at the spot where her hand patted the other pillow, and then at the short distance that would separate them. "Monique, I said I wouldn't touch you."

"I know, and a ghost can't tell a lie."

"That's what they told me," he agreed. "But this would damn well put it to the test."

"I want you beside me when I come," she said. "If we can't do it the regular way, at least we can be in bed together when it happens." She paused, then added, "If you want."

"You know I do," he said. "And I'm not supposed to be able to tell a lie, so I'm going to bank on that." Careful to stay on his side, he climbed on the bed and settled against a big white pillow. "Because I sure can't tell you no."

She smiled at that. "Good. Now close your eyes."

His brows drew firmly together. "You're kidding, right?"

"No, I'm not. This is tempting enough without me looking at you, and I'll admit I'm not comfortable with you looking at me when I'm having brain sex, either."

"Brain sex? *Another* name for it?"

Monique decided not to tell him that Nan had come up with that one. She didn't want to talk about Nanette, or anyone else, right now. She wanted to make love to Ryan. "Close your eyes, Ryan."

"I watched you last night," he admitted.

"I know, and I was too into you to let it matter. But tonight, promise me you'll keep your eyes closed. If I see you, I may try to touch you, and I'm afraid if you see me, then you may do the same. Let's just lie here, in the bed, beside each other. I'll know you're close, and you'll know I'm close. That's what I want."

"You drive a hard bargain," he said, "but okay." He slid his eyes closed, and a forest of black lashes met his cheek.

Monique's eyes had barely closed at all before she sensed him, moving over her, his heat pressing sweetly against her flesh. Brain sex. Who'd have thought?

"Kiss me, Monique."

While the voice came from the other side of the bed, the feeling, the exquisite warmth of his mouth, was right above her own. His tongue teased her lower lip, then moved inside. Monique had wondered all day what it would feel like, making love to him in her mind. It was extraordinary. Mind-boggling. Her senses were in tune to everything he was doing, his hands cruising smoothly up and down her sides, over her breasts. A sharp arrow of intense desire rocketed from her nipples to her core when he mentally pinched the tips, and she cried out with the need to come.

"Please, Ryan," she coaxed, while she let her own mind wander, and mentally flexed her hands over the broadness of his chest.

While the sensation of his kisses left her mouth and trailed sweetly down her body, his hands gently kneading her inner thighs, Monique followed her own path. She concentrated on nibbling at each flat male nipple and smiled when she heard his responding hiss of pleasurable pain. Then she moved lower, visualized tracing the chiseled indentations of his abs with her tongue before focusing on that hardened part of him that demanded her attention, while Ryan lavished equal attention on her core. In the same way that he brought her to climax with the vibrator, he described what he was going to do.

"This is me this time, Monique. No vibrators or anything else. Me. And I'm going to suck you, kiss you, nibble you and bite you, right where you want it most, until you can't take any more."

She actually sensed Ryan's mouth, sucking on the sensitive flesh at her inner thigh. She opened her legs and pushed her pelvis forward, enjoying the feel of his mouth there…burning to feel it on her throbbing clitoris.

"Nibbling you," he continued, as the intensity got stronger, and as Monique let her mind venture deeper into this pleasure…and sucked harder on his penis.

"Biting you," he said, while a burst of something that made her see stars claimed her senses…and made her take all of him, every inch of him, determined that she would make him feel everything she was feeling.

Spasms ripped through her and she cried out in orgasmic abandon as Ryan surrendered, his deafening growl of release filling her room, while the man began to fill her heart.

11

WITH TWO LADDERS propped against each side of the house, the Vicknair plantation stood beneath the Friday morning sun like an enormous square spider with skinny metal legs. Another brutal storm was on its way, expected to hit Louisiana tonight, and they had no time to spare in repairing the roof. Nan's "Be ready to work at seven," directive, issued last night, had all of the cousins except Dax and Gage already removing the tarp from the roof and assessing the gaping areas where Adeline Vicknair's beloved slate tiles were missing in action.

"Gage work late?" Jenee asked, as she and Monique labored together to straighten out the big blue sheet and fold it. The thing snapped loudly in the morning breeze while they maneuvered it corner to corner, then fold to fold, until they held a semi-neat rectangle of overlapping plastic.

"Yeah, he worked late, but he said he'd be here as soon as he could," Monique answered. She'd been up late too, having another round of brain sex with Ryan. For the past five days, he'd spent his days with Celeste and his nights with Monique. Evidently, he and Celeste had grown closer. He'd told Monique that he felt he was progressing through the steps and might actually be able to cross by Sunday. However, he'd also informed her that while he may be *allowed* to cross, that didn't mean he would. Neither claim had sat well with

Monique. Had he already become intimate with Celeste during the day, while having phenomenal brain sex each night with Monique? Was that even possible? And should it bother her that it bothered her?

She'd moved all of today's appointments to tomorrow so she could help the family before the storm, but with the limited amount of sleep she'd had this week, she didn't know how energetic she'd be for the task. However, she had to help them pull it off. The roof couldn't stand another storm, and another one was definitely coming.

Despite her fatigue, Monique eyed the roof and was glad she had something to keep her busy today—to keep her mind off the fact that she had only two days until Ryan's deadline to cross.

Two. Days.

"Well, I'm glad Gage is coming," Tristan said, backing away from the house to assess the damage and taking Monique's thoughts from her mesmerizing spirit. "We're definitely going to need everyone who can help today."

"What do you think?" Monique asked Tristan, as Jenee carried the folded tarp to the shed at the back of their property. "Will we be able to get it fixed before the storm comes?" They'd listened to the weather reports last night and that morning and knew that the gusty breeze, uncommon for Louisiana in August, confirmed the forecast. A storm—a big one—was headed their way.

"If it were a normal roof, I'd say we have a good week's worth of work left to patch those spots. But since all of the problem spots are on the steep peaks, and since slate is so much more fragile than traditional shingles, I'm betting we're looking at a month."

"But we're getting a storm tonight." Jenee walked back

around the side of the house. She'd pulled her hair in a high ponytail and looked even younger than her twenty-one years.

"I know," Tristan said. "And I also know that if those Gulf winds are as powerful as they're predicting, no tarp is going to do the trick. We've got to get this baby patched, unless we're ready for the ceilings to cave—again."

"No way," Nan declared. "Ever since he was elected Parish President and then gained a seat on the Historical Society's board, Charles Roussel has been trying to use that power to get our home. Right now, he's probably hoping the roof will cave before the Historical Society inspection and then he can force us to hand it over. Well, he can't. I won't let him. We *have* to make it through this storm. The inspection is next week."

Tristan smiled. "Hey, I'm right there with ya, Nan, but the truth is we've salvaged less than a hundred slate tiles, and we need a few thousand. How are we going to come across them in a day? And more than that, how are we going to pay for them, when every one of us has tapped out all our resources?"

"We'll do what we can," Jenee said. "Right, Nan?"

"Right." Nan strapped a tool belt around her slender hips, filling two of the pockets with roofing nails and dropping a hammer in the cloth loop on one side. "Bob Vila ain't got nothing on me." As they all strapped on similar belts, chuckling at her remark, the purr of an engine took their attention from the roof. Nan smiled.

"Oh good, now that Gage's here, we can divide up those sections into five—" Her words stalled in her throat and her eyes narrowed into slits as a black Mercedes that all of them knew well slunk down the drive, then circled wide around the biggest oak on the property. The Parish President had decided to pay them a visit.

"Look what the storm brought in," Nan muttered, as Charles Roussel, grinning, stepped out of the car.

He was no more than five-eight, only about an inch taller than Nan, Monique noted as he neared, but he had the presence of a man well over six feet. His chest was broad and powerful, biceps bulging even in his suit jacket, and his stance commanding as he stopped in front of Nanette and extended a handful of papers. "I brought you something, Ms. Vicknair."

She snatched them away and scanned the top page, while his bright politician's smile grew even larger. Monique was sure it would help Nan's disposition if the guy looked like the weasel she claimed he was. Unfortunately, Roussel's tan skin, black hair and megawatt smile was an honest-to-goodness compliment to his ancestors, and Monique would be lying if she said his campaign posters hadn't caused her to do a double-take whenever she'd passed one on Airline Highway. Cajun eye-candy, most women would say, but because of his determination to take away the home they loved, all the Vicknairs, particularly Nan, saw the guy as a different kind of candy altogether. Slimy and sour. Nan *had* admitted to Monique that she'd had one hot and heated dream where a naked and glorious Charles Roussel was the star attraction. It had enraged her that the guy could infuriate her thoroughly during the day and still somehow finagle his way into her bed via her dreams at night. Not that Nan would ever tell him; she'd only mentioned it to Monique once after a few margaritas. Monique suspected that the real reason Roussel got under Nan's skin so much wasn't just because of the house, but because she was, like it or not, attracted to the weasel.

"What now, Roussel?" Nan asked, refusing to address him by his title. He might have won the nod from voters, but damned if he ever got one modicum of respect from Nan for the victory. Monique was extremely proud of her oldest cousin for standing her ground. She sure was standing it now, her black hair waving in the breeze, high cheek bones made more prominent by her clenched jaw, eyes glittering in a color Monique would classify as why-don't-you-crawl-back-under-your-rock green.

Tristan, who could have easily intervened and taken over the Vicknair end of this conversation, given he was the oldest male Vicknair around, merely smirked and let Nanette wage this particular battle. It was only right, since she'd worked so hard the past few months to keep the feud going.

"Why, it's fairly self-explanatory," Roussel said, leaning toward Nanette as though he were scanning the paper, when in fact, Monique suspected he wanted to be closer to Nanette's impressive chest. "Based on this study by the National Home-builder's Association, they've recommended demolition for properties that stood more than six feet in floodwater after the hurricane. You see, that wasn't clean water that we're talking about, it was contaminated. Overflow from the levees, swamps, all those kind of things that had God-knows-what growing in it—that was what was in your house, and that's the reason it's going to have to come down. Safer for the community, you know. I've spoken with the city commission about it."

Nan was so enraged that Monique was surprised steam didn't literally sizzle from her pores. "You know what, Roussel?" she said, bringing her face merely inches from his.

"What's that, Ms. Vicknair?" he asked, his voice as smooth as silk, as though he were thoroughly enjoying this little game.

"I'm afraid we never got around to measuring the flood-water on the first floor, but I'm certain it never got near the six-foot mark. Since I didn't measure it, there's no way to prove whether it did or it didn't. There are no marks on the wall. And we currently have the so-called contaminated area closed off from the rest of the house until we get it properly cleaned, which we will do soon. Very soon. I'm afraid, Mr. Roussel, that you don't have a case for your city commission."

Roussel's smile faltered ever so slightly, Monique noticed. Chalk one up for Nan. Then he cleared his throat and re-grouped. "You realize, Nanette." He opted for her first name this time. "Fixing that roof will be very costly. Those are slate tiles you've got there, not exactly the cheapest thing on the block. And if you're looking at restoration, you'll want au-thenticity. That's a priority to the society. Hell, there's barely a handful of them here," he said, waving at the miniscule piles they'd manage to salvage from previous storms. What are you going to do about the rest of those spots? And what are you going to do when the winds hit tonight? That tarp worked for you last time, but I dare say it won't cut the mustard tonight."

"And I suppose you have a remedy for our little problem?" Nanette questioned. "What might that be, Roussel? Because I know you didn't come here out of neighborly hospitality."

His grin came back in full, blinding force. "As it happens, my brother is perfectly willing to buy this place today, regard-less of the damage that may ensue with tonight's terrible storm."

"Didn't know it was going to be terrible," Tristan said. "You know something we don't?"

"It's going to be windy, more windy than last week's," Roussel answered, glancing at Tristan as he spoke. "And Johnny says he'll buy the place as an addition to his property, since they're side-by-side and all. He'll pay for the demoli-tion, and give you fair market value, based on the property's current condition, of course."

"Mighty nice of him," Tristan said. "We should go over and

thank him for offering to give us fair market value, when every one of us knows the place will be worth a small fortune when it's fully restored."

"But it isn't fully restored, is it?" Roussel questioned, his tone brittle and sharp.

"Not yet," Nan said, "But we're working on it. And we aren't interested in selling to your brother, or anyone else."

"Hell, it doesn't even have a roof for tonight's storm," Roussel spat, turning on his heel and stomping toward his Mercedes. "Just wait until tomorrow. After the rest of that roof is ripped to bits, you'll beg us to take it off your hands, and the price won't be nearly so pleasing then." He paused beside his open car door and looked at the house. Monique saw it then, the admiration for the big, bold mansion, and the undeniable lust in his eyes. He wanted the plantation, not to demolish, but for his own residence. Monique knew it as sure as she knew that Nan, and the rest of them, would never let him have it.

Huffing out a breath, he called, "I'll be hearing from you tomorrow, Ms. Vicknair." But before he had a chance to enter his car, a gigantic hot-pink truck roared up the driveway. A big cloud of dust filled its wake, and the driver had no quandaries at all about bringing the massive pink beast within inches of Roussel's prized Mercedes.

Monique shielded her eyes and waited for the dust to clear, then laughed when she saw the four individuals in the vehicle. Gage had struck again, and Charles Roussel wasn't going to like it. Monique, and from the grins on their faces, the remaining Vicknairs, could hardly wait.

"What the hell?" Roussel coughed as the thick gray cloud coated his previously shiny car with good ol' Louisiana grit and grime.

"It's a truck," the sexy female who'd just jumped from behind the wheel informed him. She tossed her long strawberry mane behind her and thrust her big bosom in front of her as she waited for introductions. A brunette and a blonde, dressed identically to the driver in tight white T-shirts, hot-pink short-shorts, and tan work boots exited the passenger's side followed by Gage. His devilish smile claimed his gorgeous face, and the twinkle in his eyes showed he was more than ready to face Charles Roussel.

"President Roussel," he said, tipping his head in greeting. "What brings you out here so early? I figured you as the sleeping-in type."

"I came to talk to your cousin," Charles said, still a bit off-kilter from the pink truck practically kissing his bumper.

"You don't say. What about?" Gage asked, leaning against the pink monster, while the three females, apparently finding nothing at all interesting in the Parish President, moved to the back of the truck and began to unload bundles. "Tristan," Gage said, "why don't you help them with our supplies while I visit with Mr. Roussel here?"

"Sure thing," Tristan said, chuckling.

"What you got there?" Roussel asked, evidently realizing what the girls were unloading.

"That?" Gage asked, then shrugged. "Why, that's the best roofing team this side of the Mississippi. Triple D Roofing," he said, winking at Monique then acting as though he didn't hear her giggle. "Deidre, Dominique and Dani."

"I didn't mean who are they? I meant what're those packages they're unloading?" Roussel asked, exasperated.

Gage nodded as though he were a teacher impressed that the Parish President had asked a good question. This time, Nan did the poor job stifling a laugh.

"Well, those 'packages' as you called them, are actually the exact same kind of synthetic-slate roof shingles that were used on *This Old House* last week. You ever watch that show? Man, I love it."

The blond roofer hauled a big bundle off the truck and tossed it at Tristan. He caught it with an appreciative grin. "Nice biceps," he said, passing the small group gathered around Roussel's car and carrying the stack of tiles to the side of the house.

Gage's grin grew a little broader. "See, those slate shingles are made of recycled rubber and plastic, but they come as individual tiles. I learned about them on the show. They're eighteen inches long and twelve inches wide and have been dyed to match the antique roof slates."

"So they aren't real. They won't add to the authenticity of the house, if you're applying for historical status," Roussel quickly pointed out.

"You see, I called and asked the director of your Historical Society that very question. Seems since the older slate doesn't hold up in hurricanes and this new stuff does, the society is quite willing to accept them as restoration for the originals." This time, Gage made a big production of shrugging. "Go figure. Hey, maybe if you attended more of the society's meetings, you would've known."

"Probably pretty expensive," Roussel continued. "Bet it'll take you a while to replace the remainder of the roof after you repair those holes. You really think we want a patchwork roof on the list of historical places?" He grinned, thinking he had Gage.

He didn't.

"That was what caught my attention when I saw them on the show," Gage explained. "And it's exactly what the TV crew saw as the main appeal of the tiles. They look uncannily like the real thing, cost much less and install more easily. Shoot, we can install them with a nail gun."

Roussel, looking defeated, climbed in his car. But Gage wasn't done yet.

"Oh, and if you're worried about their lifespan, don't be. They have a fifty-year warranty, but the manufacturer predicts a one-hundred-year life expectancy. Isn't that great? With these tiles keeping us warm and dry, the Vicknair place should be here another century."

Mumbling a stream of choice words, Roussel slammed his door, then honked his horn to move the Vicknair cousins out of his way so he could circle around. There was no way he could back up, due to the big, bold pink truck blocking his path.

After he left, and after Jenee, Monique and Nan had squealed their approval of Gage's Oscar-worthy performance, Tristan held up a hand to stop the commotion.

"Okay," he said. "Where did you find the sexy roofers, and where did you get the money to pay for all of these tiles? Because even if they are cheaper than the real deal, they had to be paid for somehow. What'd you do, Gage?"

Gage smiled wryly. "Aw, hell, I didn't need to pay off that medical school loan yet anyway."

Nan's mouth dropped open. "We can't let you do that, Gage," she said, shaking her head so hard her black hair swayed like a cape around her shoulders. "We can't."

"Hey, I'm a doctor now, remember? Sure, I've only been pulling a paycheck for six months, but pretty soon, I'll be rolling in dough. Might as well use the bit I've put away to help the family."

"Gage," Monique said, "Are you sure?"

"Definitely. And the roofers were hired to renovate the

Ochsner emergency room last year. I thought about them after I saw the television show and ordered the tiles. Luckily, they were available for hire, and I was able to get the tile shipment expedited from Canada. I figure if we all work together all day and up until that storm hits tonight, we might, as Larry the Cable Guy says, Git-R-Done."

Nan's eyes glistened as she rushed forward and hugged him, then kissed his cheek. "Thank you, Gage."

"Don't thank me until that last tile is nailed. And trust me, we're going to be mighty sore in the morning. You may not be thanking me then."

"I thought you were on call this weekend," Monique said.

"Tonight I am, but I'll be okay. This is important." Gage turned toward the three women nailing boards across the roof for foot support. "Are you ready to show us what to do?" he called.

The blonde beamed at Gage, and Monique had the distinct impression that he'd already shown her what he could do, at least once.

"Bring the rest of those bundles over by the house," she yelled, "then get a nail gun and head on up. We'll have you putting these babies on in no time."

"Gotcha," Gage yelled back. Then he looked at Jenee, who looked rather jittery. "Still afraid of heights, cuz?"

"I can do it," she said, but her grin looked more like a grimace and her eyes bordered on tears.

"I know you can," he said, "but we're going to need someone to haul things to us, too. Hammers, nail guns, cutting tools. And if you could fix some lunch for us when it gets time and keep a cooler of water or lemonade at the ready, that'd be a big help."

"He's right." Tristan tossed an arm around his sister.

"That'd help us plenty. Also we don't want you tossing your breakfast where we've gotta work."

She gave him a grateful grin and nodded. "If that's okay with all of you, and you still think everything will be done before the storm, then that'd be much better for me."

"It's done then," Gage declared.

"I'll go get started on that lemonade," she said, and headed toward the house.

"Now," Gage said. "We've got seven people total to roof this thing in a day. According to *This Old House*, we should be able to finish the job with a little time to spare. You guys up to the challenge?"

"Actually, I think we may have eight people," Nan said.

"I wasn't counting Jenee when I—" Gage started, but stopped when Nan shook her head.

"I'm not talking about Jenee." Nan pointed toward the roof, where a nail gun seemed to be working at breakneck speed installing the new tiles on its on accord. Big square pieces of synthetic slate moved through the air then lined up perfectly against the preceding tile before being nailed into place, magically, by that gun.

All eyes turned to Monique for verification of who they believed was currently working on their roof, but Monique didn't see any of them. She was too focused on the muscled male, his hands moving steadily, biceps flexing and relaxing as he placed one tile in place, then another, then another, edging across the roof in quick progression.

The blond roofer, who happened to be nearest to the working ghost, stopped nailing the wooden brace and squeaked. Monique thought of it as a squeak, because it certainly wasn't loud enough to be considered a scream.

"It's okay!" Gage called up. "You're going to have to trust

me on this, Carol, but it's nothing at all to be worried about. Just a ghost who wants to help."

"Carol?" Tristan questioned. I thought you said their names were Deidre, Dominique and Dani."

"Nope. It's Carol, Adele and Dani," Gage said, grinning. "I just thought a company name of Triple D Roofing would get Roussel's attention."

While Tristan laughed, Carol's mouth formed a round O. Ditto for the other two, who had also taken notice of the floating nail gun with obvious trepidation.

"I promise there's no reason to worry," Gage reassured them. "He's a friend of Monique's."

They still looked rather shocked, but after seeing that the invisible person was as intent on completing the task as they were, they all went back to work.

Only in Louisiana.

A friend of Monique's. Monique heard the words, but didn't say a word. Instead, she found the ladder nearest the sexy male—the sexy ghost—who'd spent every night this week making her every wish come true.

Now, if she handled things right, she would do the same for him, by helping him learn to love...someone else.

12

RYAN SITUATED a large bundle of tiles beside him on the roof, which wasn't nearly as steep as it appeared from the ground—a good thing for Nan and Monique, who he assumed had never ventured into this particular arena of construction before—then proceeded to nail the next row of synthetic slate into place.

The large squares went down effortlessly, cut and nailed easily, and generated a nice, true line. If he'd known about them when he was living, he'd have used them on the house in Dothan. Ryan had inherited the home when he was in college and barely twenty. It was a massive house for a guy barely out of his teens, but then again, his parents hadn't planned on him inheriting it so soon, because they hadn't planned on dying so soon. But they had, and he did. Ryan would bet they hadn't planned on him joining the land of the non-living at the age of twenty-eight, either.

But he had.

Due to the nail gun's steady pelting against the tiles, Ryan didn't hear Monique climb onto the roof, but she was there. He knew it as well as he knew his name. With each of their nightly sessions, their bond grew even stronger. She'd become a part of him, and if he crossed over on Sunday, he'd have to let that part go. Then again, if he didn't, eventually, Monique would leave this side, and he'd be left behind. A no-win situation if he'd ever known one, and Ryan honestly didn't know what to do.

He sensed her every movement, knew her every emotion, felt her every triumph, her every hurt. Right now, she was pained, because she was about to ask him to do something that she knew damn well he didn't want to do. He stopped nailing.

"I'm not leaving," he said without turning around.

"I want—need—to talk to you, Ryan," she said, her voice very soft, extremely sexy. His entire body responded immediately to that sweet voice, some parts more than others, and he swallowed the memory of Monique giving over to earth-shattering climaxes…for him.

"What do you want to talk about?" he asked as he reached for the next tile and waited for her answer. As if he didn't know exactly what she was going to ask. She wanted him to go to Celeste. And more than that, she wanted him to fall in love with Celeste—by Sunday.

For anyone else, he'd have a patent response for the bizarre request. *Go to hell.* But this was Monique, and this was something she thought she wanted. Fine. If this was what she wanted, he'd give it to her. He was, after all, a spirit who aimed to please. The problem was, the only woman he wanted to please was Monique. Irritated, he fired the gun into another tile and secured it, then he turned around.

The fear on her face was palpable, but Ryan had no idea whether it was due to the height, or to the fact that she was telling him to go to Celeste. He swallowed and nearly groaned out loud from his desire to reach out to her, hold her, stroke that lovely golden hair beneath his palm. But he could do none of those things, so he didn't make a move. Even though he *could* touch her, she'd said no. And phantom sex had been great, but what if he did cross, and he never knew what it felt like to really stroke her hair, massage her flesh, kiss her lips? He examined those green-gold eyes, and the tinge of pink forming on her cheeks.

"You need sunscreen," he said automatically. "You all do." He'd seen the three roofer girls lathering up in SPF 30 already, but had set about his own task before making sure Monique and her family did the same. Though the slate was actually cool to the touch, the sun beating down from above was another story entirely. In spite of the deceivingly cool breeze, that sun would waste no time burning Monique's silky skin. The thought of her hurting, in any way, even if only a sunburn, didn't sit well with Ryan.

Looking taken aback, she responded, "I always wear sunscreen. And everyone else put it on, too." She gave him a soft smile, that heart-shaped mouth lifting up at one corner. "We're used to working outside on the house. It's a weekend ritual," she informed him, then added, "but it's very nice of you to remind me." She was lower than him on the roof's slope and leaned forward when she spoke. The action threw her off balance a bit and she wobbled then caught herself by placing her palms against the roof.

Ryan reflexively reached for her, hoping to steady her and praying that she didn't fall. She avoided his outstretched hand, then her eyes filled as she shook her head. "Thanks, but I've got it."

Hell, would she actually allow herself to fall off a roof before breaking that no-touching rule and reaching for him?

Ryan grimaced and grabbed another tile. He wanted to nail something. He wanted to hurt something. No, the truth was, he wanted to touch something—Monique. In fact, he wanted to press her against him and kiss her senseless, then he wanted to experience her body beneath him, more than merely in his mind, to feel her open to him completely and to push inside, to become a part of her and have her become a part of him.

"Ryan," she said, after he finished with the tile.

He didn't want to turn around, didn't want to have to watch her make the request, but he did want to look at her, so he braced his heart and turned. "Yeah?"

"I need to ask you something," she continued, her voice a little softer since the blond roofer, steadily popping her tiles into place with breakneck speed, had moved closer and paused working to replenish the nails in her gun. The result was an eerie silence, with only the faint echo of nails popping against tiles on the other side of the house, where the remainder of the family and the other two roofers were busy installing the slate.

Ryan waited until the blonde started the big red gun again before he looked directly at Monique and said what he had to say. "You want me to spend today with Celeste." Then he added, "No, I'll go one better. You want me to fall hopelessly in love with her, so I can cross over. Is that what you were going to say, Monique?"

Her jaw dropped and her eyes widened. Then she visibly swallowed and nodded. "Yes."

"You're trying to manipulate my future," he said. "What if I don't want to cross? What if I want to stay here?"

With you.

He could practically see her mind churning as she tried to choose the right words. This should be good. What would she say? *I can't give you what you want, but I know someone who can.*

"It's supposed to be incredible there," she said, sounding

as though she were trying to convince herself, instead of him. "On the other side. Everything you've ever wanted, everything you've ever dreamed of."

"You going to be there?" he asked, before he could stop the words from slipping past his mouth.

The gold in her eyes glistened in the sunlight, and Ryan's chest clenched as he realized that she was on the verge of tears.

"I'm sorry," he said.

"I'm not. I want you, too," she admitted. "But we can't. And from everything Dax has said about Celeste, I think that there may be more to her staying in the middle than helping Chloe. I'm sure she wanted to help Chloe, but I also think she was meant to stay for another reason entirely." She looked away from Ryan, focused on the brittle old tile beneath her palms. "I think she was meant to stay for you, so the two of you could do what you need to do to cross over."

"We haven't done the last step," he said. "And don't count on it, Monique. I like Celeste. During this week we've become friends. But that's it."

A ladder banged against the roof's edge to their left, and the thing creaked loudly before Tristan emerged above the edge. He nodded in their direction and called out above the echoing nail guns. "That's Ryan, I take it?"

Monique nodded. She knew he couldn't see Ryan, but she still proceeded with introductions. "Tristan, this is Ryan Chappelle. Ryan, this is my cousin Tristan."

"I know," Ryan said. "Tell him hello for me please," to which Monique relayed, "He asked me to tell you hello."

Ryan swallowed. He could help her family, but he couldn't even communicate with them directly. Couldn't communicate with them, couldn't touch her, couldn't do lots of things he desperately wanted to do. Damn, he hadn't realized the central realm was so dismal until meeting Monique. However, he'd met her now, and he knew that it was. Maybe he should go ahead and cross and get it over with. But there was that pesky matter of learning to love. However, Ryan had the sneaking suspicion he was eerily close to accomplishing that requirement, though not with Celeste.

"Monique, I brought you a bundle of tiles to set you up for this section. That way Ryan can keep an eye on you and make sure you're okay while you work." He turned his head toward the place where Ryan held his nail gun and evidently tried to judge the approximate location of Ryan's face. "That okay by you, Ryan?" he asked.

"Tell him it's fine," Ryan instructed.

"Yes, it's fine," Monique said.

"And thanks for fixing that tarp last week," Tristan added. "You saved the place, you know. We really appreciate it."

"No problem," Ryan mumbled, frustrated he couldn't simply talk to the guy.

Monique shot him a look of pity that made Ryan want to yell, then she answered, "He says it wasn't a problem."

Tristan grinned, nodded again, then climbed back down the ladder, while Ryan realized how wretched his current situation was. He couldn't have the woman he wanted, couldn't cross over and couldn't communicate with anyone who breathed, except Monique, who he couldn't touch. Hell, could things get any worse?

"Will you spend some time with Celeste today?" Monique asked. "And try to get to the last step? Friends do become lovers, you know. It happens all the time."

Yes, Ryan realized, things could get worse. But rather than pointing that out, since it wouldn't do a damn bit of good, he nodded. "If that's what you want, then sure, I will."

He waited, knowing he'd placed the ball in her court. Would it be so terrible for her to admit that she didn't want him to see Celeste or any other female, spirit or not? Would Monique tell him that she wanted him right now as much as he wanted her?

"That's what I want," she said.

And there was his answer.

"Consider it done." He turned his back to the woman who, with four small words, had effectively hurt him more than anything he'd ever experienced in life, or death.

"Do you want to talk?" she asked.

"There's nothing left to say." He grabbed the next tile and vigorously nailed it into place, then moved onto another, never looking back. He sensed her retreat, though, and listened to her edge her way to the section of roof that Tristan had prepared for her.

When he heard the first pop of a nail gun in her direction, he cast a quick glance to make sure she was holding the thing correctly and that she knew what she was doing. He'd never forgive himself if he let her get hurt. But Monique was no stranger to work, and apparently no stranger to a nail gun. She had her first row of tiles positioned and secured in no time, then moved to the next row, keeping her eyes focused on the task instead of on the ghost currently staring a hole through the female he wanted more than life. And for a dead guy to want anything more than life was really saying something.

But he did.

BY THE TIME Jenee called everyone down for lunch, nearly one-third of the roof sported new blue-gray tiles. Monique was exhausted, partly because she hadn't taken a break since she and Ryan talked earlier, and partly because she hadn't slept much all week, deciding instead to spend the majority of her nights with him. And what if, by keeping him from Celeste at night, she'd kept them from getting to the intimate stage of their relationship? Part of her was glad they hadn't got there, but another part felt she might have ruined his chance to cross over—forever.

"Are you coming down for lunch?" she called to him as she placed her nail gun against the nearest board and removed her tool belt. She waited for a response. None came. Then she looked at him, and his bemused look didn't make sense, until she realized what she'd done.

"Sorry," she said, swallowing past a hard lump in her throat. Ghosts didn't eat, didn't sleep. Why would he need to come down for lunch? "Do you want to at least take a break and come sit with us?" she asked, then shook her head again. The remainder of the family couldn't see him or talk to him, either. "Oh, Ryan, forgive me," she said, but he simply shrugged.

"No problem. I'm going to keep working, if it's all the same to you. When the roof is finished, I'll leave and head to Pensacola, since that's what you want. That is what you want, right?"

The lump in her throat thickened again, but she nodded just the same.

"And tonight?" he asked.

"You should stay—with her," she said.

"Right." He went back to the tiles.

Monique ate lunch with the family. Jenee had scooted the long pine picnic table beneath the shade of the oak and had filled their plates to capacity with tuna salad sandwiches, fresh fruit and chips. Big glasses of lemonade stood in front of every plate, with round slices of lemon floating within the clear glass and glistening drops of condensation trickling along the edge.

Staring at those droplets, Monique pictured Ryan as she'd seen him when he entered her bedroom the first night, his body wet from working on the roof, droplets trickling along that firm jaw and down the strong column of his neck. If things worked out with Celeste, Monique would never see that beautiful vision again, would only have the memory to hold onto. The thought made her stomach queasy, and she pushed her plate away.

"You okay?" Nan asked. She'd sat beside Monique at the table and leaned toward her younger cousin in that protective fashion that she was known for. Usually, the gesture irritated Monique, since she was twenty-four and could take care of herself. Today, however, she welcomed Nan's protective nature.

"No," she whispered, not wanting Gage to hear her confession and become concerned. Like most brothers, he tended to get his back up quickly when he thought anything was wrong with his sister. She didn't want to worry him now, not when the family had so much to do in so little time. "I'm not okay," she continued, when she was certain Gage and Tristan were completely engaged in flirting with the three gorgeous roofers.

"Does he still refuse to cross?" Nan whispered back, evidently sensing Monique's hesitation to voice her concerns aloud.

She nodded, then decided to tell Nanette the rest. "He's refusing, but that's not what's bothering me so much," she admitted, staring toward the house.

"If you're worried about the roof, I totally think we're going to have it done with time to spare. Just look at the progress we've made already." Nan pointed to the elegant blue-gray tiles, each one uniquely colored, but all blending to form a spectacular top on the run-down plantation.

Monique could only imagine how the place would look when they restored the rest of the house, replacing the peeling paint with a new coat or siding, fixing the broken windows, getting rid of the rotten wood and repairing the sagging porch. She imagined the eight big columns, currently a dingy gray and leaning dangerously, as sturdy, brilliant and stark white. The place could be the equivalent of Scarlett's Tara, if they only had the money and the time. But they were getting there, and the roof replacement was a key part of the restoration.

"I'm not worried about the roof," Monique admitted.

"It's your ghost, isn't it?" Nan asked.

Monique waited for Jenee to make a pass behind them, leaning over each of their shoulders to refill their glasses. "Thanks," she said, and sipped the lemonade while Jenee walked toward the guys and the roofers, who were currently quite enamored with the two Vicknair males.

"Tell me." Nan followed Monique's gaze to the house, or more specifically, to the area of the roof where the tiles were still—in Nan's view—magically being nailed into place. "Are you worried that he won't cross in time?"

Monique nearly laughed at the irony of Nan's question. No, she wasn't overly worried that he wouldn't cross in time, and she realized that with utter clarity now.

She was more worried that he would.

"I've got a lot on my mind," she said. "I've never had an assignment like this one before."

"You know, you can always ask Grandma Adeline if you can have some help. Maybe your ghost requires two mediums." Nan took a bite of tuna sandwich before continuing. "I mean, I've never heard of it happening before, but there's a first time for everything, right? I'm sure if you asked, she'd listen and see what she could do. The powers that be don't want us miserable, I'm sure. We help them out. Leave a note on the tea service asking for help. I'm sure she'll find a way."

Monique smiled. "Thanks for the suggestion, but I think

everything may work itself out. He only has the last step left to accomplish."

"Intimacy?" Nan asked, obviously remembering the list she'd helped Monique create earlier this week. She glanced at the roof. "You okay with that?"

Monique forced a smile and nodded, but she couldn't keep her eyes from watering. So she turned her attention to the sky, and a thick, black cloud cruising in front of the sun, placing all of them in its shadow and reminding them that time was a scarce commodity.

The storm was coming.

"Gotta get back to work," Gage declared. "Good job, Jenee."

Jenee beamed as she scooped up the paper plates and cups, then tossed them in a big green garbage bag she clutched in one hand.

"What do you think?" Tristan asked, tilting his head to look at the menacing cloud. "Will we finish in time?"

"We have to," Nan said, already moving toward one of the ladders. She climbed steadily upward then called toward Ryan. "We can't thank you enough for helping!"

Monique watched him nod and assumed he'd responded, though she couldn't hear him from her spot on the ground.

"Ready to get back at it?" Gage asked. "We really do need to finish up. That storm is coming, and then there's my date with Carol and Adele."

"Carol *and* Adele?" Monique questioned.

"Tristan had already asked Dani out before I had a chance, so I'm taking them out. With Dax at the beach, someone would have been left out in the cold. I didn't want that to happen, so I decided to take care of the problem myself." He actually made the statement without the slightest hint of a cat-that-ate-the-canary grin. Quite a feat.

"Bless your heart, how will you ever survive?" Monique asked, never shocked by Gage's boldly sexual take on life. True, she thought he wanted more, but he sure did take hold of physical pleasure with gusto. Which reminded her of Ryan, and the reason he couldn't cross over.

While claimant has experienced his share (and then some) of physical bonding, he refused to open his heart to love.

Two more days. She didn't want to give up her last two nights with him, but she also didn't want to fail the man she'd come to care about so deeply. He needed to take his relationship with Celeste to the next level, so perhaps they could find happiness together on the other side. Because that's what Monique wanted more than anything. Ryan's happiness.

"Come on, let's get busy." Gage nudged her toward the house. "I'm serious about that date."

"I'm sure you are," she said, dragging her eyes away from the handsome ghost on the roof. Why was he here now? Why hadn't he left to go to Celeste? How would they get to the final stage if he didn't? And why couldn't Monique bring herself to tell him—again—to go?

Because deep down, she didn't want him to.

For the remainder of the afternoon and into the evening, Monique, like the rest of the family, nailed tiles until every finger throbbed, every muscle ached and every stitch of clothing on her body was drenched in sweat. Thank goodness the thick black pre-storm cloud kept the sun from beating down as well. The heat and the pressure of having to finish were enough to make them miserable, without the added force of a Louisiana sun in the afternoon.

By seven-thirty that night, the last tile was in place, the storm was threatening and the family was exhausted. Gage and Tristan set up their plans for a late dinner with the roofers, while Nan and Jenee headed straight for the showers, and Monique faced the truth.

At some point in the late afternoon, Ryan had gone to Celeste. And he hadn't even said goodbye. As a matter of fact, he'd never ventured Monique's way again after lunch. Now that the work was done, and even thicker clouds came in to rumble and quake along with the first one, the other Vicknairs headed for the house. Monique stayed behind, scanning the roof and the spot where she'd last seen him, his powerful body maneuvering the tiles skillfully as he worked, his face intent and focused on the job and his very existence teasing her senseless. Driving her crazy with need. With desire. A desire that would never again be filled.

Ryan Chappelle was gone.

13

"IF YOU COME to make the *misere* with your sister, don't waste ya time," Inez Thibodeaux said, as Nan entered Monique's Masterpieces Saturday evening for her weekly manicure. Multiple silver and gold bangles jingled wildly as the older woman smoothed her ebony hands across the marble top on her nail-sculpting table. Inez huffed and shot a disapproving look at Monique, ignoring her employee and friend as she washed a customer's hair.

"I've never seen such a *bahbin* hanging down low. She lucky she ain't tripped over it," Inez continued. The woman was a never-ending supply of opinions, many of which were derived from her appreciation for voodoo. Right now, she ran the tips of her claw-like nails down the bold platinum streak in her bangs that provided a severe contrast to the remainder of her black-as-night hair. Her bangs were straight as an arrow, while the remainder of her hair was as curly as a corkscrew. It was an odd look, and according to Inez, obtained naturally when a voodoo chant went awry. She called the streak her "racing stripe" and Monique agreed the image suited the woman. She was a mid-sixty-year-old who had the energy of a mid-twenty-year-old, but gave Monique advice like a mid-eighty-year-old. Quite a contrast indeed, and Monique loved her in spite of her quirks…and her voodoo.

"Hi, Nan," Monique said, barely casting a glance at her sister before filling her hand with another creamy, apple-scented glob of shampoo, then lathering LuAnn Gissell's hair. "Just ignore her; she's in one of her moods." Monique bit back a smile as Inez let loose with a stream of Cajun expletives that would impress any sailor.

Monique hadn't planned on working a fourteen-hour day, but since they'd had to work on the house yesterday to beat last night's storm, she'd had to reschedule many appointments. Not necessarily a bad thing, since it'd somewhat kept her mind off the facts. Ryan had one more day to cross, one more day with Celeste and one more day until he could potentially leave Monique forever.

Yes, it was a good day to stay busy.

When Inez's cussing spree finally subsided, Nan gasped. "Inez, I don't even know what most of that means."

"Mais jamais d'la vie!" Inez exclaimed. "It mean your sister been pouting all day. And I tink she done fall for a man," she said, then muttered, "or could be a ghost?"

Monique, in the middle of rinsing the shampoo from LuAnn's thick black hair, dropped the spray nozzle and barely noticed her customer's yelp of protest when it hit her forehead. "What did you say?"

Inez, looking very smug, merely shrugged. "Sit down, *chère,* and give me dos' hands." She took Nanette's palms in her own, while Nan looked questioningly toward her cousin.

"Monique, something you want to tell me? I thought everything was taken care of."

Still apologizing to LuAnn for the sudden attack on her skull, Monique merely shook her head and wondered what in the world had caused Inez to spout that ridiculous assumption. And where did *she* come up with a ghost, anyway? Why would she think Monique was in love with a ghost? She didn't even know Monique saw ghosts, did she?

Or did she?

The voodoo charms hanging on Inez's swing lamp jingled as she swung the big bulb over Nan's hands for a better look. Did Inez know about the Vicknair plantation? Did she know about Monique? And why hadn't she said anything before? Moreover, why did she pick now, when Monique had a customer and Nanette had entered the shop—Nanette, of all people—to make her suspicions known.

"*Zeerahb*, what ya do to yo' hands?" Inez exclaimed, pulling Nanette's palms under the light and tsking loudly. "*Poo-ye-yi.*"

"They aren't that bad," Nan argued.

Inez's penciled black brows rose high enough to disappear beneath her uniquely colored bangs.

Nanette scowled. "I helped roof our house," she said matter-of-factly, "And we did a damn fine job, I might add. Survived that storm without losing a single tile, didn't we, Monique?"

Wrapping a towel around LuAnn's head, Monique nodded. "Yeah, we did a good job." She guided LuAnn to her station, as Nan added, "Even had a little help from one of Monique's friends."

Monique's steps faltered, but she recovered quickly and adjusted LuAnn's chair to style her black mane. Black and shiny and dark, like Ryan's eyes.

She swallowed hard.

"I heard there's another storm coming tonight," LuAnn said, obviously unaware of the other much more important conversation taking place between the other women in the room.

"That's what I heard on the forecast," Monique said, her mind miles away from intense storms and focused on intense eyes.

"We do need to talk," Nan said to Monique, before turning her attention back to the sassy Cajun still tsking at her cracked palms and broken nails. "And if you can't fix this, I'm sure I can go somewhere else for my manicure."

"Phfft," Inez said, waving away Nan's comment. "I can fix."

By the time Monique finished styling LuAnn's hair, Inez had Nan's hands looking smooth again and was busily trimming away her cuticles. Since LuAnn was Monique's last appointment, she plopped in the chair nearest Nan and waited for the questions to begin, though Nan's first one wasn't what she was expecting.

"Did she get onto you about your hands, too?" Nan asked.

Inez grinned so broadly that her gold molar gleamed. "Did 'em the other day," she said with pride. "Soft as silk now, dos' hands are."

Nan twisted in her seat and scanned the shop. No one was around, which appeared to be what she wanted to verify. She leaned closer to Inez and asked, her voice barely a whisper, "What did you say about a ghost?"

"Her ghost," Inez said, indicating Monique. "She don' talk to me, but she has one. And she knows it. Her *bahbin* been hanging all day."

"My lip has not been pouting," Monique protested, but Nan shook her head.

"What do you mean, she has one?"

"He's been here, watching. He was here dis morning, and I hoped he'd pass on by. But he ain't passed. Not yet. He back. He back for her." Inez paused, ran glittering gold fingernails over her voodoo charms, then squinted around the room. "Mamere tol' me 'bout your house. She tol' me 'bout your ghosts."

"What about them?" Nan asked, casting a wary eye toward Monique.

"Dat dey comes to visit dem Vicknair place, but never stay. But not dis time. He stays."

"He's been *here?*" Monique asked, as the meaning of Inez's claims hit full-force. Ryan had been here? Today? Why? And why hadn't she seen him?

"Non," Inez said. "Not really here. He's watching you, dat ghost. He's watching from afar. Dat's what *I* feel. Voodoo helps me know when I'm being watched. But he not watching ol' Inez. He watching you, child."

Why hadn't Monique thought of that? All day, she'd been miserable, knowing he was in Pensacola spending time with Celeste, wondering if they had connected emotionally. Physically. But he'd admitted to feeling something for Monique. If he truly did, wouldn't he still watch her, view her, while he was still on this side and could? Monique could feel Ryan when he was present, or when he touched her in his mind, but she hadn't felt him today—because he hadn't touched her; he'd simply watched. *She* hadn't felt him, but Inez had. And if Ryan was watching, then maybe Monique could let him know that she didn't want things to end this way, that she wanted to be with him once more, to see him again, or at least let him see her the way she wanted, before he left completely.

"I don't feel him. Is he watching me now?" she asked Inez. "Can you feel him?"

"Non, *chère*," Inez said, as Nan pulled her hand from the woman's grasp and faced Monique with wide eyes.

"What are you doing?" Nan asked her cousin.

"If I call him, he'll come," Monique said.

"But you shouldn't do that. You know you shouldn't."

"I'm not going to," Monique said, flustered. "But Inez is right. He's watching me. Maybe not right now, but he's aware of what I do while he's still on this side."

"You said he'd leave by Sunday," Nan reminded her. "That you thought he'd learn to love with Celeste and would cross on time, tomorrow."

"I know. But while he's still here, he's obviously watching me."

"So?" Nan asked.

Monique grabbed her purse from behind the counter and headed for the door. "You don't mind locking up for me, do you, Inez?"

"Non," Inez said, grabbing Nanette's hand again and holding her wrist in a death grip while she continued to work on her cuticles.

"Monique!" Nan screeched. "What are you doing?"

"He's watching me," Monique said.

"So?" Nan repeated.

"So I'm going to give him something to see." Ignoring another healthy stream of Inez's Cajun expletives, this time conveying enthusiasm for Monique's feistiness, and Nanette's shouted reminders of the Vicknair rules, Monique let the door slam behind her as she rushed out of the shop and toward her car.

The night air was hot and thick, typical for late summer in Louisiana, but since the sun had dropped completely, Monique let the top down on the convertible then started the five-mile drive home. The heated air kissed her skin and Ryan Chappelle invaded her thoughts.

He's been here.

Inez's words echoed in the night. Ryan had watched her today. What did that mean? Had he left Celeste? Had he ever gone to see her? Or what if he had, but he still thought about Monique? And if that were the case, did that mean he wasn't taking his relationship with Celeste past friendship, and therefore wouldn't cross over?

A wave of guilt flooded over her. She didn't want him to fall in love with Dax's "stunning" spirit, but if he didn't, he'd be trapped in the middle forever. Forever, as in, beyond Monique's lifetime. Forever, never to experience pleasure with a woman again.

And never to experience love.

Monique slowed the car and pulled over to the side of the road. What was she doing? Going home to seduce a ghost away from his destiny? That was what she'd had in mind, after all. She wanted him to see her, for him to know that she liked him seeing her, all of her, and then, if all of her dreams came true, he'd come back—to her.

For what? Another night of sex in their minds, without touching? How could she do that to him?

Her eyes burned. One heavy tear pushed forward then trickled slowly down her cheek. Then another. And another. Monique's neck dropped back against the headrest, and she let them all spill free. She couldn't do him that way. She wouldn't. Sniffing loudly, she let her cries claim the darkness and sobbed so fiercely that she didn't hear the other car pull in behind hers, didn't hear footsteps crunching on the loose gravel.

"Monique. Honey, you okay?" Nan asked breathlessly, opening the passenger door and plopping into the seat.

Another sniff, so loud it was a snort, wedged its way in between Monique's sobs.

"Want to talk about it?" Nan asked. "I'm assuming Inez was right. You can't get over Ryan?"

Monique nodded. "You want to kill me, right?"

Nanette laughed. "No, silly, though I may make you finish my manicure when we get home. Inez told me if I left I couldn't come back, and she only got half done." She held up her hand, displaying fire-engine-red polish on three nails.

Amazingly, Monique laughed. "Sorry."

"Don't be. She'll get over it. Besides, she isn't happy unless she's fussing. Part of her charm, I suppose." Nanette twisted in the seat to face Monique, drawing her legs beneath her then wincing when she noticed her nails. "Oh, she's really going to love me now," she laughed, holding up her index finger to show Monique the big smudge on top. Nan shrugged. "Did you have any idea she knew about our ghosts?"

"She talks about ghosts all the time," Monique said, "But she's never associated them with our family. I thought it was a part of her fondness for voodoo. Kind of makes me wonder if the reason she works at the shop has anything to do with our medium status. She lives in Manchak, and that's a good hour away."

"I'm guessing it does," Nan said. "Not that I think it matters too much. Most folks around here think she's three crawfish short of a pound anyway."

Monique laughed. "She's good at doing nails."

"Yeah, when she finishes," Nan said, again eyeing her two perfect nails, her smudged one and the seven completely bare of polish. Then she grinned, apparently happy to see the end of Monique's cryfest. "Feeling better now?"

"Yeah. I was about to do something stupid, but I thought better of it."

"Wanted to make it one more time with your ghost before he crossed, huh? A bit more brain sex?" Nan asked.

"Yeah, but I shouldn't," Monique said regrettably.

"No, you shouldn't," Nanette agreed.

Nan held up her palms defensively when Monique's jaw dropped. "Hey, I was just stating the facts." She slapped her right forearm. "Great. We probably look like the main course to every mosquito for miles. Want to put the top up while we talk?"

"Sure," Monique said.

In the time it took the two of them to snap the convertible's top in place, Monique's sadness subsided. "I'll be okay."

"I know that." Nan picked up Monique's purse from the floor. "Got your cell phone on you?"

"Yeah, it's in there. Who are you calling?"

"You'll see." Nan fished the red phone out of Monique's bag with her non-polished hand then quickly dialed a number. "Dax? Hey, it's Nan. Listen, Monique is with me and wants to ask you a question about Celeste." She handed the phone over.

"What do you expect me to ask?" Monique whispered, rather loudly.

"See if the two ghosts have hooked up today. Dax will know, and you'll stop worrying about what's happening right now in Florida."

Monique lifted the tiny phone to her ear, but didn't even have to ask the question. Evidently, Dax heard Nanette's instructions.

"Hey, I was wondering whether to call you or not," he said. "But I figured if I didn't hear from you, then you really didn't want to know."

"I didn't think I wanted to know, but Chloe and Celeste are only here until tomorrow, right?" she asked. "The end of the week at the beach?"

"Yeah, they're crossing, I guess, tomorrow. Gotta admit, I'm going to miss them."

"You care about Celeste?" Monique asked. Nan's jaw fell open, and she mumbled, "Have mercy. Him, too?"

"I care about her, but I know she's leaving so I haven't let her know. But I care about Chloe, too. She's a sweet kid. You should've seen her light up when she saw the beach. Really something." He paused, then added, "Yeah, it's going to be tough to see them leave."

"Will Ryan leave with them, do you think?" she asked, hoping he couldn't hear the trepidation in her tone.

"I honestly don't know," Dax said. "He and Celeste have spent time together and have gone somewhere every day, while Chloe sticks around here and visits with her folks. And they're gone again now, so I guess everything is progressing for both of our assignments to cross tomorrow. Actually, since Celeste was here most every night, I thought maybe they hadn't gotten, you know, romantic. But last night, she wasn't here. And tonight, she's gone again. I'm certain they're together."

Tears found their way to the edge of her eyes again, burning as they accumulated, then spilled over.

"Monique?"

Shaking her head, she handed the phone to Nan.

"Sorry Dax," Nan said. "She had to go. I'll see you tomorrow night, right?" She nodded. "Well, be careful driving back. Love you, too. Bye." She snapped the phone shut, dropped it back in Monique's purse then leaned across the console to wrap an arm around her. "You gonna be okay?"

"Yeah, I will. I need tomorrow to come and go, need Ryan to go. Then everything will be okay."

"Think you can drive home now?" Nan asked. "Or do you want to leave your car here and ride with me?"

Monique managed a smile. "No way would I leave my Mustang on the side of the road, and I've never trusted your driving."

"Hmph," Nan said, grinning in spite of the gibe. She climbed from the car and before slamming the door, asked, "Wanna race?"

"Sure," Monique said, then before Nan even made it back

to her Camaro, Monique sped away, leaving a big cloud of smoke in her wake.

Nothing like driving a fast car to make you feel better.

14

MONIQUE'S STOMACH growled as she entered the Vicknair plantation and scents of Jenee's gumbo drifted from the kitchen. But she didn't want to eat. Her eyes, feeling grainy from exhaustion, longed to close, but she couldn't sleep, either. Sleeping would end with Sunday, and Sunday would end with Ryan on the other side. Or not. And right now, she didn't know which was worse.

"That you, Monique?" Jenee called from the kitchen. "I fixed a huge pot of gumbo, and made enough rice and potato salad for an army. We're the only ones here, right now. Why don't you come help me try to make a dent in this food? You know you want some," she coaxed, leaning her head into the hall. Then she frowned and walked toward Monique. "You okay?"

"I will be," Monique said, as Nan entered the house behind her.

"Not going to eat?" Nan asked, a slight frown tugging her full mouth downward. "You really should."

"Can't," Monique said, and blinked back her tears. "I'm going to take a shower and go to bed."

"Well," Nan said, dusting her hands together, "everybody knows gumbo is better the second day anyway, so you can have a big bowl for lunch tomorrow."

"That sounds perfect," Monique said, glad that Nan under-

stood. She needed to be alone, needed to ponder tomorrow's
possibilities, needed to have a nice, long pity cry.

She started up the stairs, while Nan and Jenee went into
the kitchen. She was grateful the two of them didn't try to
force her to eat. There was no way she could swallow one bite
tonight. Her stomach was in knots, almost nauseous from
intense anxiety. She'd told them the truth. She wanted a nice,
hot shower, and then, if she could make her eyes close, she
needed to sleep. Didn't want it, but needed it, nonetheless.
Within minutes, she reached her room, entered the bathroom
and removed her clothes. Then she turned the shower on, as
hot as it would go, and stepped inside.

Hissing at the impact of the hot stream, Monique tilted her
head beneath the pulsing water and let it ease the pounding
in her skull, the pressure that had been building all day with
each and every thought of Ryan's potential crossing. She let
the tears fall freely again and listened to the echoes of her sobs
against the tile walls. Tomorrow, he could be gone, and she'd
never told him—*what?*

Monique blinked the water from her eyes and wondered—
if she had another chance with Ryan, what would she say, what
would she do? Taking a deep breath of steamy air, she let her
mind entertain that thought, to think of something more positive
than Ryan's deadline tomorrow. She picked up the round, fluffy
loofah sponge and covered it with peach-scented soap, then she
lathered her body thoroughly and thought of Ryan. Not of him
leaving, but of the way he looked at her when he spoke, the way
he excited her when he whispered in her ear, the way he mentally
caressed her body, and brought her to the edge and beyond….

RYAN STUDIED the waves capped in tips of white, gleaming
beneath the moonlight before slapping against the sandy

beach. He'd sat here, on the abandoned wooden lifeguard stand, last night and watched the shadows of ships passing in the distance, the occasional seagull swooping low to the water then high to the heavens, people—lovers—walking arm-in-arm and laughing, hugging, embracing love and embracing life. Now he'd do the same tonight, watching what he desperately wanted to have—with Monique.

"Are you okay?"

He turned toward the voice, its sweet cadence a welcome reprieve from his thoughts, and nodded.

"Trying to make sure I'll remember everything," he said. But it wasn't the sand and sea that he was worried about forgetting. Or missing. How could he cross over and leave Monique here? And if he didn't cross now—if he consciously made the decision to stay in the middle from this point on—didn't that mean he'd be stuck here forever? Ultimately, although it would presumably be years down the road, she would cross, too. Then he'd be here without her, without anyone who mattered.

Celeste sat beside him, as she'd done last night, and stared out over the water. They'd only met a week ago, yet he'd shared so much with her, and she'd done the same. Celeste, as Monique had said, was a very unique spirit and an extremely attractive woman. He turned toward her, saw the mouth that seemed always to carry a hint of a smile, the dark eyes sparkling in the moonlight and those long golden spirals of hair, lifting in the Gulf breeze and making her appearance downright angelic. She was stunning, beautiful in fact. But she wasn't the one he wanted. And he wasn't who she wanted, either, though she hadn't confided who was.

Their situation, both of them waiting to cross over, had forged a bond that Ryan suspected would last an eternity.

He'd spoken freely of his lust for life, of his attempt to make the most of his time on earth, and of how those efforts had turned fatal fourteen months ago. He'd told her of Monique, of the way she'd touched his soul, and of his inner suspicion that he might have fulfilled his requirement for crossing—with her. And wasn't that something? That perhaps he'd finally learned to love, but if he truly did, then he'd be forced to enter another dimension and leave her behind? And if he did love her, why hadn't the light appeared again? What did that mean? And if what he felt for Monique wasn't love, then what was?

"Are you watching her?" Celeste asked.

Ryan shook his head. He'd been watching Monique sporadically all day, but a frisson of fear kept him from viewing her now. He supposed it was because each glimpse of her increased his desire to see her, talk to her, touch her. It'd taken every ounce of willpower he possessed not to go to her a little while ago, when he'd seen her crying.

In fact, he had been about to leave Pensacola and join her within the tiny expanse of her car, when Nan had arrived and comforted her sister. Thank God. Ryan had no doubt he wouldn't have been able to sit that close to her, to see her in so much distress, without reaching for her. And at that moment, he knew she'd have let him.

He couldn't do that to her. She didn't want to hurt her family, didn't want him to touch her for fear she'd reciprocate, and break that rule. And if he had gone to her, he didn't know if that blatant truth would have stopped him from having what he so desperately wanted to experience before he crossed over… making love, physically rather than mentally, to Monique.

"I've watched my love all day," Celeste admitted, her words barely whispered against the salty breeze.

Ryan knew there was a reason she wouldn't divulge the

name of the man, though he couldn't imagine what it was. He suspected the reason Celeste called him her love rather than her lover was because she had never confessed her feelings to the man. Did she regret that? And, Ryan wondered, would he regret never telling Monique?

"Personally," she continued, "I think if we only have one more day to see them, even if from a distance, we shouldn't waste a minute." She smiled, but a heavy tear trickled down her cheek, glowing in the luminescence of her aura. "I'm going to him," she whispered. "He's sleeping, and perhaps, he'll never know I was there. But I'm going to him tonight. I want to watch him while he sleeps and carry that vision with me when I cross."

Ryan turned toward her, but she was gone. And she was right. If he only had a limited time to see Monique, even if from a distance, then he shouldn't waste a minute. True, she sensed him when he was present. But he'd been watching her from afar, and she hadn't seemed to tell. Why shouldn't he take advantage of that blessed ability while he still could?

He closed his eyes and thought of her, and the vision that came before him took his breath away.

"Monique."

She looked tired, upset. Ryan's chest clenched. Her green-gold eyes were red from crying, and her mouth formed a slight frown, as though she were holding back more tears. Entering her bathroom, she closed the door and removed her sandals. Then she slid her hand beneath her golden waves to massage the back of her neck.

She wore a forest-green halter dress, and it displayed her lovely shoulders, creamy and white. He'd noticed throughout the week that even though her work required her to wear a Monique's Masterpieces black jacket to protect her clothing from bleach and perms and color, she hadn't let that stop her from wearing incredibly sexy clothing underneath the blousy smocks. Today had been no different. And Ryan was extremely grateful as he viewed the way the fabric hugged her beautiful curves.

Ryan ached to kiss those shoulders, that mouth. He ached to kiss away her tears. But he couldn't.

While that thought tore at his soul, he saw that her hand hadn't merely massaged her neck; she'd unknotted her dress, and it fell to the floor, with the golden privacy veil instantly taking its place.

His throat went dry. How could he cross and leave her behind? She turned the shower on, twisting the knob to the hottest setting, then stepped inside. The golden veil blurred slightly from the shower's steam, but he could still see her, her head tilting back to accept the brunt of the water's force. It sprayed her face, trickled down her neck to beneath the golden covering and to the beautiful body he'd seen nearly every night this week.

Then, while Ryan watched in agony, she began to cry, her tears joining the water and her sobs piercing the night, and his heart.

"Monique."

If he went to her now, wouldn't it be worse? She was hurting; he was hurting. And he was leaving. But she thought he was leaving because of Celeste.

After sucking in great gulps of air, she closed her eyes and seemed to mentally calm her thoughts, her head nodding slightly as she covered the large round sponge with a body wash and worked it into a lather. Though he couldn't see beneath the veil, he could see her face. She was progressing past the sadness, moving past the pain, and remembering the pleasure.

Remembering him.

MONIQUE CLOSED her eyes and used the sudsy sponge to trace the path that Ryan had taken several times during their interludes, placing the foamy ball beneath one ear, then dragging it across her neck to the other, and recalling his whispers there. Then she moved it across her collarbone and could almost feel the memorable sensation of his mouth across her skin. She slid the loofah slowly to one breast, rubbed it over her nipple and imagined Ryan standing at the foot of the bed and watching her. She visualized that moment when she wanted him to see her, all of her, and the way his eyes grew even darker, even more intense, when he drank her nudity in.

She sucked in a gulp of pre-climax air as she moved the foaming sponge to the other nipple. Oh mercy, merely thinking about Ryan was going to make her come. She rubbed the sponge harder over her breast then edged it to the aching spot between her legs. Guiding it to her clitoris, she instantly remembered Ryan's words.

This is me, Monique, my mouth clamping down and sucking you until you can't take it any more. Sucking and nibbling and biting, until you can't hold on, until you have to let go and set that spiraling, burning, maddening tension free...

Monique dropped the loofah and burst into tears. She couldn't. She was so close, but she couldn't let go, not without Ryan.

"Help me," she whispered, water pelting her flesh while her heart broke into pieces.

"If I weren't dead already," a deep, husky voice said through the thick, heavy steam, "this would officially kill me."

"Ryan." She opened her eyes. Through the clear shower curtain, he was easily visible, standing in the center of the room. Without regard to the water spraying the floor, she pushed the vinyl curtain aside and stared. "You're really here."

His grin crooked up on one side, and his eyes moved over her body. "Yeah, I'm really here, and you're really wet. And really naked."

"You can see me?" she asked, taking in his appearance as she spoke and not making any effort whatsoever to cover her nudity. She wanted him to see her. She wanted him to want her, enough that he would remember her forever, even on the other side.

"The veil disappeared as you moved that sponge across your breasts. You were thinking of me when you touched yourself, and you wanted me to see."

"I was," she admitted. He wore a black T-shirt and extremely faded jeans that hugged his thighs tightly and didn't do anything at all to hide the bulge between his legs. She wanted him. And yet…

"You're crossing over, aren't you? Tomorrow?"

"I believe so."

"So," she said, swallowing hard. "You've fulfilled the requirement?"

He didn't speak this time, but nodded.

Monique fought the stab of pain at that. He'd found love? With Celeste? And yet he was here with her, and according to Inez, he'd been watching her today.

"I don't want to talk about that now," he said, his voice thick with emotion. "I didn't come to talk about crossing." He smiled slightly, grabbed two towels from the shelf on her wall and placed them on the wet floor. "Here. Let me fix that." While Monique stood spellbound, he reached in front of her and angled the nozzle away from the floor, so Monique's naked body still received a good portion of the spray, but the remainder hit the tiled wall of the shower, instead of the bathroom floor. "That's better. If water started pouring through to the kitchen, Nan might get upset."

Monique smiled at that. Nan would get more than upset, and she suspected he knew it. "If you aren't here to talk about crossing," she said, watching as he backed away from the shower, taking great care not to touch her in the process, "then why are you here?"

His hair was damp and wavy from the shower spray, and his upper torso was drenched, but he didn't seem to notice. Monique, however, did. His T-shirt stuck to his beautiful frame and highlighted his biceps, pectorals and abs, almost more than the luminous glow surrounding his body. He was breathtakingly handsome, and he was making her burn deep inside. It'd been a long, long time since a man had touched her there. And while Ryan had given her the best orgasms of her life, he hadn't been able to join with her completely, become one with her, make her feel whole. She wanted that, and she wanted it with him.

"I want—need—more than brain sex," she said honestly.

"I know. I do, too," he said, still looking her over. "But the reason I came has nothing to do with the rules, or with my crossing. I saw you, Monique. I saw you crying, and I saw you stop what you were doing. You were nearly there, nearly over the edge, and you stopped. Why?"

Suddenly chilled, she backed up so the hot water sprayed her body like a warm blanket. "I couldn't do it without you."

He visibly swallowed, the beautiful column of his throat pulsing in the process. "That's what I thought," he admitted. "And that's why I came."

"Why?"

"You couldn't do it without me, but I'm here now."

"You want me to—"

"Think of me touching you," he said, "while you touch yourself. And," he added, again swallowing thickly, "let me watch."

Could she do this? Could she actually stand within this hot stream of water, lather up that sponge and masturbate while he watched?

She blinked, saw the way his dark eyes had that intense heat, that wicked fire, burning in their depths. Tomorrow he would cross, and she'd never see that passionate fire again.

"Won't it—isn't it hard on you? Watching? When I'm losing myself completely, but I can't help you do the same? It isn't fair. I can't do you that way. I mean, brain sex won't give us everything we want, but at least you won't be left unsatisfied."

"Monique," he said, his voice raspy.

"Yes?"

"After I cross, you'll still need *this*. You'll still live a normal life with normal desires, normal needs. Let me see you doing it this way, and I'll convince myself that this is the way you'll find pleasure until I meet you again on the other side. I'd rather remember this, than think of you being pleased by someone else."

"But I don't want anyone else," she blurted.

"A lifetime, *your* lifetime, probably still has a way to go. You'll find someone else along the way."

"But—"

"Let—me—watch. Please, Monique. Let me." The words were spoken so intensely, so powerfully, that they sounded almost like a command. He wanted this, truly he did, and she wanted to give Ryan everything he wanted.

Starting now.

Monique reached down and picked up the loofah, squeezing away the excess water and covering it with more peach-scented body wash. As before, she placed the foamy ball beneath one ear and eased it across her throat to the other, but this time, she didn't imagine Ryan looking at her. She saw him, his chest rising and falling slowly in an obvious attempt at control.

"Tell me what you feel, Monique." He took a step toward the shower, not close enough to touch her, but close enough that the mist from the water made his luminous aura blur at the edges.

Monique had never done anything in her life like this, but that didn't mean she wouldn't do it, for him.

Only for him.

"I feel your mouth, placing soft, wet kisses here," she said, as the sponge crossed her collarbone then edged toward her right breast. She turned the sponge so the abrasive edge crossed her nipple, then she moaned and rubbed it back across the burning tip. Back and forth, back and forth. Then she moved to the other breast and did the same.

"Tell me."

"Your teeth," she said, her own voice husky now from her aroused state, "gently pulling at my breasts, taking my nipples between them and giving me the sweetest, most delicious sensation. Nearly painful, but blissfully so."

He cleared his throat. "Monique."

"Yes?"

"I can't take much more," he admitted. "I want inside you so bad it hurts. Come for me. Let me see you come. Now."

Determined to grant his every request, she eased her legs apart, then slid the foamy ball directly to her clitoris and began to rub it slowly, sensually.

"Your mouth," she whimpered, "sucking and biting and nibbling, while I feel my insides whirling out of control. Deep inside, I'm aching for more, wanting your long, hard length filling me so badly that I want to scream. You're getting me ready for it. You want me to come hard, fiercely, intensely, before you put yourself inside, so you work my clit with your mouth. Kissing me there, then sucking, then finally clamping down hard and—" Her body tensed turbulently, then her climax claimed her completely, making her scream, making her cry out in pleasure, while Ryan moved closer, those dark black eyes looking into hers as she soared over the edge.

Monique's eyes flickered closed for the briefest of seconds, and when they opened, he was gone.

15

THUNDER BOOMED loudly and a slanting rain beat against Monique's bedroom window with maddening force, as though fighting to find its way inside. Lightning, trying to one-up its vigorous counterparts, crackled fiercely as it bore to earth, splitting the sky in two and illuminating everything in its path, until it collided with something close enough to make the big house shake. Close, but not nearly close enough for Monique. She wished the biggest bolt of jagged electricity would set its sights on her, come right through her window and take her out of her misery. Send her to the other side.

Send her to Ryan.

Merely an hour ago, he'd been here, close to her, inches away, in fact, and about to reach for her. Monique had seen it in his eyes, had welcomed it and had made up her mind; she wasn't going to stop him this time. She wanted him to touch her, and she wanted him to do more, to do everything. More than that, *she* wanted to touch him. And wouldn't you know, the minute she mentally decided to toss those rules straight out the window, he disappeared.

Why?

Had he sensed her resolve cracking? Had he known she was about to give up the Vicknair heritage for him? Or had someone, or something, pulled him away at precisely the moment that Monique would have given herself to him?

She'd never know. Because—she glanced at the clock—in fifteen minutes, midnight would come and go, and Ryan's last day on this side would arrive. Would he cross at midnight, or would he remain throughout the next twenty-four hours and cross tomorrow night? Again, Monique didn't know, and she probably never would.

Yesterday she'd vowed that if she ever got the chance to see him again, she would try to find out as much as possible about the mesmerizing male. She'd never wanted to know anything personal about ghosts before, but with Ryan, she wanted to know everything.

What did he do when he was alive? What were his favorite hobbies? His favorite subject in school? And the question that had caused her the most contemplation—how had he died? But when she'd been alone with Ryan, she hadn't thought to ask him anything at all. In fact, the entire situation had revolved around her, and that stung.

Monique leaned up and soundly punched her pillow. Maybe Pierre had had it right after all. Maybe she was a tease. But she hadn't meant to tease Ryan; she wanted to give him everything, to make his dreams come true, assuming his dreams included her. He'd said he believed the requirement had been fulfilled, but if it had, why hadn't he crossed? And if it had, why had he come here to be with her, instead of staying with Celeste?

Chalk that up to yet another thing Monique didn't know.

She punched her pillow again, then jumped when another bolt of lightning collided with something nearby. A transformer? Probably not, since the red lights on her clock showed the power was still on. Probably a tree. In any case, the storm was showing Louisiana and the mighty Mississippi who was boss. Monique only wished she had the authority to do the same. She'd love to tell the powers that be what she thought of their rules.

Flipping over in the bed, she pitched her voice to the ceiling and bit back tears. "We were so close," she said. "And I want him so much. You know I do. I give you everything, help the spirits, and all I want is to be with Ryan." She swallowed thickly past the lump building in her throat. "One time. Why couldn't we have one time, so I would know, and so I could remember, until I see him again on the other side? Is that too much to ask, for everything I give up? To let me be with the only man I've ever wanted? Really be with him, touching him, and feeling him touch me."

She listened to the loud Winchester chimes echo from the grandfather clock in the sitting room. Midnight.

Would Ryan cross now?

Another round of thunder and lightning burst forward with a vengeance. "Can't anyone up there let me break those rules? Just once?" she yelled toward the ceiling, but her words were overpowered, once again, by the roaring thunder outside. "Can't you give me permission?" Monique whispered, while her tears formed jagged paths down her cheeks to the shells of her ears. She slid her fingertips over her face to remove the moisture, but more tears followed in their wake.

The last chime seemed louder than the others and noisily proclaimed that Ryan's day of crossing had come. Monique closed her eyes in defeat.

Then her neck started to burn.

Her eyes popped open.

"No." But she recognized the familiar tingle and knew exactly what it meant. A new assignment. Which meant her old assignment, Ryan, had crossed over.

"No!" she yelled, throwing the covers aside and sitting up in the bed. Before her feet even hit the floor, the burning moved beyond her neck to settle in her chest and make her nipples ache. She stood while her flesh flamed, the fire raging forward from her chest to blaze through every limb. Her breathing hitched and every nerve ending tingled in anguish. Anguish, because she knew what the burning meant, and anguish, because Ryan was gone.

She crossed the room, her bare feet stinging as though she were walking on hot coals. Why was the burning so intense already? It wasn't as though she hadn't started moving, heading toward the sitting room where she had no doubt another letter awaited.

Another letter. Another ghost. A ghost that wasn't Ryan.

She didn't want to go. She wanted to ignore the summons and make the powers that be suffer for a change, but she was the one suffering. Her body scorched so fiercely that she could barely make her way down the stairs. Gripping the handrail and gritting her teeth at the fiery sensation in her palms, she stumbled down the stairwell.

Thunder shook the house as Monique battled the intensity of the summons. Why was it burning so much? Was this her punishment for nearly breaking that damn rule?

"I—didn't—do—it," she spat, even her throat aflame. She'd had a severe case of strep throat last winter, and the pain had been so intense that she'd cried with every swallow.

This was worse.

"Why?" she asked, then moved a hand to her throat when the single word seemed to rip its way out. So she silently added, *Why tonight? Why another ghost already? And why couldn't I have Ryan, just once?*

The sitting room was aglow from Adeline Vicknair's

fringe-embellished lamp, the one that always remained lit, even when the power was out. It was a constant reminder that Grandma Adeline was nearby, and that the cousins could be summoned at any time.

Like now.

In front of the red velvet settee, the gleaming silver tea service sat prominently in the center of the mahogany coffee table. And in the middle of the silver tray, as Monique had known it would be, a lavender-tinted envelope with her grandmother's swirling penmanship identified a name along the outside.

Monique.

She moved forward, her feet still aching with every step, until she could plop down on the settee and reach for the envelope bearing her name. The moment her fingertips touched the stylish linen paper, the familiar icy waterfall of coolness quenched her searing flesh. Normally, she'd have felt relief from the sensation; tonight, however, she only experienced pain. She didn't want to help another ghost. She wanted Ryan. But, as always, she'd do what she had to do, and the first thing she had to do was open the letter.

Monique ran her finger beneath the edge of the envelope and, like every other time, listened to the soft crack of the paper giving way as it opened. And, also like every other time, Adeline's flowery perfume filled the air as Monique withdrew the letter.

A single page.

One page? A summons always consisted of three pages. The handwritten note from Grandma Vicknair, the sheet of rules and the original memo sent from the powers that be. Monique withdrew the pale-purple page, its edges scalloped in the trademark style of Adeline Vicknair's stationery. Where were the rules? And the memo?

She carefully unfolded the paper and read the two words written in her grandmother's swirling script in the center of the page. Two words. Nothing more. But if those words meant what Monique suspected…

Permission Granted.

"Oh, my," Monique whispered, as she sensed a masculine presence enter the room.

"Ryan?" she questioned, turning on the settee to see him standing in the doorway, grinning broadly. Her heart leapt at the sight. He was beautiful, and he was hers.

For how long?

"They've given us tonight," he answered her unspoken question.

Thunder boomed outside, and Monique flinched. "Tonight?" she asked, regaining her bearings. "And we can touch? We can do—everything?"

"To your heart's content," he said, his dark brows flicking wickedly and that delicious smile crooking up on one corner. "I believe it's mighty late, ma'am, and you should be in bed."

"Oh, yes, I should." She shot a look at the tea service, and the envelope that was slowly but surely fading away. "Thanks," she whispered, then gasped when his big, strong arms slid beneath her and hauled her powerfully against his muscled frame. He was so warm—hot—exhilarating. Her hands moved instantly to his face, framed his jaw, pushed through his hair. She was trembling, shaking in his embrace from the raw pleasure of being so close, of wanting him so much, of having one night with Ryan. Touching him. Feeling him. Joining completely with him.

While her body shivered in shocked delight, he carried her out of the sitting room and up the circular staircase to the second floor and her bedroom, cradling her close to his heart. Monique had the sudden image of Scarlett, in Rhett's arms, thrilled that he was about to have his wicked way with her. Lucky Scarlett.

Lucky Monique.

"I wanted you so much I cried," she admitted, when he placed her almost reverently on the bed. "When you left, I thought I'd never see you again."

"I couldn't stay," he said, taking a hand to the lace edge of her emerald gown. The warmth of his fingers made her tremble with need. "I was going to take you, right there, in the shower, but I couldn't. I didn't want to do anything to hurt you or your family. You were about to let me, and I wouldn't have been able to say no. So I did the only thing I could—I left." His wide palms moved lower to cover her breasts, and he squeezed them gently, while she gasped in sheer pleasure. "It was the hardest thing I ever had to do."

"Ryan, we only have one night," she said. "I don't want to go slow. I want to see you, all of you, and I want to watch you come inside of me."

His jaw clenched tight. "Monique, I want you so badly it's killing me, but if I don't keep things slow, then I'm afraid I won't be able to control myself. It'll be hard and hot and intense, and probably rougher than you want, and I don't want to hurt you."

His honesty touched her soul and the intensity behind his words told her exactly what she needed to hear. He wanted her as badly as she wanted him.

"I've been a long time without a man, too," she said. "And I've never had you inside me," she added, as the pressure of his hands on her breasts made her gasp. "So, hard and hot and intense, rougher than you think I can handle," she said, letting her mouth curve in a seductive smile, "is exactly what I want."

Her body lifted from the sheet as his hands slid away from her breasts to grip the edge of her nightgown, pull it apart and rip the thin fabric away. Her panties were next, and he tore the flimsy material from her body, tossed it to the floor, then wasted no time putting his hand between her thighs and pushing one finger, then two, deep into her core, while his thumb started a maddening assault on her clit that had her convulsing in pre-climax shudders.

"You're as hot, as tight, as I knew you'd be," he said, his voice hungry with need. "I've dreamed of touching you, Monique, burned to touch you."

"Yes, Ryan. Yes." Her words quivered with the intensity of her desire.

"Is that what you want, Monique? Is that where you want me? I need to—have to—hear you say it."

She reached for his pants, pressed her hand against the hardness encased in his jeans and nodded. "Yes, Ryan, please. Now."

He slid his fingers from her burning center, but instead of removing his clothes, he eased her to the edge of the bed, then lowered to his knees. Massaging her inner thighs with shaky hands, he gently spread her legs apart. "There's so much I want to do with you," he said. "And I've wanted to taste you for way too long, Monique." Then he pressed his mouth to her clitoris and kissed her softly. "Oh, Monique," he whispered, then gently kissed her there again.

"Ryan," she whimpered, reveling in the warmth. He ended

the intimate kiss and licked her aching center. Monique held her breath and focused on every sensation. Ryan, licking her, sucking her, driving her closer and closer to the edge. When her stomach dipped and that spiraling, tingling wave of desire began to burn toward the very spot where his mouth was torturing her so thoroughly, he pulled back, looked up at her with those wicked dark eyes.

"I want you. In you," he said, standing, while her body quivered in anxious anticipation. He stood and removed his clothes, quickly casting the T-shirt aside, then following suit with the rest of his clothes. Monique noticed that, as before, he wore nothing beneath his jeans. He was long and hard and thick, and she wanted him deep inside. She took a breath, totally preparing to tell him, again, what she wanted. But he didn't need additional instruction. Before she uttered a word, he eased her legs apart, settled his length against her wet opening, then clenched his jaw. "Hard," he said, gritting his teeth. "That's what you want?"

She nodded, then screamed with ecstasy when he pushed every incredible inch inside, deeper than she'd ever been touched before, and filled her completely. Her cry ripped from her chest and blended with the thunder claiming the sky outside, and it forced Ryan to stop, holding himself still, while her muscles clamped tight around him.

"Monique, tell me this is what you want. I need to know. I—don't want—to hurt you."

"It is," she said, and she felt his fingers slide between their bodies, find her clitoris and begin working their magic. She came almost immediately, as soon as he touched the throbbing nub, and she tightened like a vise around him, her convulsive spasms sending him completely over the edge.

He yelled, deep and low and guttural, a primitive growl that filled her senses, almost as much as he filled her core, pushing in, pulling out, holding her legs apart as he thrust harder and harder, and as her muscles started to tighten again, the spiraling desire building and building, moving toward that spot where his body penetrated hers, where he found the pleasure he'd needed for over fourteen months, the pleasure he was finally getting…with her.

The elation of knowing she was satisfying him pushed her over the edge again, and as the thunder boomed outside, Ryan joined her, his massive body convulsing fiercely through his release, and his eyes telling Monique everything she needed to know. *She'd* given him this. Even if she lost him today, and she feared that she would, she'd also given him the pleasure he needed, the pleasure he deserved and, she hoped, she'd given him a memory that would traverse the boundary between the living and the dead.

Their bodies shuddered post-climax, and he hugged her close, until the tremors subsided. Then he rolled over on his back, carrying her on top of him and smiled against her cheek.

"I'd planned on being gentle the first time."

Monique laughed softly. "Sorry I messed up your plans. Maybe next time?"

He nodded, stroking a hand down the length of her back. "I've wanted to hold you like this all week, to touch your skin, kiss your lips." He placed a soft, tender kiss against her mouth. "Touch your silky hair." He brought his hand up her back and twined it in the length of her hair, then moved it to his face and inhaled. "Peaches."

She smiled. "You like peaches?"

"I can honestly say I like everything about you, Ms. Vicknair," he said, nuzzling her ear. "Even after I left your bed at night, I watched you sleeping," he admitted, his voice barely above a whisper as he nibbled her tender lobe. "I saw your face relax when you had pleasant dreams, tense when you had unpleasant ones."

She remembered a couple of extremely passionate dreams that she'd had and wondered if he'd seen her then. "Can you tell when I dream of you?" she asked and felt his smile against her cheek.

"You moisten your lips, then you gently push the covers down your body and move your hands over your flesh. You touch yourself, the way I wanted to touch you, but you never climax that way."

"I couldn't," she admitted. "I didn't want to do that without you."

"I wanted to touch you so badly, to kiss your mouth, to run my fingers through your beautiful hair."

Remembering Pierre's "sand" comment, Monique raised her head and looked into Ryan's eyes. "What color is my hair?" she asked. "I mean, if you had to describe it, how would you?"

He ran his long fingers through her hair and tilted his head to one side as though contemplating what to say.

"Can you see it, in the darkness?" she asked, but she assumed he could. In spite of the storm, moonlight spilled in from her elongated windows. Plus, Ryan's own luminescence cast the entire bed in a sensual glow. Surely he could see her hair. But how would he describe it?

"I see you perfectly," he said. "And your hair is the exact color of the brilliant light that guides souls to the other side. If I do cross today, when I see that light again, know that I'll be thinking of the way it mirrors your beauty. If I cross, Monique, my last thought will be of you."

She swallowed, touched beyond measure. "One more question."

"Okay." He moved his hands down her body, massaging her back as he passed, then cupped her bottom so her center arched forward, and his hardness nudged the apex of her legs. "What's the question?"

She'd love to take advantage of that thick hardness that was so near her aching core, but they only had one night, and she didn't want to regret not asking him again.

"How did you die?"

16

MONIQUE'S QUESTION hit Ryan with the same shocking sensation as tumbling, freefalling, at the equivalent of a hundred and thirty miles per hour, hurling from the sky directly toward the ground below.

He knew that feeling well.

One minute he'd been watching Monique pleasure herself in the shower, the next he'd fled the scene, afraid of what he would do when she opened her eyes. Then an hour later, he'd received that message from Adeline. He and Monique had been granted one night before he crossed. And now that he'd finally touched her, had her, claimed her as his own, she'd thrown yet another twist into this wild night.

Other than briefly recounting the details to Celeste, he hadn't discussed his death since that day fourteen months ago, when living on the edge had swiftly become plummeting over it. Though Adeline, and the others on that side, knew what had happened and discussed it freely, Ryan preferred to avoid the topic altogether. He'd been blessed, he reasoned, when Adeline informed him that the medium assigned to his case had no desire whatsoever to know how he died. Despite that, he'd felt an urge to tell Monique a few nights ago, when they'd discussed his past, but she'd stopped him, said she didn't want to know.

But now she did.

He looked into those green-gold eyes, examined her concerned features. Concerned, for him, and concerned about the reason behind his existence in the middle.

"Dax thought, because of the way you were willing to work on that roof in the storm, that you might have died doing some sort of extreme sport," she said, and Ryan nearly laughed at the dead-on accuracy of her brother's suspicion.

Ryan had watched Dax this week, seen him interact with Celeste, Chloe and the little girl's parents, and witnessed the expert way in which he kept the interaction upbeat, in spite of the fact that their daughter was dead. The family's last week together had been a positive experience, thanks to Dax. Ryan had been impressed. Now Dax had added another feather to his cap. He'd used the limited knowledge he had about Ryan and completely hit the nail on the head.

"When you told me you tried living life to the fullest, but went overboard with it, I figured Dax was right," Monique continued.

"He *is* right," Ryan said, running the pad of his finger across Monique's lower lip as he spoke. "I died skydiving."

"How did it happen?" she whispered, that sweet mouth moving against his finger, before she kissed it softly. She snuggled closer, as if she knew how difficult this was.

Ryan pulled the sheet over her and welcomed the sensation of her warm flesh cloaking him, giving him the strength he needed to speak words he'd never said before.

The story of his last breath.

"I had six thousand jumps behind me when we boarded the plane that morning. Basically, I was very comfortable in the air and never had the least bit of difficulty. I packed my chute, both the primary one and the reserve, and knew that everything was in order. Except—" He paused, recalling Mike's face.

"Except?" she asked.

"I didn't typically jump in the rain, and that morning it was raining. We—my best friend and I—kept thinking the storm would pass, but it only got stronger." His chest tightened at the memory. "Any other time, I'd have nixed the jump and come back another day."

"But why not that day?" Monique asked, leaning away from him so she could look into his eyes when she spoke. She ran her fingertips down his jaw, cradled his face. "Or would you rather not talk about it?"

"No," he said. "It's okay." Truthfully, he didn't want to talk about it, ever. But he also didn't want to deprive Monique of learning everything she wanted to know about him, his life and his death. "I had a friend from high school, Mike Haggerty, who envied the way I lived after my parents died. We shared an apartment in college, and Mike was with me when I got the call about their car accident. He was the only one who seemed to understand what happened to me after their death."

"That you wanted to get more out of life than your parents had," she said.

He nodded. "Yeah, but like I told you before, I went overboard. I decided there was nothing I would miss out on, no matter what. If there was something I wanted to try, I tried it. If there was something I wanted to buy, I bought it. Now, don't get me wrong, I worked hard, too."

"What did you do?" she asked, and he grinned.

"I owned a roofing company."

She punched him in the chest. "Seriously? And you didn't feel compelled to mention that when you were out there putting those tiles on at twice the speed of the rest of us, including those roofers?"

"Hey, I can't let you in on all my secrets, and I was trying to impress you."

She giggled. "It worked."

"But anyway," he continued, "I started my own business, something Dad had always wanted to do, and I traveled around the globe trying my luck at pretty much every extreme sport known to man. However, once I jumped out of a plane, I was hooked. Every Saturday found me skydiving. Six thousand jumps, and all of them near-perfect."

"What went wrong that day? I'm guessing it had something to do with your friend, Mike?"

"It was his twenty-ninth birthday, and I told him I'd take him anywhere he wanted to go for his birthday. He wanted to go skydiving. He'd been before, a few times, but didn't have nearly the number of jumps under his belt. That was why I thought we should turn back when the rain started to fall."

"But Mike didn't want to turn back?"

"It was his birthday, and he wanted his present on the actual day," Ryan said, grinning. "He isn't known for patience."

"Isn't?" she questioned. "Mike is still on this side?"

Ryan nodded. "He's married now and has a kid on the way. I'm happy for him, really, I am."

"What did Mike's birthday jump have to do with your death?" She scooted up on his body and propped her arms on his chest, like a child in school, waiting for the teacher to give the answer to a question. Except Ryan was fairly certain she wouldn't like the way this story ended, even if she'd already read the last page.

"Mike jumped first," he said. "Looking back, I realize that he'd never jumped in the rain before. It's a different sensation, and it tempts you to do things you wouldn't normally do. The impact of hitting the rain at a hundred and thirty miles per hour tends to mess with your reasoning. I guess it messed with his."

"What did he do?" she asked.

"He waited too long before pulling his chute. If the chute had been packed correctly, it wouldn't have mattered that much, but it wasn't. It came out tangled and was completely useless."

"But you said Mike lived."

"He did. He remembered what to do and cut the chute free, then pulled his reserve in time to make a safe landing, rain and all." Ryan closed his eyes, saw that tangled chute again, dark green and menacing, like a gnarled claw, reaching through the sky.

"What happened to you?"

Ryan opened his eyes, saw her searching them for answers, concern etched on her features.

"What happened?" Monique repeated, while the rain beat against her bedroom window, reminding him of that fatal rain, that fatal day.

"His primary chute sailed away, into the sky, and into my chute. Mike was so anxious to get it out of the way so he could use the reserve that he forgot to check for other jumpers. Forgot to check for me." Ryan grinned uneasily. "Hell, all of those jumps before, over six thousand of them, but I didn't stand a chance when that loose chute caught hold of mine. The two tangled, and I plummeted. Didn't stand a chance."

"Oh, Ryan. I'm so sorry." Her lower lip trembled slightly, and she visibly swallowed, her emotion palpable.

He chuckled, but the sound was cold even to his own ears. "Don't be. I blacked out way before I hit the ground and didn't feel a thing. One minute I was in the land of the living, the next I was in the middle." He squeezed her against him, "Hey, if you're weighing different ways to go, that one isn't so bad." He touched his finger to her mouth, rubbed it across her lower lip. "And it wasn't a completely negative experience. The jump started out oddly exhilarating, more than any other I'd ever experienced, because of the rain."

"Because of the rain?" she asked, the gold flecks in her eyes glittering in the subtle darkness. "How?"

Smiling, Ryan rolled her on her side. "I'll show you." He trailed the back of his fingers down the column of her throat, across the swell of her left breast, then lower.

"Have you ever felt the back side of a raindrop?"

She shook her head.

"Think about it. A raindrop is tear-shaped. The round fullness at the bottom is what we usually feel, when it lands on our skin. But when we jumped that day, we were behind the rain, hitting it full speed, so that the top of each drop, that pointed tip at its peak, snapped against our skin. But there wasn't just one droplet, there were thousands. And we passed through the shower, while they pinged against our exposed skin like tiny wet needles." He leaned over her, smiled. "I'll show you."

MONIQUE HELD her breath as Ryan nuzzled her throat, then pressed a warm, wet kiss against the slope between her neck and her shoulder. Before his mouth moved away from her skin, however, he bit her flesh, making her gasp, then he sucked the tender spot and kissed it again.

"The top side of a raindrop," he murmured, while her insides fluttered. "When they touch you, they touch you everywhere." His mouth moved a fraction, toward the center of her throat, and he kissed, bit, sucked and kissed again.

"Lots of tiny, wet pinpricks," he continued, before moving lower, to the top of her sternum, and repeating the process, while Monique melted at his touch.

"Look at the window, Monique," he said, before starting on her right breast. Kiss. Bite. Suck. Kiss.

She inhaled deeply, held it while he edged his way toward her nipple. "Oh, Ryan."

His lips curved into a smile against her breast, and he looked up at her, his black eyes glittering with desire. "Monique."

"Yes?"

"Look at the window."

She turned her head and focused on the elongated glass, the way the moonlight shimmered through the curtain of rain, the shadow of the magnolia branches forming a leafy dome above the driveway in the distance. Then Ryan moved to the other breast and kissed, bit and sucked the burning point, and she lost all interest. Monique closed her eyes and enjoyed the feel of his mouth massaging her nipple, his teeth grazing the tenderness, his kiss making her stomach quiver and her uterus clench in anticipation.

"Monique." His mouth moved over her sensitive breast as he spoke.

"Mmmm?"

"Look at the window."

"Oh. Right," she said, like a kid whose attention had wandered during her teacher's lesson, and oh, what a lesson this was.

He chuckled softly. "Watch the way the rain hits the glass and imagine it, feel it, touching every inch of your skin. Like this." Another kiss, then a pinch-like bite on the outer swell of her breast combined with the vision of the rain, pinging against the window, before running down its length.

With the Mississippi River on the other side of the levee,

a natural breeze almost always sent the rain toward the house at a slant. Now was no exception. It collided with the glass in little pinpoints, the way Ryan's mouth collided with her skin, an almost painful sensation. With the quick, sharp bites to her flesh followed by a blissful sucking, then a final kiss, before he repeated the process again and again.

As the rain continued to pelt the window, Ryan continued to pelt her skin. He made his way to her stomach now, yet while his mouth concentrated on her abdomen, his hands pushed against her thighs, opening them wide and preparing her for what she knew would come.

The storm picked up, rain fell faster against the window, yet Ryan was unhurried in his pursuit of his goal, moving in an excruciatingly slow but direct path toward the very part of her that could feel each bite, each suck, each kiss. She wanted to feel that there.

She wanted to feel Ryan there.

He was so close, directly above her aching center, and covering her with small, quick, sharp bites, while the wind whistled outside the window and the rain came in even harder. Each droplet hitting the window intensified the sensation of his mouth against her flesh.

Monique couldn't take any more.

"Ryan, please. Don't wait."

He didn't. He moved directly to her clitoris and bit it while she writhed, then he sucked and kissed the tenderness, while Monique closed her eyes and saw stars. She fisted her hands in his hair through her climax, then pushed him away from her center and gazed into his deep, dark eyes.

"The tip of a raindrop," he said, then added huskily, "The last thing I felt before I died."

And with that thought, that he'd experienced something so

unique, so exhilarating, and then lost everything, Monique knew what she wanted to give him now.

"Let it be me this time. I want the last thing you feel before you cross to be me."

Wordlessly, she moved away from him and guided him to her previous position, lying on his back, his head resting on the pillow. Then she leaned over him and kissed his forehead, the bridge of his nose, his mouth. Ryan moaned as she moved to his neck, nuzzling it the way he'd nuzzled hers.

"You're beautiful," she whispered against his skin and remembered when she'd called him that before, the way he'd laughed, and she smiled.

Easing her way down his muscled chest, she did her best to make sure no part of him remained untouched by her kiss. If the last thing he'd felt before death was the stinging rain, the last thing he'd feel before crossing would be her adoring kisses.

And she did adore him, truly.

Moving between his legs, she paused to look at him, his arousal so hard, so ready for her touch. She kissed him there, at the tip, then placed soft kisses around the swollen ridge, then down the entire length. Soft, wet kisses while his entire body tensed beneath her touch. Then she opened her mouth and took him inside. Ryan's low growl filled the night. She drew him in deep, eased him out slowly, drew him in deeper, eased him out even slower.

His hands fisted in her hair. "On top of me," he directed. "Now, Monique."

She gave his manhood another kiss, then did as he asked, moving above him until she was pressed against the end of his erection, then she guided him inside. She kept things slow and deliciously rhythmic, easing over him. His eyes, heavy-lidded and intensely aroused, drank her in, and Monique made certain she gave him a vision to remember.

Moving her hands to her hair, she pushed her fingers through its length while she thrust her breasts forward and tilted her head back, all the while relishing the feel of him, long and hard within her. Up and down, in and out. She moved a hand to one breast and pinched her nipple, rolling it between her thumb and finger while Ryan watched. The pain of it brought back the tantalizing pain of his raindrop simulation, and she envisioned him again, biting and kissing and sucking her everywhere.

Monique had wanted to keep this slow, but she couldn't. He felt so good, and she wanted to feel him pulsing within her, wanted to hear him yell through his release. She leaned forward, let her hair fall around her face like a curtain and braced her hands on his broad chest, then she moved her hips at a hard, frantic pace, enjoying the friction, relishing in the fact that, for now, he was inside her, filling her completely.

For now, they were one.

Her release hit her hard, and she screamed through the intensity, while Ryan's hands clenched around her hips and drove her down his length one last time, hard and fierce and forceful. Then his fingers squeezed, and he set his climax free.

Monique collapsed on top of him, closed her eyes and smiled against his chest while he stroked his hands up and down her spine. "Ryan."

He kissed the top of her head. "Yeah?"

"I love you."

His entire body went rigid beneath her, his hands stopped moving.

Monique opened her eyes, and to her amazement, his aura had strengthened. Then she realized that throughout their lovemaking, it had been barely visible at all, merely a faint light surrounding him as she touched him, pleased him, loved him. But now, it glowed brilliantly, almost painfully.

"Ryan?" she asked, leaning back to see his face.

He shifted, rolled her on her side and brushed a luminescent finger down her cheek as he spoke.

"It wasn't Celeste," he said, while the thunder outside intensified, and the rain beat harder against her window. "Though I don't think you really believed it was. Surely you knew, surely you felt it, didn't you, Monique?"

She swallowed, and nodded. God help her, this was what she wanted, so why did it hurt so much?

"Not Celeste or anyone else, ever. They were right when they didn't let me cross, Monique. I'd never learned to love before." He swallowed thickly. "But I have now, and you were right. The last thing I'll remember this time…is you. I love you, Monique, with every bit of my soul, I do."

"Oh, Ryan," she whispered, leaning toward him to feel him against her one more time.

But her face only met the cool satin of her pillow, and as the storm died outside her window, the dawn of painful reality left a hollow space in her soul.

17

"IT'S MONDAY," Nan said. Wearing a bright-yellow sundress with a red scarf tied around her waist and matching sandals, she was the picture of summer, dazzling and radiant.

Monique, on the other hand, had opted for black. Black earrings, black necklace, black dress, black sandals. Black world. Everything seemed very dark, very empty, very…bleak. Without Ryan.

When she received no response to her statement, Nan continued, "You don't work on Monday."

"I do today," Monique said, finding the only black coffee mug in the house and filling it with coffee—black. She sat at the table and ran her palms down the side of the cup while she contemplated entering the real world again, her regular routine, without Ryan on this side. Truthfully, the only thing she had to do at the shop was Inez's hair, since they scheduled their own treatments on Mondays, when Monique's customers and Inez's customers knew the shop was closed. However, Monique planned to stay at the salon even after she finished with Inez. She wanted to be alone, wanted to think, wanted to wallow in her misery.

She wanted Ryan.

"Tristan got an assignment last night," Nan said, apparently trying to make another attempt at conversation.

Even though Monique really didn't want to talk, she was curious about Tristan's latest ghost. Ghosts were the family's destiny, after all. "During the night?" she asked.

"Yeah. I got up to get some juice and found him leaving the sitting room. This one is a little girl who was in that LaPlace apartment complex that burned last week. Tristan actually helped put out that fire and said that two people died. Evidently, the man crossed over okay, but this little girl needs to tell her grandmother goodbye. Tristan is planning to visit the woman today to help her cross."

"That's nice," Monique said, then sipped another bitter gulp of coffee. No sugar today. She wasn't in the mood for anything sweet.

"And Gage said he's started hearing someone crying. He says it's still very faint, but he should get an assignment soon."

"That's nice," Monique repeated.

Nan topped off her cup of coffee then moved to sit across from Monique at the table. "I wish I didn't have to go to the school today," she said. "I think you could use some company, but we've got that teacher in-service day before classes start next week, and I can't miss it." She frowned, sipping her coffee. "This is going to sound strange, coming from me, but I'm sorry he crossed. If he had stayed, though, he would have been caught in the middle forever. You did the right thing, convincing him to go."

"It wasn't convincing him to cross that was the problem," Monique said. "It was teaching him to love. And I did. Except he didn't fall in love with Celeste." Her throat tightened, but she forced the words through. "He fell in love with me."

"Oh, honey, I'm sorry," Nan said, as the kitchen doors swung open and Dax, dressed in a dark suit and royal-blue tie, entered the kitchen.

"Back to business as usual," he said glumly, opening the cabinets in search of breakfast. He withdrew a box of instant oatmeal, ripped two packages open and dumped them in an oversized bowl. Then he added water, put it in the microwave and turned to look at them. "Guess you can't keep the dream going forever, huh?" He sounded as miserable as Monique felt.

"Talking about the beach?" Nan asked.

"Yeah," he said, withdrawing the bowl from the microwave. Then he mumbled, "That, too."

Monique sipped her bitter coffee and eyed her younger brother, obviously as disheartened about Celeste's crossing as she was about Ryan's. "You okay?" she asked.

"I will be," he said, and flashed her a sweet smile. "Going to miss them though. Celeste and Chloe."

Nan looked from Monique to Dax. "You know, I bet the two of you will get a break from ghosts for a while. Surely Grandma knows that you've both had a couple of tough weeks." She took her mug to the sink and poured the remainder of her coffee down the drain.

"Why don't you go away for a few days?" she continued. "Both of you. The roof is ready for inspection, and Dax, you've got more vacation time, don't you? Monique, you can ask some of the Metairie stylists if they can take your appointments this week, right? I mean, I feel like you both deserve a break, and I'm betting Grandma Adeline will give you one. This will probably be the best time for both of you to go somewhere, maybe take a trip to Biloxi and hit the casinos for a few days. Or go to Grand Isle and relax. Forget about ghosts for a while."

Forget about ghosts? Forget about Ryan? Not in this lifetime. And from the look on Dax's face, Monique guessed he was thinking the same thing about Celeste. But she knew

Nan was only trying to help, and she didn't want to hurt her by telling her how ludicrous her idea was.

"I've got too much scheduled this week to take off," she said. "And it's too late to call the girls from Metairie. I'm sure their books are filled with customers there." She noted Nan's frown and added, "But it was a nice thought."

"Yeah," Dax said. "I had to add all of last week's appointments to this week's schedule, so there's no way I can take a trip now." He ate a few spoonfuls of oatmeal, but then stood and took the unfinished bowl to the sink. "Besides, I'm wanting to stay busy this week."

Monique gave him a reassuring smile. He was right; staying busy would help them get through the emotional aftermath of Celeste and Ryan crossing over. And if she was going to get busy, she planned to start right now. "Speaking of work, I've got to get to the shop. Hope your in-service day goes well," she told Nan.

"Thanks," Nan said, scooping up her planning books and her purse from the counter. She took one step, then stopped when her cell phone started beeping out "Jolie Blon." Dropping the purse and books to the counter, she fished it out, then answered, "Hello."

Monique watched as Nanette's eyes widened. "Yes, we're ready. I can be here this afternoon. No problem. Okay. Thank you for calling." She disconnected.

"What?" Dax asked.

"The Historical Society is sending over a man to inspect the roof this afternoon." She looked from one of them to the other. "We did do a good job, didn't we?"

"A damn good job," Dax said. "You want me to come back and be with you when they show? I can move my schedule around again."

"No. Basically, I don't have to do anything, but let them look at our handiwork." She had an odd expression of part-excitement, part-trepidation.

"It'll pass inspection," Monique said. "It has to."

"Yeah. And then, more than likely, they'll give me the next hurdle for us to climb. But at least we'll be one step closer."

"And Roussel will be one step further away." Dax smirked.

"Exactly." Nan nodded for emphasis as she dropped the phone back in her purse and prepared, once again, to leave. "You guys have a great day. I'll call and let you know what happens with the roof." She left the kitchen, and Monique stood to follow.

"And I hope your day goes well, too," Monique said, giving Dax a soft kiss on the cheek on her way out.

She heard his reply through the sound of the back door slamming against the frame.

"You, too, sis. I hope your day is great."

Within minutes, she had her Mustang cruising at a nice pace along the familiar curves of River Road, levee on her right and an eclectic mix of houses on her left. Modern homes mingled with antebellum plantations, with trailers and shacks interspersed throughout. Some were in prime condition, others were barely standing. Life and time had affected each one, some adversely, some favorably; it all depended on the circumstances behind the family and the home.

Life and time had affected her, too, and Ryan. His life, taken from him so quickly, and her time, the time she still had to endure before she saw him again.

She neared one of the largest plantation homes on the stretch of asphalt between Montz and Ormond. It was in the barely standing category, in about the same condition as the Vicknair plantation, minus the new roof. Would it ever be the same again?

And would Monique ever be the same again?

She turned off River Road to head toward her shop and wasn't surprised to see Inez's old green Plymouth Fury parked outside, the voodoo charms capturing the sunlight as they dangled from the mirror. At least Inez would be more comfortable at the shop this week, with no more ghostly visits from Ryan.

Monique parked next to Inez's clunker, turned off the ignition, then sat for a moment to think about last week and this weekend. Thank goodness it wasn't raining. She needed a little time before she felt raindrops on her skin and remembered Ryan's interpretation of the other side of a raindrop. Maybe the powers that be could hold the rain at bay for a while, at least the rain around her small portion of Louisiana.

Deciding she might as well officially start her day, she climbed from the car and entered the shop to find Inez leaning over the shampoo bowl dousing her black mane *and* a large portion of the floor around the sink.

Monique hurriedly dropped her purse at her station. "I'm only five minutes late," she said. "Couldn't you wait before you tried to flood the shop?"

Inez cackled, then lifted the sprayer to Monique, only she forgot to turn the thing off and ended up drenching the front of Monique's dress.

"It's a good thing you're the best nail sculptor around, lady," Monique said, turning the powerful spray back toward Inez's head. "Or you'd be fired."

"Phft," Inez said, swiveling around so her head faced the ceiling and her hair flopped into the sink. "You all talk, *chère*—" She put a wet finger on Monique's lower lip. "—and your *bahbin* is still hanging."

"Well, forgive me if I'm not going to apologize for pouting. I'm having a rough day." Monique squirted a glob of conditioner in her hands and ran it through Inez's hair.

Inez tsked loudly, then opened her big black eyes wide. "No ghosts today," she said matter-of-factly.

"You're right. None today," Monique said, inhaling the apple fragrance while rinsing Inez's hair. She turned off the faucet and squeezed the excess moisture away, then grabbed a white towel from the stack behind the counter.

"It'll be okay," Inez said, patting Monique's hand as she secured the towel around her head.

"I know," Monique admitted, and forced a smile. "But it's going to take a little time." She guided Inez to her station then located Inez's color, jet-black.

Evidently realizing Monique wasn't in the mood for talking, Inez sat silent while Monique concentrated on coloring her hair and didn't say a word until Monique prepared to section off Inez's trademark platinum streak to keep its color.

"Go on an' change it, too," Inez said. "All black."

Surprised, Monique looked in the mirror. "You sure? You've had your racing stripe for as long as I've known you. It'll change your look."

"I'm sure, *chère*. Tired of same ol' ting."

"Okay," Monique said, blending the platinum section into the bulk of her hair and distributing the black color over the pale strands. "I sure hope you don't change your mind."

"No." Inez closed her eyes while Monique finished the color treatment.

In less than an hour, Monique moved Inez to the shampoo bowl for a rinse. She sprayed a small amount of water into her hair then lathered the color before rinsing it away.

Monique had worked with hair long enough to know something was wrong, and she feared she knew exactly what it was. "Oh no," she whispered.

"Hmm?" Inez said, as Monique quickly wrapped her head in a towel.

"Inez, you've never mentioned having any trouble with your hair taking color before. You would've told me if there was a problem, right? I mean, well, are you taking any strong medications or anything that could have made the chemicals react—adversely?" She was horrified at what had happened to Inez's beautiful hair. Sure, Monique's color treatments were always a little off when she had a spirit coming, but never like this. Oh, how Monique hoped she wasn't responsible for *this*. The thought of taking care of another ghost now made her feel sick.

Inez jumped up from the chair and hurried to the nearest mirror, unwrapped the towel and let it fall to the floor.

"Mais, jamais d'la vie!" she exclaimed, eyeing the hair that, even wet, was undeniably red. And Monique knew, if it was that red when wet, it would only be more vivid when dry.

"I'm so sorry," Monique said, chewing on her lower lip and wondering if there would be any way to fix the flamboyance of Inez's head now.

Inez lifted her hair to make sure the entire bounty was the same gaudy hue, then she looked at Monique, and her round face split into a grin. "S'okay, *chère*. I wanted change, and *gar ici*, change I got. And dis my fault, too. Not jus you. I only mess up my hair one time, when I got me a color right after I did a big chant. An' I did a chant dis morning."

"A chant?" Monique shook her head while Inez plopped in the chair at her station. Trying not to panic at the hideous mess on her employee's head, she grabbed a brush and gently worked it through Inez's flaming hair. "What do you mean, Inez?"

"Voodoo. I did a chant dis morning, one Mamere taught me, to help keep bad tings from you today. I know you were some kinda sad, but I forgot about da color."

"I burn when a ghost is coming, and you mess with your body's natural chemicals when you play around with voodoo," Monique said, thinking that they were more alike than she had ever realized before.

"Ahh," Inez said, though Monique didn't know if she was really paying attention. She seemed very intent on examining, and apparently admiring, her hair.

"You're really okay with this?" Monique asked, amazed.

"Yes." Inez smiled again.

"Really?" The jingling bell on the salon door announced that someone had entered. "Oh dear, I forgot to lock it. I'll be right back."

"I like it," Inez muttered, as Monique left her station to see what their visitor wanted. She hated turning a customer away, but she really hadn't planned to do anyone's hair after finishing with Inez. She wanted to stay in the shop and mope. Maybe this customer would be willing to come back another day. She started toward the front of the shop, but halted when her phone began to ring.

"Wan' me to get it?" Inez asked.

"No, I'll get it," Monique said, then called out toward the waiting customer, "Just a minute. I'll be right there." She picked up the ringing phone. "Hello?"

"We did it!" Nan yelled. "We passed!"

Monique smiled—she'd *so* needed some good news today. "That's wonderful, Nan. I can't believe it. We did it, didn't we? All of us together." *And Ryan.*

"We sure did. Gage was here when I got the news. He came over because he thinks he is going to get an assignment tonight; he said he's heard ghosts all day. Well, one ghost, and he said it's a woman, and it's a stronger pull than usual. Guess this place is going to stay busy."

"A stronger pull?" Monique asked, remembering how strong a pull Ryan had when he came. Was Gage getting a ghost that would affect him like Ryan affected her?

"Yeah. I'm sure he'll tell us more after she comes. But anyway, you're the first one I called, so I need to keep spreading the word. Isn't this amazing, Monique?"

"Very amazing," Monique agreed, then remembered what Nan had said this morning. If they passed the roof inspection, the society would probably give them another chore to verify they were working toward restoration. "Nan?"

"Yeah," Nanette said, still excited.

"Did they give you another task? Not that I mind working, but I'm curious what we'll be doing next."

"Yeah, they did," Nan said, but she didn't sound too down about it. Then again, neither was Monique. They'd passed the first hurdle; now they'd simply keep going. "Our first floor has to get tested. We've got to clean it up and let them certify we've removed the contamination."

Monique instantly pictured the sludge that had seeped into the house on the majority of the first floor. This was not going to be a little thing. "How long do we have?"

"Two months, and in the meantime, we may actually get some money from the society to help us in our efforts. They really seem to think we can do it, in spite of Roussel being on their board."

"And they're right," Monique said, catching Nan's enthusiasm. "We *can* do it."

"Okay. Well, I'm off to call everyone else." Nan disconnected.

Monique turned and continued toward the front of the shop. "Can I help you?" she asked, rounding the wall that separated the lobby from the work area.

With his back to her, a man was looking at the products displayed on the shelves across from the register. He was tall, with dark hair and broad shoulders. She swallowed. From the back, he resembled Ryan. Was her mind merely playing tricks on her? Probably. How would she ever get back to a normal life when she'd never have what she wanted?

"Do you need some hair products today?" she asked, then froze when he turned.

"I wondered if you take walk-ins," he said, and stepped toward her, flashing that sexy smile as Monique fought to control her racing heart. Was she imagining this? Yes, she had to be. But he looked so…real.

"Ryan?"

"Because I'm very interested in walking in," he said, moving even closer. "Walking in, living in, existing in—in this side, in your life, in your heart."

"It can't be," she mumbled, while his hand reached out to cup her face. "You—crossed over."

He shook his head and tilted her face toward his. "No, I didn't. I met with Adeline, and with practically everyone else that matters over there," he said. "But I didn't cross." He smiled. "Evidently, there's a provision for people like us."

"A provision?" She inhaled the scent of him and examined the beautiful column of his throat, and that exquisite throbbing in the side, his pulse. *Mon dieu*, he was real.

"According to the powers that be," he said, "should a ghost find his soul mate while dwelling in the interim, then the two shall have the chance to bring their souls together, on this side. To live together, until death—true death—do they part." He paused, then added, "With one condition."

"What's that?"

"I can't go back to my old life, can't even attempt it. I *did* die, after all. The powers that be made me promise I would be content to start life over, and they made certain I knew that I would never be able to go back to the life I had before. If that was okay, then I could stay, start my life anew…with you. Which is exactly what I want, Monique, if you want it, too."

"Oh, Ryan!" she yelled, jumping into his arms and kissing that lovely pulse at his throat.

"Mais, jamais d'la vie!" Inez yelled, rounding the corner with her hands waving in the air. "Das him?" Then she gasped. "No, you no ghost?"

"Not anymore," Ryan said.

"Cho! Co! True?"

"Yes, it's true, Inez," Monique said, hugging him tightly. "It is true." She kissed him, melted into him, absorbed his touch. She squirmed against him, determined to get as close as possible.

To never let him go.

"You did dis?" Inez asked, when Monique broke the kiss. The older woman held up a lock of her flaming hair. "Or was it my voodoo?"

"I didn't do it," Ryan said, grinning.

She shrugged. "S'okay. I want change, and I like my voodoo, even wit da kinks. An' I tink he'll like it."

"Who?" Monique asked.

"My ghost," Inez said proudly, then grinned. "The one who comes when I dream—" She winked prominently. "—you know, *dos'* dreams."

Monique's mouth fell open, then she looked at Ryan.

"Oh no, it wasn't me visiting her," he said, holding up his palms defensively. "She must have garnered another ghost's attention."

Inez wiggled her dark brows, which reminded Monique that they'd have to color her brows, too, if she were going to keep the ridiculous shade of red, and Monique suspected she was, since she thought "her ghost" would like it.

"How many stay in the middle and play fantasy man?" Monique asked her own fantasy-come-true.

Ryan grinned, shrugged. "Hell if I know. I'm not concerned about that anymore. From now on, I only plan to fulfill one woman's fantasies."

"Good," Monique said, leaning up to kiss the mouth she adored, the ghost—correction—the man she adored. Then she looked into his eyes and gasped. "Oh, wow."

"What?" he asked.

"They're so…blue."

* * * * *

*Ryan will keep Monique satisfied for a while,
but there's another Vicknair who needs to learn
there's more to life than meaningless sex.
Don't miss the excitement when Gage finds himself
tangling with a ghost—and a woman—
he won't be able to forget.
Look for GHOSTS AND ROSES,
available July 2007,
wherever Harlequin Blaze books are sold.*

Mediterranean Nights

Join the guests and crew of **Alexandra's Dream**, *the newest luxury ship to set sail on the romantic Mediterranean, as they experience the glamorous world of cruising.*

A new Harlequin continuity series begins in June 2007 with
FROM RUSSIA, WITH LOVE
by Ingrid Weaver

Marina Artamova books a cabin on the luxurious cruise ship **Alexandra's Dream**, *when she finds out that her orphaned nephew and his adoptive father are aboard. She's determined to be reunited with the boy...but the romantic ambience of the ship and her undeniable attraction to a man she considers her enemy are about to interfere with her quest!*

Turn the page for a sneak preview!

Piraeus, Greece

"THERE SHE IS, Stefan. *Alexandra's Dream*." David Anderson squatted beside his new son and pointed at the dark blue hull that towered above the pier. The cruise ship was a majestic sight, twelve decks high and as long as a city block. A circle of silver and gold stars, the logo of the Liberty Cruise Line, gleamed from the swept-back smokestack. Like some legendary sea creature born for the water, the ship emanated power from every sleek curve—even at rest it held the promise of motion. "That's going to be our home for the next ten days."

The child beside him remained silent, his cheeks working in and out as he sucked furiously on his thumb. Hair so blond it appeared white ruffled against his forehead in the harbor breeze. The baby-sweet scent unique to the very young mingled with the tang of the sea.

"Ship," David said. "Uh, *parakhod.*"

From beneath his bangs, Stefan looked at the *Alexandra's Dream*. Although he didn't release his thumb, the corners of his mouth tightened with the beginning of a smile.

David grinned. That was Stefan's first smile this afternoon, one of only two since they had left the orphanage yesterday. It was probably because of the boat—according to the orphanage staff, the boy loved boats, which was the main reason David had decided to book this cruise. Then again, there was a strong possibility the smile could have been a reaction to David's attempt at pocket-dictionary Russian. Whatever the cause, it was a good start.

The liaison from the adoption agency had claimed that Stefan had been taught some English, but David had yet to see evidence of it. David continued to speak, positive his son would understand his tone even if he couldn't grasp the words. "This is her maiden voyage. Her first trip, just like this is our first trip, and that makes it special." He motioned toward the stage that had been set up on the pier beneath the ship's bow. "That's why everyone's celebrating."

The ship's official christening ceremony had been held the day before and had been a closed affair, with only the cruise-line executives and VIP guests invited, but the stage hadn't yet been disassembled. Banners bearing the blue and white of the Greek flag of the ship's owner, as well as the Liberty circle of stars logo, draped the edges of the platform. In the center, a group of musicians and a dance troupe dressed in traditional white folk costumes performed for the benefit of the *Alexandra's Dream*'s first passengers. Their audience was in a festive mood, snapping their fingers in time to the music while the dancers twirled and wove through their steps.

David bobbed his head to the rhythm of the mandolins. They were playing a folk tune that seemed vaguely familiar, possibly from a movie he'd seen. He hummed a few notes. "Catchy melody, isn't it?"

Stefan turned his gaze on David. His eyes were a striking shade of blue, as cool and pale as a winter horizon and far too solemn for a child not yet five. Still, the smile that hovered at the corners of his mouth persisted. He moved his head with the music, mirroring David's motion.

David gave a silent cheer at the interaction. Hopefully, this cruise would provide countless opportunities for more. "Hey, good for you," he said. "Do you like the music?"

The child's eyes sparked. He withdrew his thumb with a pop. *"Moozika!"*

"Music. Right!" David held out his hand. "Come on, let's go closer so we can watch the dancers."

Stefan grasped David's hand quickly, as if he feared it would be withdrawn. In an instant his budding smile was replaced by a look close to panic.

Did he remember the car accident that had killed his parents? It would be a mercy if he didn't. As far as David knew, Stefan had never spoken of it to anyone. Whatever he had seen had made him run so far from the crash that the police hadn't found him until the next day. The event had traumatized him to the extent that he hadn't uttered a word until his fifth week at the orphanage. Even now he seldom talked.

David sat back on his heels and brushed the hair from Stefan's forehead. That solemn, too-old gaze locked with his, and for an instant, David felt as if he looked back in time at an image of himself thirty years ago.

He didn't need to speak the same language to understand exactly how this boy felt. He knew what it meant to be alone and powerless among strangers, trying to be brave and tough but wishing with every fiber of his being for a place to belong, to be safe, and most of all for someone to love him....

He knew in his heart he would be a good parent to Stefan. It was why he had never considered halting the adoption process after Ellie had left him. He hadn't balked when he'd learned of the recent claim by Stefan's spinster aunt, either; the absentee relative had shown up too late for her case to be considered. The adoption was meant to be. He and this child already shared a bond that went deeper than paperwork or legalities.

A seagull screeched overhead, making Stefan start and press closer to David.

"That's my boy," David murmured. He swallowed hard, struck by the simple truth of what he had just said.

That's my *boy.*

"I CAN'T BE PATIENT, RUDOLPH. I'm not going to stand by and watch my nephew get ripped from his country and his roots to live on the other side of the world."

Rudolph hissed out a slow breath. "Marina, I don't like the sound of that. What are you planning?"

"I'm going to talk some sense into this American kidnapper."

"No. Absolutely not. No offence, but diplomacy is not your strong suit."

"Diplomacy be damned. Their ship's due to sail at five o'clock."

"Then you wouldn't have an opportunity to speak with him even if his lawyer agreed to a meeting."

"I'll have ten days of opportunities, Rudolph, since I plan to be on board that ship."

* * * * *

*Follow Marina and David as they join forces
to uncover the reason behind little Stefan's unusual silence,
and the secret behind the death of his parents....*

Look for From Russia, With Love *by Ingrid Weaver
in stores June 2007.*

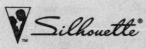

REQUEST YOUR FREE BOOKS!

2 FREE NOVELS PLUS 2 FREE GIFTS!

HARLEQUIN®

Blaze®

Red-hot reads!

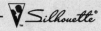

SPECIAL EDITION™

COMING IN JUNE

HER LAST FIRST DATE

by *USA TODAY* bestsellling author
SUSAN MALLERY

After one too many bad dates, Crissy Phillips finally swore off men. Recently widowed, pediatrician Josh Daniels can't risk losing his heart. With an intense attraction pulling them together, will their fear keep them apart? Or will one wild night change everything…?

Sometimes the unexpected is the best news of all….

HARLEQUIN®

Blaze™

COMING NEXT MONTH

#327 RISKING IT ALL Stephanie Tyler
Going to the Xtreme: Bigger, Faster, Better is not only the title of Rita Calhoun's hot new documentary, but it's what happens when she falls for one of the film's subjects, undercover navy SEAL John Cashman—the bad boy who's very, very good….

#328 CALL ME WICKED Jamie Sobrato
Extreme
Being a witch isn't easy. Just ask Lauren Parish. She's on the run from witch-hunters with a hot guy she's forbidden to touch. Worse, she's had Carson McCullen and knows *exactly* how good he is. Maybe it's time to be completely wicked and forget all the rules.

#329 SHADOW HAWK Jill Shalvis
ATF agent Abby Wells might be madly in lust with gorgeous fellow agent JT Hawk, but she's not about to do something stupid. Then again, walking into the middle of a job gone wrong—*and* getting herself kidnapped by Hawk—isn't the smartest thing she's ever done. Still, she's not about to make matters worse by sleeping with him. *Is she?*

#330 THE P.I. Cara Summers
Tall, Dark…and Dangerously Hot! Bk. 1
Writer-slash-sleuth Kit Angelis is living a *noir* novel: a gorgeous blonde walks into his office, covered in blood, carrying a wad of cash and a gun and has no idea who she is. She's also sexy as hell, which is making it hard for Kit to keep his mind on the mystery….

#331 NO RULES Shannon Hollis
Are the Laws of Seduction the latest fad for a guy to snag a sexy date, or a blueprint for murder? Policewoman Joanna MacPherson needs to find out. Posing as a lonely single, she and her partner, sexy Cooper Maxwell, play a dangerous game of cat and mouse that might uncover a lot more than they bargained for….

#332 ONE NIGHT STANDARDS Cathy Yardley
A flight gone awry and a road trip from hell turn into the night that never seems to end for Sophie Jones and Mark McMann. But the starry sky and combustible sexual heat between the two of them say they won't be complaining…. In fact, it may just be the trip of a lifetime!

www.eHarlequin.com

HBCNM0507